# That Day
# by the Creek

# That Day by the Creek

## A Novel About the Sand Creek Massacre of 1864

John Buzzard

CLADACH
Publishing

THAT DAY BY THE CREEK:
A NOVEL ABOUT THE SAND CREEK MASSACRE OF 1864
Copyright ©2016, John Buzzard
Published by:
Cladach Publishing, PO Box 336144 Greeley, CO 80633
www.cladach.com

Cover art: Scan#H.6130.37 "Battle of Sand Creek" oil painting by Robert
Lindneux, 1936. Used with permission of History Colorado.

Library of Congress Cataloging-in-Publication Data
Names: Buzzard, John, 1966- author.
Title: That day by the creek : a novel about the Sand Creek Massacre of 1864
    / John Buzzard.
Other titles: Sand Creek Massacre of 1864
Description: Greeley, CO : Cladach Publishing, 2016.
Identifiers: LCCN 2016009741 (print) | LCCN 2016015892 (ebook) |
    ISBN 9780989101479 (pbk. : alk. paper) | ISBN 9780989101486 ()
Subjects: LCSH: Sand Creek Massacre, Colo., 1864--Fiction. | Cheyenne
    Indians--Fiction. | Arapaho Indians--Fiction. | Chivington, John M. (John
    Milton), 1821-1894--Fiction. | Colorado--Fiction. | GSAFD: Western
    stories. | Historical fiction.
Classification: LCC PS3602.U983 T53 2016 (print) | LCC PS3602.U983
    (ebook) | DDC 813/.6--dc23
LC record available at https://lccn.loc.gov/2016009741

ISBN-13: 9780989101479
ISBN-10: 0989101479

Printed in the U.S.A.

## Dedication & Acknowledgements

I would like to dedicate this novel to my father, who not only taught me to walk in the ways of the Lord, but who also instilled in me an appreciation of our history in the American West. As a child I recall asking him about a picture of the Sand Creek Massacre I saw in a book. He explained that the charging cavalry were not always the good guys as depicted in the John Wayne movies.

I'm also grateful for the editing skills of Catherine Lawton and Christina Slike of Cladach Publishing for helping me streamline the multi-facets of this historical event into novel format.

# Table of Contents

# Prologue

## THE LAST SAD RITES
Denver, Colorado
October 7, 1894

O n the day of Colonel John Chivington's funeral, chaos reigned in Denver. In front of the Trinity United Methodist Church, over three thousand people shouted, pushed, and tripped over each other to get a look at the approaching hearse. Police in their new blue uniforms and white gloves struggled to keep the street clear. Their overzealous whistle blowing only added to the confusion. A small group of Indians dressed in traditional robes stood in silent protest. Their mere presence, a reminder of a time better left forgotten, upset some folks.

Even on tiptoe I couldn't see over the other reporters. A crunch of wheels announced the hearse halting in front of the crowd. As I turned to ascend the church steps for a better view, the crowd surged backward, knocking me to the sidewalk. I nearly panicked. Several sets of feet stumbled over me, and my palms burned from scraping the concrete. I tried to get leverage and regain my feet.

A baritone voice boomed, "Hey, watch out for that fellow on the ground."

An older gentleman in a charcoal-gray suit and Stetson hat stood over me. Beside him was a tall Indian in a black suit and white collar. He had short-cropped, salt-and-pepper hair. Both men extended a hand to help me up. The Indian's wrist bore a nasty scar.

"Thank you, gentlemen." My voice was shaky. I inhaled deeply, replaced my derby on my head, and tried to recover some poise.

"Are you all right there?" The older man spoke with a distinctive drawl. He looked six-feet tall, about a hundred-sixty pounds. Bags drooped under his blue eyes and jowls hung. Even so, his face was pleasant; he could be everyone's favorite grandfather. His bolo tie had a horseshoe slide clip, and his brown belt had a silver buckle with the silhouetted head of a Texas longhorn. In his left hand he carried a dog-eared Bible.

"Yes, I'm fine." I wiped my right hand on my pants then extended it. "I'm Hugo Parsons, with the Chicago Daily News."

"I'm Joshua Frasier," said the first man, grasping my hand in a friendly shake. "And my friend here is Pastor David Pendleton."

"Pleased to meet you."

"Likewise." Pastor David's voice was soft and deep. But his handshake was a vice around my palm. I tried not to wince. Never in my life did I expect to meet a church leader who was an Indian.

Organ strains wafted through the church door like a call to assemble inside. But I didn't want to lose the moment's opportunity, so I blurted, "Say, Mister Frasier. Did you know the colonel?"

He hesitated and glanced at Pastor David. "Yes, I knew him. But I haven't seen him since the war."

"So you served with him? In what capacity, if I may ask?"

"I was his regimental chaplain. But it sounds like the service is about to begin. We should go in and find our seats."

"Yes, sir. Say, would it be possible to meet you here afterwards? For my article I'm going to need a brief interview with someone who knew the colonel."

Again Mister Frasier briefly hesitated. "All right, Mister Parsons. I'll meet you back here after the service."

"Great. And thanks again for saving my neck."

The two men headed up the stairs. I, on the other hand, stood rooted, taking in the magnificent exterior of the church. I had overheard another reporter say the red and gray masonry stone was rhyolite from Castle Rock. The gothic architecture was reminiscent of European cathedrals yet somehow fit this high-plains city. Each pointed peak seemed to reflect the grand mountains rising to the west. The stone steeple piercing the air was the highest tower I had ever seen.

On the steps, several veterans in outdated uniforms greeted Mister Frasier in what I assumed was an informal reunion. He passed through one of the three archways onto the porch where four ruffians in rumpled suits and straw hats stood. *Corn-fed good-old-boys*, I thought, *all in need of a shave*. One of them shoved another and said, "Go on, Scooter, let's see if you can handle him."

Scooter, or whatever his name was, looked to weigh well over three-hundred pounds. His suspenders held up his pants over his barrel belly. He stepped in front of Pastor David before he could enter the narthex.

"Hey, Chief, where do you think you're going?"

"I'm going to attend the funeral," David said calmly.

"I don't think so. You see, boy, this is a white man's church. Why don't you go back to your tribe over there on the curb?"

The other three laughed.

"I can't." David grinned slightly. "I'll be at the service."

"Maybe you don't understand English so good. I told you—"

"That's enough," roared a red-faced Mister Frasier. He glared at Scooter. "Maybe *you* don't understand. What my friend is trying to tell you is that if you don't get out of his way there might be two bodies going to the graveyard today."

"What's all the fuss about?" A burly policeman stepped in between Mister Frasier and Scooter.

"Apparently, these citizens are concerned about who enters their church," answered Mister Frasier, staring at the fat thug.

"So, you're particular about who enters your church, are you?"

Scooter glanced at his friends but got no help from them. "No, sir. We were just funnin' is all."

The policeman pressed the end of his nightstick into Scooter's belly. "Well, your funning is over. You lads find some other place to sober up, or I'll find one for you."

Without another word, the four ruffians hurried down the steps through the mourners.

"Thank you, officer," said Mister Frasier, more calmly now. "I keep hoping such hostility toward Indians will go away, but nothing really surprises me."

"I'm afraid there will always be that one percent who refuse to change." The officer held the nightstick behind his back and kept an eye out as the men passed the group of Indians on the street. Then he nodded to Mister Frasier. "Good day to you, sir."

Once inside, I made my way to the overhead gallery reserved for the press, eager for a better view of the stained-glass windows and the impressive wall of organ pipes. I took one of the few remaining seats. Straight across from where I sat, on the opposite wall and behind another gallery, light shone through a beautiful rose window. On the adjoining wall, a massive stained-glass window of an angel shone down on the crowd. Notes from the brass pipes resounded off the high stone walls. The main floor of the sanctuary was reserved seating only. Mourners without seats had to stand in galleries where they jostled for a glimpse of the casket.

I spotted Mister Frasier in a pew, with head bowed and eyes closed, clutching his Bible. Everyone else chit-chatted, waiting for the service to begin. I decided Mister Frasier was a man to be admired. He came to the rescue of a stranger, defended a friend with righteous indignation, and displayed reverence in the Lord's house.

The pall bearers set the casket upon a dais surrounded by an arrangement of white flowers. Draped over the coffin was a blue and silver Masonic apron bearing a square, a compass, a triangle, and a red cross of the Knights of Templar.

A Mendelssohn string quartet accompanied Henry Bromwell, whose baritone voice sang a caliginous descant he had written for the occasion:

> *Direful Death, thy gauge of terror*
> *Spares the hearts of mortals never.*

*Shall thy weapon smite forever?*
*Who shall pass thy square tremendous?*
*Who confront thy maul stupendous?*
*Who deliver or defend us?*
*Blessed death! Thy shrouded portal*
*Open towards the realms immortal.*
*There the loved and lost are found.*
*Glory be to God eternal!*
*Glory to the Word supernal!*
*There the capstone lost is found.*

The senior minister, Doctor Robert McIntyre, stepped to the pulpit wearing a purple and white alb. I found his white hair distracting, the way it stuck out like a wild tumbleweed. After a long, loud prayer, he opened his heavy black Bible to the second epistle of Timothy chapter four, verses seven to eight. Stretching to his full length, he bellowed:

> *I have fought a good fight, I have finished my course, I*
> *have kept the faith: Henceforth there is laid up for me*
> *a crown of righteousness, which the Lord, the righteous*
> *judge, shall give me at that day: and not to me only, but*
> *unto all them also that love his appearing.*

Removing his glasses, Doctor McIntyre looked over the congregation before he began. Then, "In seventeen years of ministry, I have preached hundreds of funeral sermons and used this text a score of times, but never has it applied with such appropriateness as today. I never in my life knew a man who represented the soldierly element in Christianity as perfectly as did the man we are here to honor. As a pioneer, as a spiritual warrior, as a path finder, and as a patriot, he exemplified a Christian man."

Here and there a sob rose from the mourners.

With emotion in his voice and tears in his eyes, Doctor

McIntyre continued. "The hero of Glorieta is gone from us. He was a man who walked the streets of this town as such a superb figure, that those of us who saw could not but admire. As life ebbed from his body, as the cancer took its toll, the eagle eye began to take on film, and the always-firm hand became weak and unable to perform its duties. He knew the end was near. And now he lies here before us, preaching a more eloquent sermon than he ever did in life. The Chivington we love still lives in the Lord. We shall see him again. Hero, patriot, father, and friend—farewell! Good-bye for a little while, till in some kindlier clime you bid me good morning."

Behind the podium sat several distinguished men, including former Governor John Evans. Some of them got up and spoke as if Chivington was America's greatest hero since George Washington. The Masons opened the casket and, as the organ resumed, mourners filed by to view the thin body of an old man with a long, white beard.

With relief, after the service, I stepped outside into the fresh air. However, the scene outside the church and along the street remained tense. The veterans I had seen before exchanged heated words amongst themselves. The Masons watched from a distance. Even the town citizens seemed to be bickering with each other.

Mister Frasier and Pastor David met me on the front steps and we proceeded down the crowded sidewalk. Pastor David silently followed Mister Frasier and me.

"How can I help you, Mister Parsons?" Mister Frasier asked.

"Please, call me Hugo."

"Very well. Call me Josh."

"Well, sir ... I mean Josh ... I was hoping you could shed some light on the enigmatic life of the dearly departed."

"Like what?"

I looked around to see who might overhear us. "From what I understand, Colonel Chivington was a great figure in this nation's history," I practically shouted.

"Was he now?" Josh grinned slightly.

"You disagree, then?" I asked loudly with a smirk.

Josh gave me a curious look. "Hugo, the Lord doesn't take kindly to gossiping or ill talk of folks. Truth be told, though, the colonel was not a figure to be admired."

A fat young man with brass buttons on his vest that appeared to be spring loaded, pointed at Josh. "I heard what you said. You're wrong. The colonel was a great man who made this state a safe place to live for decent folks."

"Did you know him?" Josh asked the man.

The man, whose sweaty hair stuck out from under his derby, didn't hesitate. "No, I did not, but in grammar school I learned about all the great things he did." He yanked his arm away from his thin wife who was pulling at it and trying to get his attention with a pleading look.

By now a crowd had gathered around us. "The colonel was not a hero. The press has got it all wrong," said a large man in a sergeant's uniform.

A sniveling little man who wore a private's uniform said, "He was the greatest officer the army ever had, and he should've been president."

Another slight man with a derby and glasses, whose sideburns connected to his mustache, declared, "He was a man of the cloth!"

"He died with blood on his hands!" shouted a woman.

The scene developed into a shove-and-shout match. Police officers ran to the scene to break up the melee.

*Hard to believe these people just came out of a church!* I thought.

The small group of Indians remained at the street corner. A few people hurled ugly insults at them, but they remained stoic and silent. A lone tear ran down the cheek of one Indian woman.

"Dear God, how I hate that," said Josh, angry again.

"I wonder who they are," I inquired.

"They are Northern Cheyenne. Probably off the Tongue River Reservation in Montana," answered Pastor David, which reminded me of his presence.

"Where are you two from?" I asked.

"That part of Indian Territory now called Oklahoma," answered Josh. Pastor David nodded.

"Oh yeah. The land grab in '89. Where will the Indians go when it all becomes Oklahoma?" I sincerely but stupidly wanted to know.

"They'll be sent to a dirt-poor reservation like the rest of them. You've really got a lot to learn, haven't you?" snapped Josh. Then, "I apologize, Hugo. Didn't mean to bite your head off. There are just some things I can't get used to. Don't want to get used to."

"It's okay. You're right. I do have a lot to learn. Look, is there some place private we can talk? It's getting close to lunch time. I'll buy."

"That won't be necessary," said Josh. "I'm staying at the Stockmen's Inn, planning to look into purchasing some local acreage to graze my herd. How about joining David and me for lunch as our guest? Come on, let's take that trolley."

One of Denver's new electric trolleys took us to the Colorado Stockmen's Association, essentially a private club and hotel for ranchers—members and their guests only. Wagon-wheel chandeliers and electric lanterns hung from the lobby ceiling. As they entered, Josh, who led the way, stopped briefly to gaze at the portrait of the club's founder, T. Wright Mendenhall above the giant fireplace mantel. The head-and-shoulders photograph of the late, great cattle baron sporting a handlebar mustache, three-piece suit and ten-gallon Stetson seemed to watch us as an attendant took our coats and hats then seated us in the café. We ordered steaks with all the trimmings. The fragrance of roast beef and fresh-baked bread set my mouth to watering.

"I'm curious," Josh said. "Why did you want to agitate those people?"

I tapped my pencil on the table. "Because, sir, I needed a scoop. Reading about a fistfight that broke out at Chivington's funeral would be more interesting than reviewing the eulogy. As the saying goes in my profession: 'If it bleeds, it leads'."

"You think I've got a story that bleeds?"

"I figure you've got a story that will refute a lot of that smarmy bunk we heard at the funeral."

"You certainly have a way with words." Josh spoke with sarcasm. "What is it you want to know?"

"Well, to start with: Why did you attend the funeral?"

The question seemed to catch him off guard. "Because I served with him."

"But you never liked him."

"Well, I wouldn't say never. And I have forgiven him."

"Forgiven him for what?"

Our steaks arrived. The waiter filled our coffee cups. Josh still didn't answer. I took a bite of steak and pressed on. "Were you with the colonel during … you know?"

"You mean was I with him that day by the creek?" Josh stared at his food.

"Yeah, that's what I want to know."

He silently chewed a bite of steak. Finally he answered, "Yes, I was with him."

"How did a man of God end up there?"

"How did any of us end up there?" Josh met my gaze. "It wasn't anything we had planned on."

"How could God allow such a terrible thing to happen?"

Josh and Pastor David exchanged a quick look. David didn't speak a word, but listened intently as he ate.

"I asked that very question thirty years ago." Josh set down his fork. "Maybe you *should* hear my story. It will take some time."

"I'm in no hurry." I cut another bite of the juicy beef. "Tell me about the first time you met the colonel."

Josh leaned back in his chair. "It was in 1856 when I first saw the Reverend John Milton Chivington preaching at a church I happened to be visiting near my hometown of Westport, Missouri, which nowadays is called Kansas City. What nobody knew at the time was that the preacher had received a death threat by some pro-slavery members in the congregation. When Reverend Chivington stepped to the pulpit, he looked at us with angry eyes as dark as coal. He was a giant of a man. He slammed down two pistols next to his Bible. I'll never forget what he said. With a voice that boomed like thunder, he declared, 'By the grace of God and these two revolvers, I am going to preach here today!' And he did. When it was all over, those slavers who made the threat sulked out of that church like whipped dogs."

I chuckled. "When was the next time you saw him?"

"Six years later, when I was inducted into the army."

"Go ahead and start from the beginning."

"Well, thirty-four years ago, in the east, the winds of war were blowing. I moved out west. I arrived at Fort Wise a broken-hearted widower. Little did I know the Lord was about to guide me through a difficult lesson on how he can make something good come out of a tragic event."

Once Joshua started his story, there was no stopping him. I took notes and still managed to thoroughly enjoy the memorable steak dinner. He furnished me with far more than enough information for an article.

In the following pages I am going to tell you Joshua Frasier's story as he told it to me, a true account.

# Chapter 1

## TRAIL'S END
### SEPTEMBER 1860

There in the middle of the prairie, in the southeastern corner of Colorado Territory, Brother Uriah signaled the wagon train to halt. He yelled, "Welcome to Fort Wise! This is the end of the line for you missionaries."

From his wagon, Joshua Frasier took in the scene. It seemed as if hundreds of people had moved to a city that wasn't built yet. Actually there were thousands of people, if he included the number of Indians in the Arapahoe camp visible to the south. A few completed fort buildings stood here and there, but mostly innumerable tents, tepees, and covered wagons. The fort had no walls, and its dirt streets teemed with all sorts of men: Indians, Mexicans, pioneers, soldiers, and mountain men. Drunken laughter and banjo music wafted from a saloon. Mules led by soldiers moved heavy rocks from the nearby riverbed, evidently for use in the numerous construction projects within sight.

"Looks like chaos," mumbled Josh to himself.

Brother Uriah, his black hair framing a face that sported a thick shaving scar across the chin, was the muscular trail boss from Boston. He worked for the Methodists, guiding and protecting new missionaries to their posts. He thanked the captain of the wagon train and told him this was where his party would remain. The captain led the remaining fifty wagons to the north bank of the Arkansas River to make camp. They would be pressing on to Santa Fe the next day.

Nearby was a simple white church complete with a steeple and cross. Next to it stood a one-story stone administration building with a sign that read, "Cheyenne & Arapahoe Methodist Mission." Out of that building walked a sickly-looking white man and a tall Indian. Josh recognized the Indian. The white man wore a dirty black stovepipe hat that matched his suit. He coughed into a yellow-stained handkerchief.

Uriah brushed the dust off his knee-high boots then announced, "Folks, this is the mission director, Reverend Huelskamp. And this is his aide, Walking Elk."

Walking Elk stood head and shoulders above any other man at the fort. He also wore a soiled black suit and a dome-shaped felt hat with a round, flat brim.

"Brother Uriah, it is good to see you again," said Reverend Huelskamp.

"Good afternoon, Reverend." Uriah then introduced each of the new arrivals to the reverend and Walking Elk. "Reverend, I would like you to meet Oscar Devenish and his wife Eliza, Eli and Shirley Sullivan, and this young man is Joshua Frasier," said Uriah.

Josh shook hands with Walking Elk. "We met at Wesleyan University in Connecticut when you were there recruiting for the board of foreign missions. Isn't your name Sampson Wapiti?"

"That's the white-man's name the board members gave me. We're less formal out here. I'm glad to see my words had some effect," said Walking Elk in a deep voice. "Many of the Christians I spoke to believed their only duty was to warm a pew on Sundays. God bless you for coming to help my people."

Reverend Huelskamp enthusiastically shook hands with each of the new arrivals. He looked surprised when Oscar Devenish, instead of greeting him, angrily exclaimed, "Reverend, I would like to speak with you about the conduct of this Joshua Frasier while in Pennsylvania." The severe appearance of the man—with receding hairline, beard reaching his chest, holding a hoe as if it were a walking stick—matched his tone.

"Brother Oscar, not now," Uriah warned.

Rather than answering Oscar, the thin reverend hacked into his handkerchief then spoke to the group. "Ladies and gentlemen, welcome to our mission at Fort Wise. As you can tell, our little corner of the prairie has become a busy hub. You arrived just in time, as things are about to get busier. Recently, Congress sent the Indian Affairs commissioner to meet with all the regional tribes. You can see how large is the Arapahoe tribe camped to the south." He waved his arm in that direction. "Imagine another whole tribe of Cheyennes here as well! Remember the Lord said, 'The harvest is plentiful, but the laborers are few.' Never has this been more true than it is here at Fort Wise. I'll let you to get some rest, then in the morning I'll meet with all of you and explain more. Brother Uriah, could you have them at the officers' mess for breakfast at seven o'clock?"

"They'll be there."

That night, Josh lay in his bedroll listening to the noisy saloon. Michelle, his wife of three months, had died of smallpox only a month before. When he finally drifted off to sleep, he dreamt of her dark eyes and her long red hair that she let hang loose at bedtime.

At sunrise, he suddenly awoke. Uriah the trail boss was kicking the bottom of his feet.

"C'mon, Josh, get some coffee. There's something I want to discuss with you before we meet with Reverend Huelskamp." Uriah grabbed the coffee pot off the campfire and poured a cup.

Josh crawled out from under his covered wagon and stretched his cramped legs. He sat facing south, sipping from the hot tin cup. The Arapahoe camp covered more area than he had noticed the night before. Their lodges—decorated with hunting scenes—filled the entire bottom of the Arkansas Valley and a large herd of ponies grazed peacefully.

"Quite a view, isn't it?" said Uriah. "Take it all in while you can. In fifty years I bet those Arapahoes will all be gone. The arrival of the Indian commissioner cannot be good for the Indians."

"Why is the camp so smoky?"

"The women are making smoke with green leaves on their fires to ward off the mosquitoes and flies. But I didn't wake you to discuss Arapahoe insect control. Look, you're going through a painful experience right now. I need to know if your head is clear enough for this situation. If you don't think you can handle it, I'm sure the Board of Commissioners would understand if you returned to your mother's farm in Missouri. Heck, the staff at St. George's could even assign you to a church in New England if you want. Besides, you know the rule about having a wife."

"Brother Uriah, let's get something straight; I didn't come all the way out here just to turn around and go back to New England. Wife or no wife, I'm going through with this."

"Reverend Huelskamp will have the final say on that. He'll be the one to give you an assignment—if he keeps you."

"Where do you go from here?" Josh changed the subject.

"I'll head north to Fort Laramie and wait for the next arrival of replacements for our Willamette Mission in Oregon. Then I'll return by ship to Philadelphia and start the whole journey all over again."

Uriah then woke the others sleeping in their wagons. With a touch of humor he said, "Rise and shine! Try to make yourselves presentable as best you can."

"I am always presentable, Brother Uriah. The state of my attire should be the least concern of the ungodly heathens," said Oscar in a patronizing voice.

"For crying out loud, Devenish! Do we have to listen to your moralizing so early in the morning?" Josh said, staring into the fire.

"You two had better cease-and-desist or you'll find yourselves being sent home," warned Uriah. "Brother Oscar, unless you want a tomahawk between your eyes, do not refer to the Indians as ungodly heathens."

"That'd be some improvement," Josh muttered as he got up to leave.

The interior of the officers' mess added a touch of civilization to the frontier fort. For the missionaries, just being indoors for the first time in two months was a welcome relief. (One boat had taken them from Pittsburgh to St. Louis, and a smaller steamer had brought them to Independence.)

The windows of the officers' mess were adorned with white lace and set in creamy-yellow painted walls. Inside, Reverend Huelskamp greeted each of the new arrivals. Josh chose to sit near the Sullivans. After Michelle died, they had made sure he had a hot supper at the end of each day's journey. The Devenishes, though, were a different breed. Oscar had the warmth of a glacier and his wife Eliza could give lessons on snobbery to Queen Victoria. Their Puritan tactics in responding to the Great Commission lacked any kind of love for the people they were sent to serve and save.

The trail-worn group greeted their breakfast of scrambled eggs, bacon, biscuits and pancakes as if it were a savory feast. Josh's older traveling companions ate slowly, taking small bites. In contrast, Josh poured syrup over a stack of pancakes and devoured them.

Reverend Huelskamp sat at the head of the long table and began his orientation.

"Good morning to you all. Ladies and gentlemen. Again, welcome. You've all been thoroughly screened by the Board of Commissioners and I have complete faith in their judgment. Until now my staff consisted of only four people, myself included. Our task is daunting, so I'm pleased that you have answered the call.

"Obviously we are here to lead the Indians to the Lord, but their bellies must be fed and their medical needs met before that can happen. The Methodist Mission works closely with the army and the OIA—the Office of Indian Affairs, that is. We are still in the process of relocating from our old site upstream. Adding to the confusion, the OIA commissioner, since arriving here, has ordered all the plains tribes to assemble in this place, even though many of them do not get along. We have an ongoing problem with government employees and civilian contractors cheating the Indians and enslaving them with whiskey. Many of the Indian women are degraded, because their warrior husbands loan them out to the soldiers in exchange for a bottle.

"But enough of that for now. Let's get down to brass tacks, folks. I want to know your background and why each of you feels the Lord has led you here. Mister Sullivan, let's start with you."

"Both my wife and I were grammar school teachers in Lancaster, Pennsylvania. We are proud to be at your service, Reverend," stated Eli Sullivan in a pronounced oratorical voice.

"And at some point you heard the Lord calling you to educate the children of the Cheyenne and Arapahoe people?" asked the reverend.

"Indeed we have," declared Eli, who looked much like the bearded presidential candidate, Abraham Lincoln.

"Then we have a place for you," said Reverend Huelskamp, smiling. "As you can tell, Fort Wise is still under construction and it is my desire that a schoolhouse be built for the Indian children."

The reverend turned to Oscar. "And you, sir? What about you?"

Propped against the table next to Oscar was his hoe. His intense blue eyes grew wide. "My name is Oscar Devenish and this is my wife Eliza. I will teach these heathens the science of farming. A nomadic lifestyle can no longer be sustained in the Nineteenth Century. With the Bible I shall point them to the Lamb of God, and with this hoe I will show them a means of saving their famished bodies. Government annuities indeed! Remember, the apostle Paul said if someone doesn't work, neither should he eat.'"

Obviously Reverend Huelskamp was not immune to Oscar's knack for annoying people. "Brother Oscar, I hope you are not planning on dabbling in Indian affairs. Please leave that to the appropriate government agency. Expansion westward has all but depleted the traditional hunting grounds of the Indians, and I can assure you living on assigned reservations and receiving annuities is not their choice."

He turned to Josh, and a concerned look settled on his face. "How about you, young man?"

Josh had his mouth full of pancakes.

"Me?" he muttered, feeling his face heat up. He finished chewing and swallowed. "I have a teaching certificate from Wesleyan University. When Walking Elk paid a visit to the campus, he spoke of a need for the Bible to be translated into Cheyenne."

"Yes, that is correct. But ... you are aware of the Board of Commissioner's requirement that men are to be married? Brother Uriah has informed me of your loss. I am truly sorry. And I know this gives you a handicap. However, nobody else is able to perform the translation duties. Do you think you can handle the task?"

"Yes, sir. I excelled in my Hebrew and Greek studies."

"How were your grades in Greek?"

"*Aristi.*"

Reverend Huelskamp grinned. "Very well. Other missions have made exceptions, so I'll go out on a limb. You'll find the Algonquian languages just as challenging as your college courses. There's another thing, though. Being as fresh out of school as you are, how are you set financially? We've seen many people come out here with good intentions but unprepared for the cost."

"My father-in-law ... that is, my late wife's father, was a man of means and donated a generous sum of money for our mission."

"Well, that settles it then. Your skills will be most useful here."

"Thank you for giving me this chance. The Lord sent me to witness to the Cheyennes and I will remain with them—wherever they may be." Josh piled three more pancakes onto his plate.

"Hopefully the mystery of their whereabouts will soon be resolved." Reverend Huelskamp stopped abruptly as two men entered the dining area—a frail, nervous man in a new brown suit and a weathered mountain man.

The mountain man was a tad less than six feet and clad entirely in fringed buckskin. A wiry red beard covered his hatch-shaped face. Out from under his crumpled slouch hat bushed wild flames of red hair. A large Bowie knife, sheathed in fringed leather decorated with Cheyenne beads, hung from his belt.

The man in the suit appeared in his late twenties, prematurely bald. Gruffly he stated, "We're a bit behind schedule, Reverend. We were getting last-minute instructions from Uncle Alfred ... uh, I mean Judge Greenwood. I'm his personal aide and assistant chief of staff."

"Have we met before?" Reverend Huelskamp asked, hinting for a name.

"No," the commissioner's aide answered, avoiding eye contact.

"Will the commissioner be available this morning?"

"I don't think so. ... Sir, this is Mister Ogle—"

"The name's Peter Ogle, but everybody in these parts knows me as Porcupine Pete," said the mountain man. He vigorously shook hands with the reverend, then took a seat at the far end of the table. "We've met before, though it's been a coon's age."

"Ah, yes, we met when I first traveled the Oregon Trail. How have you been, Porcupine? I remember saying a few prayers for you back then. Did it do any good?"

"You're darn tootin' it did." Porcupine scraped a generous portion of scrambled eggs onto a plate and grabbed two biscuits with his dirty hand. "My horse played out on me near Chimney Rock, and I walked pert-near twenty miles before a wagon train found me. Got snowed in at Cucharas Pass in the winter of '51. The snow plumb buried my cabin and I had to boil the broth out of my boots to keep from starvin'. Lord only knows how I out-ran them painted devils in the Blackfoot country. They wore nothin' but moccasins and war paint. I guess the good Lord figured I needed my scalp more than they did. Believe me, they had plenty already."

Eliza Devenish fanned herself as if she were about to faint. "Oh, dear me!"

"Then there was the time I found myself on the edge of a cliff wrestlin' a grizzly b'ar bigger than—"

"Ahem!" the commissioner's aide interrupted and returned the conversation to the subject at hand. "After the assembly of the plains tribes, Commissioner Greenwood wants to meet with the Cheyennes and Arapahoes to discuss some modified conditions of the government's treaty. Two army messengers went out three weeks ago to find the Cheyennes, but they haven't returned."

"And they're not likely to, either," interjected the reverend. "If they didn't get lost, they may have bumped into a band of hostile Kiowas."

"That's the only kind of Kio-ways there is," offered Porcupine. "You're prob'ly right, Preacher, since they have a war party approachin' from the east."

"The Kiowas have a war party coming here?" The commissioner's aide asked in alarm. "In heaven's name, man, why didn't you tell me this before?"

Porcupine calmly chewed a biscuit. "You was wantin' to know if I could find the Cheyenne fer you. I don't recollect nothin' said about the Kio-way. Besides, you wantin' Kio-ways to break bread with Cheyennes ... what did you think was gonna happen?"

"I guess we didn't consider that. Well, this news advances the timetable considerably. Reverend, would you accompany Mister Ogle to find the Cheyenne camp? My uncle says Black Kettle trusts you. He'll move his people here if you tell him to."

Reverend Huelskamp surveyed his dining companions. "I am too old to be riding across territory full of hostile Indians while looking for the friendly ones. Perhaps one of my new volunteers here would be willing to accompany Mister Ogle and speak to Black Kettle with Christian love on behalf of the Methodist Mission."

Porcupine grinned at again being called "Mister Ogle."

But the commissioner's aide desperately and pleadingly turned to the pilgrims. "Will any of you gentlemen go?" Oscar and Eli turned whiter than milk and imperiously refused, their wives beside them shaking their heads as well.

"What about you, Flapjack?" Porcupine addressed Josh, who sat alone, no fearful wife beside him.

"Well, I don't know. I'm sort of on probation."

"I made no mention of a probationary period, Brother Joshua," said the reverend with finality. "Mister Ogle—that is, Porcupine—is more than capable of finding the Cheyennes, but they will be hesitant to return to the agency headquarters. I would like someone from the mission staff to help alleviate their fears. Should the Board of Commissioners consider recalling you, having the experience of such a task would work in your favor."

Josh cut into another syrup-smothered pancake with his fork. "All right, I'll go."

"Is this young man satisfactory?" the reverend asked Porcupine.

Porcupine smothered a biscuit with honey and answered, "That boy is green as grass, but he's got more bark on him than them other two cream puffs."

The commissioner's aide said, "It's settled! I'll inform Uncle Alfred." He rose and ran from the building like a spooked jackrabbit.

"Come on Flapjack, let's get you geared up so we can skee-daddle before things get too hot around here." Porcupine wiped his hands with the tablecloth.


Josh led Porcupine back to the missionaries' camp. When they reached Josh's covered wagon, Porcupine set about taking inventory of everything that came with it. The items were mostly wedding gifts.

"You got some real nice things here. But they won't amount to a hill-o'-beans on the trail. Might fetch a fair price at the trading post, though. Them oxes can still be recruited. Come on, let's head over there."

"What do you mean by recruited?"

"Meaning after Jack fattens them again, he can sell them at a higher price."

The perimeter of Fort Wise was a giant square with only the buildings on the north line complete. The fort's administration building afforded a place for people to conduct business. Bent's

Trading Post was situated on the northwest corner, between the north line and the church.

In front of the trading post, they found Indian Affairs Commissioner Alfred Greenwood and Reverend Huelskamp waiting for Porcupine. The commissioner's entourage lingered in front of the administration building.

"In heaven's name, Reverend, where is the commanding officer?" asked Commissioner Greenwood.

"Sorry, Judge, I am not his caretaker. Maybe he overslept."

Judge Greenwood explained, "I brought with me a shipment of annuity goods and gifts from Washington, but they will not be distributed to any of the tribes until the Cheyennes are here."

"This is Joshua, my new associate who I told you about. He'll accompany Mister Ogle in finding the Cheyennes," said the reverend.

"Pardon me, Preacher, but we can't go no place until this boy is properly outfitted. So if y'all will excuse us." Porcupine gave a mock salute and led Josh into the trading post.

The stone-and-log building held all the necessities for life on the frontier. A large rack of elk antlers hung over the door. An Indian man in his thirties with black shoulder-length hair and pock-marked face stepped out from behind the counter.

"Flapjack, I'd like you to meet Jack Smith," said Porcupine. "Jack's pappy has been livin' with the Blackfoot, Sioux, and Cheyenne long before I got here, and I've been here darn near forever. He speaks the languages of them three tribes plus Mexican."

"You mean Spanish?"

"That too," affirmed Porcupine.

Josh shook hands with Jack. "The name's Joshua. I'm pleased to meet you."

"Likewise." Jack didn't sound as tough as he looked. "Where are you off to?"

"I'm not sure."

"We's headin' north lookin' fer yer mama's people." Porcupine said, gazing at the collection of firearms.

"The buffalo are getting harder to hunt, so you'll probably find them along the Republican River," said Jack. "What will you need, Porcupine?"

"Flapjack here has got a fine Conestoga wagon filled with goods—and four oxes to boot."

"A Conestoga and oxen, huh? Let's have a look."

After an hour, Josh exchanged most of the items he had brought from the east. He held on to a silver thimble he had given Michelle in lieu of an engagement ring. He would have given her a ring, but the Puritans in her community insisted all gifts had to have a practical use. He also kept the saddle and tack he had brought from his mother's farm near Independence, Missouri.

In return for the other items, he acquired a fine bay gelding, a pack mule, plenty of nonperishable foods, a Colt .44 Dragoon with a holster, and a Sharps 1853 hunting rifle. Jack had given him more than a fair trade.

Outside they found Commissioner Greenwood, a well-fed man with bushy sideburns, waiting. Three Comanche chiefs were approaching him. Expressionless, the chiefs shook hands with the commissioner. One chief simply stated, "Christ is over us, and we should be good children."

Excited to see a Christian Indian, Josh started to introduce himself, but stopped when he heard Greenwood's angry response.

"You have not been good children, and your constant attacks along the trail prove me correct. No gifts or annuities shall be given to the Comanche."

Josh kept his thoughts to himself, then, and saddled his horse.

While strapping on his Walker-Colt .44, Porcupine shook his head. "If'n a war party of Kio-ways ain't enough, this danged fool has to go rilin' the Comanches."

# Chapter 2

## FRIENDLY ENOUGH INDIANS

After Josh and Porcupine rode ten miles up Adobe Creek, they stopped to build a campfire and rest. Porcupine smoked his corncob pipe and recollected to Josh his life on the frontier.

"The army hired me as a guide durin' the war with Mexico. We stopped fer chow somewhere in Chihuahua, and the cook put a tortilla in my left hand while the cap'n put a letter of termination in my right. I'll be dog-goned if'n that cook didn't take the tortilla back. Later, while huntin' buffalo, I was recruited fer what was called a scientific expedition into Oregon Territory. It was led by Cap'n Fremont himself. While we camped at Klamath Lake, in the middle of the night a war party of Modocs attacked us. I tell you, I became a God-fearin' man that night. Right there in that pitch-black forest, with them screamin' devils makin' my hair stand on end, I asked Jesus into my heart."

Using his saddle as a back rest, Porcupine squirmed a bit to make himself comfortable and then continued his story. "During the march south the next night, I stepped on a porcupine. Nocturnal, I think they're called; night is when them critters come out. Anyways, that's how I got my name. The chief of scouts, Kit Carson, was the first to call me Porcupine Pete. Them quills went right through my boots and they hauled me outta there with a travois and horse. There was nothin' fer me to do 'cept read the Good Book all the way to Californy."

At dawn, Porcupine prepared biscuits, bacon, and coffee. "Get outta that bedroll, Flapjack, we've got a lotta hard ridin' to do." After breakfast, they mounted their horses and continued up the creek.

During the ride, Josh told Porcupine his story. "My getting religion wasn't as dramatic as yours. I was seventeen and sitting in church with my mother and brother on a hot Sunday morning when it dawned on me that I had never said the sinner's prayer. The pastor was preaching on an entirely different subject. I wasn't really listening. When the service ended I went to the altar and said that prayer."

"What about yer pa?"

"What about him?"

"You said you was a sittin' thar with yer ma and brother. Where was yer pa?"

"As far as I'm concerned, I never had one."

"I see." Porcupine scanned the low ridges of the prairie. "How did you get yerself out here?"

"I felt called to pursue a teaching degree from a Bible school back east. I worked as a blacksmith's apprentice and saved every penny. At the shop I met dozens of frontiersmen on their way down the Santa Fe Trail. I couldn't get enough of their stories about life amongst the Indians. Eventually I found myself praying for the Cheyennes. They're the tribe I wanted to be with. With God opening the appropriate doors, I went to Wesleyan University in Middletown, Connecticut. That's where I was recruited for the ABCFM."

"What's that?"

"That's where I went to Bible school."

"No, I mean what's them confounded letters?"

"Oh, the American Board of Commissioners for Foreign Missions."

"That's a mouthful."

"You're right," Josh agreed then continued. "At a Wednesday night service, Walking Elk spoke to the student body about the needs of the Cheyennes and his words hooked me. The next morning, I submitted my name for missions work out West. I was interviewed by an ABCFM panel at St. George's United Methodist Church in Philadelphia. I had never seen such a big church. The building dates all the way back to the days of the British."

"I take it you passed the interview." Porcupine watched the trees to their left and the endless prairie before them.

"Yeah, I was selected, but the board required me to get married first before going on the expedition."

"That's not a bad idea. Havin' a wife along is a comfort and helps keep a fella from fallin' into temptation. I'm no Bible thumper; but I believe ol' King Solomon said that he who finds a wife finds somethin' good and gets favor from the Lord."

Josh drew a deep breath. "That's pretty much what they told me. Don't know, though. I mean, why would God give me a wife only to let her die on the trail?"

Porcupine reined his horse to a stop and became serious. "Look at the fancy rig you got now and them new guns yer totin'. Did you get the money from shoein' horses? No, you didn't! You married into it. Did you get all that expensive silverware and dishes you used fer tradin', all by yer lonesome? Nobody knows why she was called home so soon, but even I can see that if 'n it weren't fer her, you'd be nothin' but a barefoot greenhorn."

Josh lowered his head. "Yeah, I guess you're right, but I figured Michelle and I would start government reforms on the Cheyenne reservation together."

Porcupine gently heeled his horse into walking forward again. "What's this about gov'ment reform?"

"Back East, I learned that the Indian tribes there have their own governing bodies. For example, the Iroquois tribe has a confederacy with elected council members and a chairman. They even have their own court system. Why can't that work out here? The Cheyenne reservation should govern itself. Indians would be subject to tribal law and the whites to territorial law. Indian towns could be established with functioning municipalities, schools, and churches. If it can be done in the eastern states then it can be done here. Brother Uriah grew tired of me talking about those dreams, but I didn't care. If I have any say in it, the Cheyennes will not become extinct like smaller tribes along the Missouri."

"And just how is you a plannin' on doin' that?"

"The selection board told me that the Indian agents will often hire the missionaries for certain positions, because we can be trusted. Career government bureaucrats are more likely to cheat the Indians than we are."

"That's true, if'n the agent ain't out to grease his *own* palms."

Josh thought for a moment. "I know I can't make any changes overnight, but if I could get one of those government jobs it would be a start. Maybe someday I could work my way up to becoming an agent. Then things would get done."

"An ambitious fella, ain't ya?"

That night they camped at a bend where the creek turned to the northwest. In the morning, after filling their canteens, they continued due north, leaving the creek behind. They kept a constant vigilance for Indians among the scrub grass, friendly or otherwise, and spoke very little. When they saw a cloud of dust on the horizon late in the afternoon, Porcupine signaled Josh to halt.

"What is it?" Josh asked in a loud whisper, feeling uneasy.

"Horses, but I can't tell how many. They're probably gettin' watered at Rush Crick, which is where I was plannin' to camp." Porcupine pulled from a fringed buckskin scabbard one of his two Hawken rifles. He handed the lead rope of his mule to Josh. "Hang on to Number Six and stay put until I get a hundred yards ahead."

Josh wanted to pull out his own rifle, but couldn't as he held the ropes of two mules and the reins of his horse. He watched Porcupine move farther and farther ahead. In the hot sun, sweat ran from under his hat and down his neck. The animals swished their tales at pestering flies. He wished he had a free hand to hold his canteen.

Porcupine disappeared over a draw. After five minutes, he appeared again and motioned Josh to come.

"Are they Kiowas?" Josh asked when he caught up.

"Nope."

"The Cheyenne?"

"Them neither."

"Then who?"

"Coupla white fellas I ain't seen before, with six Indian horses. They sure look outta place. Prob'ly headin' fer one of them mining camps." He removed his hat and scratched his head. "When they make camp and pasture their herd, we'll ride in and I'll say howdy. You don't say nothin'. I need you to look like one tough hombre. Pull yer hat down low and hold yer rifle up."

When the afternoon shadows grew long, Porcupine and Josh moved in. Outside a wooded area marking the course of Rush Creek, the six Indian horses grazed on grass and green leaves. Porcupine pointed to a brown-and-white pinto. "I've seen that one before." They proceeded with caution and soon smelled smoke from a campfire and heard two loud voices laughing and talking. Porcupine's Hawken lay across the front of his saddle. Josh felt his skin crawl but held the Sharps as instructed.

The two strangers sat by a campfire near the water's edge. One handed a whiskey bottle to the other, who poured some into a tin coffee cup. Startled to see the sudden appearance of two visitors, they jumped to their feet.

"Ah, good afternoon," said the shorter, pudgy one. He was dressed in gray trousers and a tattered dirty coat separating at the seams. His derby hat looked as if it had been discarded by a tramp. The only quality thing he wore was a pair of Mexican riding boots.

"Afternoon. I'm Porcupine Pete."

A brand new Henry repeating rifle leaned against a tree trunk. Another was in a scabbard attached to a saddle draped on a log. No side-arms were visible.

The shorter one quickly glanced at the Henry against the tree then back at Porcupine. He sported a full mustache, but the rest of his face was covered with razor stubble. He nervously wiped his hands on the front of his coat. "I'm Joe Blackburn and this here is Nate Talbot."

Talbot flashed him an angry glare.

Blackburn continued, "We just got out … ah, well, that is, we ran into some trouble with the sheriff in Salina. Didn't we, Nate?"

"That's right! He accused us of running a rigged game. Shoot, it ain't our fault those cow punchers can't play cards." Talbot's voice rose to a high pitch. He was thin, had long brown hair pulled back into a ponytail, and wore an English flat-cap. The city clothes he wore had probably been thrown away by the same tramp who once owned Blackburn's derby, and his black boots were smeared with horse dung.

"What're you doin' in these parts?" asked Porcupine.

Blackburn said "Mining" at the same time Talbot said "Horse trading." Blackburn moved his fingertips side-to-side in front of his mouth and glared at his friend. "What we meant is that we're heading for the mining camps around Denver and we'll need to sell some of them horses in order to file a claim."

"Uh huh." Porcupine grunted. "Have you boys seen any Kio-ways around here?"

"No, we ain't. Can't say we've been looking for 'em neither," said Talbot.

"We came out here from Fort Wise and the word goin' round is that the Kio-way is on the warpath," said Porcupine.

"Kiowa on the warpath?" Panic rose in Talbot's voice. "Dog-gone-it, Joe, you said there weren't no hostiles between Fort Riley and Denver."

"Ah, shut up. Can't help it if situations change," said Blackburn.

Porcupine continued, "So if'n you boys got somethin' that belongs to them it would behoove you to make a bee-line to Denver before the sun gets hot in the mornin'."

"Much obliged." Blackburn nervously tipped his hat.

Porcupine reined his horse to the left and headed upstream. Josh followed silently. Before they were out of ear range, they heard Talbot whine, "Why did you have to tell them our real names? How come you didn't use the names of them other fellas in the jailhouse?"

"I couldn't think of their names right off," yelled Blackburn.

"And everyone thinks I'm the dumb one."

"Ah, shut up!"

The voices faded and after a mile, Porcupine halted. "We'll stay here fer the night."

Josh dismounted and asked, "What do you make of those two?"

"I think they're a couple no-goods makin' their way to the gold fields. Those are stolen Kio-way horses. And I'll tell you somethin' else, that pinto belongs to a Cheyenne warrior named Sleepin' Wolf. That don't make no never mind to the Kio-way, they stole it fair-and-square and they're gonna be lookin' fer it."

Josh thought for a minute. "You mean that pinto and those other stolen horses could bring the Kiowas here?"

"That's exactly what I mean."

"Shouldn't we keep riding?"

"Can't do it, Flapjack. These animals are plum tuckered out, and so am I. If'n them Kio-ways come this way they'll most likely follow the trail of the two jaybirds downstream and bump into them first. It's best we keep a cold camp tonight."

They ate a dreary meal of salted beef and hardtack washed down with canteen water. The animals remained packed, saddled, and picketed near the stream.

It was a long, sleepless night. They propped themselves against tree trunks about ten yards apart, but couldn't see each other. They listened for the slightest sound. Josh's hungry stomach sounded like someone moving furniture on a wood floor.

Just before sunrise Josh heard horses pass by on the other side of the creek. They continued traveling to the northwest. When all was quiet again, Josh moved over to Porcupine. "What do you make of that?"

"Probably them jaybirds with the stolen horses, but I'd like to make sure before we ride out into the open."

"Do you want me to ride over to their campsite and make sure?"

"Yeah, but wait till there's more sunlight."

An hour later, Josh mounted his horse and retraced the route back to the strangers' camp. A quarter mile away, he tied the horse's reins to a tree branch and set out on foot with his rifle. Before long he found the vacant campsite. He snooped around looking for nothing in particular then strolled over to three large trees growing close together on the far side to see what was beyond them. Now in the middle of the trees, he only saw more cottonwoods that followed the course of the creek.

When he turned around to cross the empty campsite again, he heard horses heading his way. He remained in the trees trying to figure the last time he had felt this scared. Four Indian warriors rode into the campsite and came to a halt. They wore hare-bone breastplates, breechclouts and bison hair pieces. War paint covered their stern faces, and each carried a single-shot rifle.

Josh didn't know his heart could beat so loud.

He barely breathed as the warriors slid off their bareback horses and knelt to examine the fresh tracks. Five minutes later, forty more mounted warriors arrived. The four scouts showed the others what they had found and pointed to the northwest. They loudly spoke to one another and one glanced toward the grouping of trees where Josh stood. Since the large group of warriors stood between him and his horse, Josh became even more anxious. But at that point, a scout discovered warm coals in the fire pit and they all leaped on their horses and galloped away.

Josh exhaled and gave a prayer of thanks. Cold sweat soaked the back of his shirt. Failing to wait and see if others guarded the rear, he ran across the campsite and the quarter mile to his horse. Relieved, he found the brown bay nonchalantly munching on grass. When at last he rode into his own campsite, he found Porcupine lying behind a log with one of his rifles, watching the far bank.

Josh jumped off his horse and crouched next to the mountain man. "I saw a bunch of armed Indians where those two fellows were staying."

"Yup, I seen 'em. They was Kio-ways all right, because my left ear was tinglin'. If'n they was Comanche it would've been my right. It's a good thing we come across those two scoundrels to keep them painted devils off our trail. Come on."

Back on their horses, they dashed across the creek and entered a draw. They made good time riding over one grass-covered hill after another. Then Josh took the lead ropes of both mules and went on ahead so Porcupine could watch for anyone approaching their rear. They plodded along the rest of the morning in this fashion, seeing only mule deer and grouse.

At noon, Josh saw people riding horses off in the distance ahead of him. Other horses pulled travois. They also rode north, but at a slower pace than Josh. As he got closer he saw they were Indian women and children with a few old men.

Some older boys on swift ponies left the group and rode circles around him while making playful whooping sounds. With each pass they came a little closer and Josh worried they'd try to take his supplies. The mules pulled their ears back and rolled their eyes. He made his way into the midst of the women riders who held the lead ropes of their pack horses. The women looked at him with curiosity then at each other, laughing. A distinguished-looking old chief with long gray hair rode to their right and watched Josh carefully. Josh noticed one attractive young woman wearing a plain red robe who glanced at him briefly with a look of indifference. Her long hair was not braided like the other women. A girl of about two years of age sat in front of her on a pony.

Five minutes later, Josh noticed the woman's pony had closed the distance to his horse. The red-robed young lady was at his immediate right staring straight ahead. Josh wasn't sure, but he thought she may have given him a second glance by only shifting her eyes. Their horses pressed against each other. She gave Josh an angry look and lifted her right hand that held the bridle's single rein, implying he should watch where he is going.

"Hey, what's going on here?" Josh demanded. "You weren't

anywhere near me and then you purposely guided your horse to bump into mine!"

Their knees touched but she looked straight ahead as if nothing happened. Josh held his tongue; he really didn't mind it that much. With sidelong glances he studied her full face and almond-shaped dark eyes. Behind those eyes must lie some secrets. Her face—though toughened by prairie winds—was somehow beautiful.

"I have a feeling you're really not angry." He knew she couldn't understand him. In this distracted state, Josh felt something heavy strike him across his left shoulder. There was Porcupine, glaring at him and holding a coiled rope.

"Ouch! Dog-gone-it, Porcupine, what did you do that for?"

"Fer bein' a pea-brained flatlander who doesn't have the sense God gave a goat, that's what fer. We was suppose to avoid contact with the Indians until we found the Cheyenne camp."

The Indian lady in the red robe reined her pony away from the two white men.

"Now look what you did. What's the problem, anyway?" asked Josh. "These Indians seem friendly enough."

"These are Kio-ways, that's the problem. Look around ya, Flap-jack. Do ya see any warriors?"

"No."

"That's because they were that bunch we were hidin' from this mornin'. These here are their wives and kinfolk. After they catch those two jailbirds, they'll be goin' to wherever this group is headin'."

"Sorry, I didn't think about that." Josh looked around. They were now completely surrounded by the women and older boys. "How do we get out of here?"

"Wiggle out as best we can. There's only one more creek before the Republican and that's where they're prob'ly headed. Maybe, if'n we get far enough ahead, we'll lose 'em before dark."

As Porcupine and Josh tried to break away from the group, several women blocked their way. The one in the red robe flashed Josh a look of concern then concentrated on the trail ahead. The old chief rode next to them and spoke in Kiowa while using sign language.

"He says we should ride with them," Porcupine interpreted. "There's plenty of bad Injuns about, and we'll be safe with them."

"What bad Injuns is he talking about?"

"To a Kio-way a bad Injun is a Cheyenne."

"Isn't that good news? After all, we're looking for the Cheyennes."

"Well, I sure ain't gonna tell no Kio-way chief that! Not yet. Guess I'm gonna have to tell him sooner or later, but I'll do it tactfully. Careful what you say, his English may be better than he's puttin' on."

The chief held his hand horizontally and made a wavy motion then hooked his index fingers on the sides of his head like horns.

"Tomorrow or the next day they'll move east with the warriors and hunt buffalo and then they'll have plenty of robes to trade." The mountain man also made signs. "I told him we'll camp with 'em tonight, but we'll keep movin' north in the mornin'."

Late afternoon, they reached a creek that ran lazily through groves of cottonwoods. Clear water rippled over its sandy bottom. Porcupine had Josh stand back while some of the women removed the heavy packs and saddles off the tired animals. The mules grazed with their herd, but the horses were picketed nearby.

An older woman gruffly ordered the girl in the red robe to offload a tepee from a travois. Josh moved to help her, but Porcupine called him back. "Don't even think about it. Fer you to do a woman's work would be an insult to her and an embarrassment to yourself."

"So what do we do?"

"We do what the Kio-way men do; not a darn thing."

Some of the children approached and pointed to their open mouths.

"I think they're hungry," observed Josh.

"I never knew an Indian who wasn't. Can't really blame them, though; I've been thar plenty a' times myself." Porcupine grabbed a leather bag of salted jerky and handed out the pieces. "Well, by golly, there is somethin' we can do! Let's go bring in some fresh meat. This'll be a good time to try out yer buffalo gun."

Josh retrieved his Sharps rifle and a box holding ten .52 caliber cartridges wrapped in nitrate-treated paper. With a satchel draped over one shoulder, he followed Porcupine across the creek to the spur of a hill. A large herd of elk moved through a draw and headed toward the water.

Porcupine picked out two large bulls with wide racks and assigned one to Josh. "Get that one to the right who's munchin' on the grass. Let me know when yer ready." He was lying prone on the ground aiming the Hawken.

"They're both munching on grass."

"Well, dag-blame-it, you do know which one is to the right don't you?"

It was the first time Josh had ever loaded a rifle from the breech. With the round in place, he took aim. "Ready."

"When I count to fer, go ahead and shoot."

"Four?"

"Okay, on three then."

The Sharps kicked hard, but Josh saw both elk knocked off their feet before black powder smoke shrouded the immediate area. "By golly, Flapjack, you got 'im. That was one fair piece a' shootin'."

"Thanks. You did pretty good yourself."

"Huntin' game in these parts is easy, but them days are closin' fast. In fact it's gettin' downright impossible fer the Indians as their land keeps disappearin'." Porcupine reloaded the Hawken with a ramrod. With the gun ready, he started back to camp.

"Aren't we going to field dress those elk?" Josh asked.

"Nope, the ladies will take care of that too."

At the camp, Porcupine told the head matron where the two elk were located. She assigned a group to take a couple of pack horses and retrieve the game. The girl in red was also ordered to go. She glanced at Josh when she passed, but did not smile or speak. By now she had put the robe away and wore a gray thread-bare dress and deer-hide leggings that sagged at her ankles.

Porcupine and Josh made their camp near the creek, a hundred yards from the nearest lodge. Josh built a fire and put on the coffee pot.

"I'm goin' over to the chief's lodge to jaw with him a spell," said Porcupine.

Josh poured himself a cup of coffee and sat on a fallen tree trunk. Lo-and-behold, ten of those Kiowa ladies came to pay him a visit. Josh looked for the red-robed one, but she was not among them. They brought large portions of raw elk meat on sharp sticks. Fresh-roasted meat was good, but with bread it was even better; so they pestered Josh for any additional food in the packs. Remembering what Porcupine had told him, he said, "I won't cook you anything, but you're welcome to whatever ingredients I have." They didn't understand a word, but gathered flour, cornmeal, and yeast.

After an hour of frenzied work, the ladies served Josh fire-baked bread and roasted elk. He enjoyed the bread but found the meat grossly underdone. Afraid of giving offense, he refrained from returning the bloody meat to the fire. The women sat around the campfire talking and laughing as they ate. For dessert, they each filled a spoon from Porcupine's jug of blackstrap molasses. Afterwards, they thanked Josh and returned to their camp.

Josh was attempting to reorganize the packs when the red-robed girl walked by. She didn't acknowledge him. Not wanting to miss an opportunity to speak with her alone, though, he impulsively reached out and grabbed her hand. She pretended to be angry but only half-heartedly tried to pull away. When Josh let go, she didn't leave. She asked him a question in her language, and Josh figured she wanted to know why he had stopped her.

He motioned for her to sit next to him on the fallen tree and offered her meat and bread. Cautiously, she accepted. While eating, she grunted and belched her thanks. He liked her shiny black hair, untied and hanging down to her waist. Around her neck she wore a crude wooden crucifix on a leather strand. Mustering his courage,

Josh patted the tree trunk to his right, indicating he wanted her to sit closer. She touched her chest with her right hand and didn't budge. Josh moved to the left, then she did likewise.

Before the strange game could progress, Porcupine returned from the chief's lodge, where a similar dinner had been served. "His name is Chief Sitting Bear. He says they're stayin' here until the warriors return. How're you two gettin' along?"

"Oh, just dandy, I guess." Josh felt awkward. "It would be nice if we could communicate. I don't even know her name."

Porcupine tilted his head and studied the Indian girl. He tapped his left middle and index fingers with the ones on his right and then pointed at her. With her right hand closed, she held it above her head and quickly extended her fingers, and then repeated the motion in front of her mouth. Then she made other gestures like a bird flying away.

"Shoot, even a mule-headed Missourian like yerself could figure that out. Sunflower. That's her name. Says her child's name is Little Dove." Thinking again, he asked her, "Is you Kio-way?"

"That doesn't even make sense in English," said Josh.

"Hush." Porcupine held up his two index fingers and moved them from his right eye to the back of his right ear, and asked, "Kaui-gu?"

Sunflower swung her right hand toward her chest.

"That means 'No'. Don't know why they can't turn their head side to side like everyone else," said Porcupine.

Sunflower moved the edge of her right index finger across the top of her left one in a single cutting motion.

"Cheyenne," interpreted Porcupine.

"She's Cheyenne? Maybe she could lead us to their camp!"

Porcupine folded his arms while shaking his head. "She ain't here by choice, Flapjack. More than likely she belongs to one of them Kio-way braves. It's a sad fact, but to these Indians, women are nothin' but property to be traded, like horses. Oh, they would never sell one of their own. But Lord help an Indian maiden who is captured by an enemy tribe."

Sunflower told them of her background and Porcupine translated: "She says she was married to a half-breed French trapper whose mother was a Pend d'Oreille. They lived with his mother's tribe far to the north where she was terribly abused. There were some black-robe missionaries livin' with the Pend d'Oreille, and she accepted their faith. No matter how bad the beatings, she always found comfort in Jesus. After the spring thaw they moved south. When she was with child, the trapper traded her and a horse to the Kio-ways fer a prettier Ute squaw."

"Ask her if she'll meet me here tomorrow," said Josh.

"Now hold on there. Come tomorrow we ain't gonna be nowhere around here, 'cause we're leavin' at first light. It's gettin' dark. I'm gonna have one last look round the camp."

When Porcupine left, the woman in charge came over and ordered Sunflower back to the Kiowa camp. Sunflower scurried away.

That night Josh slept soundly near the campfire. At sunrise he felt Porcupine kicking the bottom of his feet. "Get up, Flapjack. Take yer horse and bring them mules in, so we can get 'em packed and on our way."

Josh pulled himself back into the saddle and rode to the section of prairie where the Kiowa ponies grazed. He had gathered the mules and was starting back toward camp when he caught sight of riders far to the south. He hurried to rejoin Porcupine.

He found Sunflower waiting for him. Jumping out of the saddle he greeted her with a smile. "Good morning!"

She handed him a piece of hot-off-the-fire elk meat on a stick.

Porcupine was bridling his horse. "Eat it and get yer mule packed. We need to hightail it outta here before unwanted visitors arrive."

"I don't know if I can pack that fast. Visitors are almost here."

"What?" exclaimed Porcupine. "You love-struck knucklehead, what are you talkin' about? If you saw somethin', why didn't you tell me?"

"I just did."

"Well, forget the pack. Get back on your horse and let's scoot."

"Too late." Josh took a deep breath, trying to remain calm. Sunflower pressed against him and he reached his arm around her. She was trembling. *No wonder*, Josh thought. She likely suffered plenty of abuse from her male owner as well as laboring as a slave for all the warrior wives.

Into their camp rode four mounted warriors, each with a leveled rifle.

# Chapter 3

## TEPEE ETIQUETTE

J osh recognized the four warriors as the same scouts he had seen the previous morning. Their faces remained painted and they shouted unintelligible orders. One of them let out a high-pitched yell, evidently signaling others behind them to hurry.

"Don't make any sudden moves," Porcupine warned.

Pandemonium broke out in the camp when the other warriors arrived. The families enthusiastically welcomed the men, but the warriors focused angrily on the two strangers. In the confusion, Sunflower's daughter, Little Dove, ran to her mother's side. Porcupine and Josh found themselves surrounded by forty-four hostile warriors, all pointing weapons at them.

The women frantically tried to clarify that the visitors had treated them well, but the women's words had little effect on the warriors. The chief came out of his lodge and chastised his men and their sub-chief.

"Ol' Sittin' Bear is givin' them boys quite a tongue lashing," explained Porcupine. "He's tellin' them how we fetched game fer their wives and kids while they went searchin' fer them stolen ponies."

The warriors lowered their weapons and listened to the heated discussion between the chief and the leader of the war party.

The chief wore a magnificent bonnet of eagle feathers and carried his peace pipe. "Where are the stolen ponies, White Bear, and where are the thieves who took them?" Porcupine interpreted for Josh.

White Bear wore a head piece made of red-dyed porcupine quills. Red war paint covered the lower half of his face and the right side of his head was shaved. The front of his left shoulder sported a yellow hand print. "We had the thieves within sight. Then many soldiers appeared from the north. There was no choice but to let them go and for us to return."

"Blue coats from the north?" Sitting Bear wondered out loud. "They must be protecting the white men who are obsessed with those yellow rocks. I have learned there are also many soldiers to the south on the Arkansas."

"Yes, that is where these two came from. We followed their tracks all night." White Bear glared at Josh. "Why did they ride in this direction?"

"I have smoked with this man called Porcupine, and he tells me he is on business for the Great White Father. All tribes are to meet on the Arkansas before the first snow. He is on his way to inform the Cheyenne. Our bands under the leadership of Little Mountain are in that area now, but I have not received word if they will go to the fort peacefully. I have given this man my word that the Kiowas will not harm him or his companion."

"Did you promise his friend my Cheyenne squaw?" demanded White Bear.

Before Porcupine could translate, the warrior grabbed Sunflower and threw her to the ground. "Go back to my lodge, Cheyenne dog, and I will deal with you later."

"Leave her alone." Josh tried to shove the warrior chief, but he didn't budge.

*What have I done?!* Josh thought. *This guy is solid as an oak.*

"Lord help ya, look what you've gone and done. Now you gotta fight him!"

"But I don't want to fight him!"

"Well you started it, so do yer best or he'll beat you to a pulp."

Enraged, White Bear attempted to grab Josh the way he had Sunflower, but received a busted lip for his effort.

"Nice goin', Flapjack. Make him madder than he already is."

Veins bulged on White Bear's forehead as he reached his boiling point. He tried to get Josh in a bear hug, but Josh threw a couple more jabs to his face and ducked.

The other warriors gathered round and loudly made wagers.

"Don't let him get a hold of ya, or he'll squeeze yer gizzard through yer gullet. And don't go fer yer gun, or they'll kill us both," shouted Porcupine.

The two fighters faced each other, moving clockwise then counter-clockwise. Several warriors jokingly taunted their leader. Josh kept backing away until someone pushed him into the arms of White Bear. That was exactly what the warrior chief wanted. His muscular arms tightened like a noose. Josh's face burned and he could feel himself growing faint. The Indian was greasier than a slab of bacon and smelt of smoke. With a desperate gasp of air, Josh head-butted White Bear in the face so that his nose matched his lip. That did the trick. White Bear grabbed his nose, trying to ease the pain.

Josh wanted to end the fight immediately, so he did the only thing he could think of. He launched a kick that planted the pointed toe of his boot under White Bear's breechclout. The warrior went cross-eyed, dropped to his knees, and then fell forward. He no longer held his nose.

The warriors became silent. Three of them went to aid their injured leader, but the chief ordered them to stop. White Bear rolled on the ground in pain, hardly breathing. The chief grabbed Sunflower by the arm then pressed her against Josh.

"That settles it. She's all yours, Flapjack!" Porcupine cackled.

Sunflower pointed to her daughter while speaking frantically. White Bear managed to sit upright. Blood ran from his nose and lip, and his face was swelling. He let out a string of angry words.

"He says you won the Cheyenne woman, but the little girl still belongs to him," said Porcupine.

Chief Sitting Bear acknowledged this to be true.

Still panting and shaking like a two-dollar scaffold, Josh wanted to know, "What do they mean 'I won her'? This thing you told me about, where they trade women like horses, is wrong. Little Dove is Sunflower's daughter, and she's coming with us."

He walked over to where the little girl stood with a group of women and tried to lift her. Immediately, three warriors strung arrows and forced him back. Still on the ground, White Bear seethed with anger and brandished a large knife. This did little to alleviate Josh's fear.

Sunflower looked directly into Josh's eyes and spoke. Porcupine translated freely. "She says very noble, but right now yer heart is bigger than yer brain." He let out another cackle and slapped his knee. "But she says if'n the little girl must remain here with the Kio-way, then by golly, so will she."

Sunflower gripped the front of Josh's shirt and conveyed with her eyes she wanted to leave with him and return to her people. Josh gently pulled himself away from her and pointed to the mule while looking at White Bear.

"No," the warrior chief shouted then spoke in Kiowa.

"Says he's got plenty of pack horses already," said Porcupine.

Slowly Josh unbuckled his gun belt and wrapped it around the large revolver in its holster.

White Bear refused it as well.

"He says he can't hunt with that hog leg. I would tell him he could kill an enemy with it, but he's likely to use it on you," said Porcupine still chuckling.

"I'm glad you find this amusing." Josh put the gun belt back on and walked to his horse. Reluctantly, he pulled his Sharps rifle from its scabbard and tossed the saddlebags over his shoulder.

The warriors whispered excitedly amongst themselves.

Josh returned to where White Bear sat, and presented the rifle to him. White Bear returned the knife to its sheath and stood up, wincing. He took the rifle from Josh and felt its weight then peered through its sights while aiming at a tree.

Josh offered a bandolier holding nine rounds.

White Bear grabbed the bandolier and nodded his approval.

The women released Little Dove and she ran over to her mother who knelt and hugged her. Josh reached into the saddlebags again and pulled out a box of ammunition. "I'll need a horse for them to ride." Porcupine translated.

White Bear grabbed the ammo. He then instructed a teenage boy to bring one of his many horses, with a bridle. The boy brought Josh a buckskin pony. White Bear walked to his tepee, admiring his new rifle.

"Dog-gone, Flapjack, you sure put that White Bear in his place. I'd hate to fall asleep during one of yer sermons."

"Maybe we should get going," suggested Josh.

"Maybe yer right. I'll get them mules packed while you take care of the ladies."

Josh threw a blanket on the pony's back and helped get Sunflower and Little Dove situated. Mounted and ready, Josh and Porcupine started north again. Sunflower showed them a trail that led directly to the Republican River. She rode in the middle to converse with Porcupine and still be next to Josh. After their midday meal, Josh let Little Dove ride with him. She gripped the saddle-horn and exclaimed over various animals and birds of the prairie. The little girl especially liked it when the horses accidentally flushed out pheasants. At one point, Josh noticed Sunflower had two large scars across each arm, and he asked her about them.

Sunflower spoke in Cheyenne. Porcupine translated, "She slashed 'em when her father was killed during a raid against the Utes." Then he added, "They do that fer some reason."

During the ride, Josh found sign language easy to learn and had limited conversations with Sunflower while saying the words in English. Sunflower did the same in her dialect. They made surprisingly fast progress learning each others' language.

In the late afternoon, they reached the river and made camp. Porcupine handed Josh his older Hawken rifle. "You can use this until we get back to the fort. Now let's go scare up some grub."

In a shady area under some cottonwoods, they found a three-point buck and two does drinking from the river. Porcupine aimed his Hawken and it roared like an angry dragon with a burst of flame and smoke. After a few seconds, the air cleared and they saw the buck lying still while the does loped up a hill wagging their short white tails.

"Should I have Sunflower bring a mule and haul it out of here?" Josh asked.

"You get the mule and haul it out yourself." Porcupine gave Josh a curious look. "We're not in the Kio-way camp no more, so you can go back to pullin' yer weight. And if'n yer gonna make her yer wife, you better learn what love is."

"Whoa, wait a minute! You're going mighty fast. I didn't say anything about making her my wife!"

"Then why did you start a fight with White Bear? That girl must have gotten to you somethin' fierce fer you to take on a killer like that."

Josh leaned back on a tree with his hands on top of the musket's muzzle. "I don't know why I did that. I was scared something fierce, but next thing I knew, I'm fighting that big Kiowa brave. It was like David and Goliath; somehow I felt I had help."

"You needed help. Did you see that yellow hand print on White Bear's shoulder? That means he's killed an enemy in hand-to-hand fightin'. He's killed more than one that way."

"The right side of his head was shaved. What does that mean?"

"That don't mean nothin'. He does that to keep his hair from gettin' tangled in his bow string. Now go fetch us a mule while I clean that buck."

Sunflower prepared a dinner of roast venison and beans. Josh said the blessing and Sunflower made the sign of the cross. After about ten minutes of concentrated eating, Josh's strength revived. "Which way do we go tomorrow?" he asked.

Porcupine paused between ripping off bites of the lean meat that had been wrapped around and roasted on a stick, resembling a turkey leg. He talked as he chewed. "We'll follow the river downstream, which should lead us right to the Cheyenne camp. I reckon we'll get to it in a day or two."

"How can you be sure?"

"I can't."

After the meal, Sunflower explained that the Cheyenne call themselves "Tsistsistas," and Porcupine said, "There's no English word fer it. Roughly, it means The People."

The next afternoon, when they caught sight of the Cheyenne camp far to the east, Sunflower perked up. For three winters she had not seen her people, she told them.

The huge circular camp straddled the river with hundreds of bleached buffalo-hide tepees. All the entrances faced east. Five warriors with lances rode out to investigate the newcomers.

Like the Kiowas, the Cheyenne warriors wore only breechclouts and moccasins in the late summer heat, but their faces were not painted and their hair was braided and wrapped in pieces of dried buffalo skin. They surrounded the visitors, who came to a halt.

Sunflower explained who her father had been and why the white men were here.

The warriors recognized her. One warrior told them to follow him into the camp. Another galloped ahead, summoning the chiefs to the meeting lodge.

They rode through the camp single file, Sunflower and Little Dove behind the lead warrior, Porcupine behind them, and Josh at the rear. The other warriors remained outside the camp watching for additional unannounced company. Everybody in the camp stopped their activities and stared at the visitors, while dogs ran and barked.

Josh breathed a prayer of thanks. Meeting Sunflower, overcoming White Bear, and arriving at the Cheyenne camp gave him a sense of providential care he hadn't felt since Michelle had died.

The large tepee of the chiefs sat on the south bank of the river. Painted a light orange, pictographs of bison and horses decorated its exterior. A red-sun patch was sewn at the rear.

The visitors dismounted and handed the reins to boys, who

watered the animals. The warrior told them to wait while he went inside.

Porcupine studied Josh's face. "Have you ever been invited into a tepee before?"

"Nope, can't say that I have." Josh pushed his hat back.

"All righty then, here's a quick lesson on tepee et … et … What's the word I'm a lookin' fer?"

"Etiquette?"

"That'll do. When we're invited in, we go to the right, and Sunflower must come in after us and go to the left according to their customs. Don't sit unless yer asked to and then you better do it. Eat everything they give you, tail and all. Don't pass between someone and the fire. Only the old folks can start a conversation, so say nothin' unless one of 'em speaks to you first. Last of all, when the head chief empties his pipe, it's time to leave."

The warrior returned and invited them in. Porcupine entered ahead of Josh followed by Sunflower, who carried Little Dove. A group of tribal leaders sat cross-legged on buffalo robes around a small fire with the smoke drifting out the small opening above. The two chiefs sat at the far end of the tepee, so they could see all who entered. Behind them hung an American flag between two lodge poles.

White Antelope was the oldest man in attendance. His braided, gray hair framed his deeply creased face. He wore traditional fringed buckskins, and his shield depicted his many coups. The other chief was Black Kettle, who wore a white shirt with a black vest and upon his head sat a rumpled top hat.

During the long ride, Porcupine had explained to Josh that Black Kettle headed the Council of 44, the central governing board of the Cheyenne tribe. Although respected by the tribe as a whole, the warrior societies received him coolly for agreeing too easily to government treaties that were never honored. The warriors still considered White Antelope their war chief, though it had been many winters since he last participated in a raid against the Kiowas.

Fortunately for Josh, both chiefs spoke English. White Antelope invited the visitors to sit at his left. "Porcupine, many snow falls have passed since we last smoked to honor our friendship. Yet today it is not friendship you have come here to discuss. But first, who is this young man you have brought to our camp? And how did you bring the woman Sunflower back to our people?"

After introducing Josh, Porcupine said, "I think Sunflower can tell her story better than me."

Black Kettle's hair was parted on the left and he wore a long shirt and buckskin leggings. When his mouth was closed it formed a lazy 'S' and no one could tell if he was smiling or frowning. He looked over at Sunflower and gave her permission to speak.

In the tribal language, she told about the abusive Pend d'Oreille she had married and then her days as a slave to the Kiowa. When told of Josh's fight that had set her free, the elders and chiefs laughed.

Sunflower was dismissed to visit the lodge of her mother's family. Josh's eyes followed her until he realized White Antelope was addressing him.

"White Bear is a mighty warrior who has more than one white man's scalp on his lance. Not long ago, our scouts heard the scalp dance of the Kiowa long into the night when there had been no war between our tribes. Yet the woman called Sunflower tells us you defeated this man without a weapon. How is this possible?"

Sweat ran down Josh's face in the hot tepee. "It wasn't something I did on my own. I think God helped me." There was no breeze though the bottom edge of the lodge skins were rolled a foot off the ground for ventilation and smoke was escaping from the hole at the top of the tepee where the tips of the lodge-poles were bound. Josh mopped his forehead with his sleeve, and waited.

The chiefs nodded. Black Kettle spoke. "Yes, you speak of the Great Spirit told to us by the Black Robes. The Great Spirit who created the earth, sun, and stars who we call *Ma'heo'o*."

"This woman of our people, whom you saved, tells us you wish to live among us and to speak further of *Ma'heo'o*," said White Antelope.

"That is true. I wish to learn the language of the Cheyenne and share my knowledge of the Great Spirit."

"For you to go against the warrior White Bear for one of our women shows that the Great Spirit dwells in you and no doubt his words are upon your lips. From this time, you will be known as Black Robe. After we speak with Kicking Horse, I am sure he will give his niece Sunflower to you as a wife," said White Antelope.

"Hold on there. Sunflower should be able to decide—" Josh felt Porcupine's elbow compacting his ribs.

Porcupine bared a large grin of yellow teeth and said to the chiefs, "Black Robe says he gratefully accepts Sunflower and won't slip under the blankets with her until he weds her proper in the lodge of the Great Spirit."

"Black Robe is a man of virtue. It is settled," said Black Kettle. "Now let us speak of the reason you have come. What news have you brought to our camp?" The elders all looked intently and expectantly at Porcupine.

"There is a fella sent by the Great White Father from the East who's now at Fort Wise with many gifts. His name is Greenwood and he is chief over all the Indian agents. He demands the Cheyenne gather at the fort post-haste. Yer kin, the Arapahoe, are there now. He has many gifts fer the whole lot of ya."

"I know this Greenwood," said Black Kettle. "He gave me this flag of your nation when I was in Washington."

"Well, I'm sure he'll be tickled pink to see ya."

Black Kettle's lazy-8 lips twisted into an unmistakable smirk. "I do not think Commissioner Greenwood will have pleasure at seeing me. It is not my friendship he seeks. His gifts are merely a way to placate us into ceding more land."

The elders spoke earnestly to each other, then White Antelope asked, "Why does Mister Greenwood wish us to leave here while we still hunt the buffalo?"

"I ain't exactly sure." Porcupine squinted one eye while speaking to the chiefs. "I got a notion he wants to jaw with you about a new treaty."

One of the council elders rose angrily to his feet. "For ten winters we have abided by the Fort Laramie Treaty and remained between the South Platte and Arkansas Rivers. As the whites crossed our land on their way to the mountains, we kept silent. Now they settle on our hunting grounds and their chiefs want a new treaty."

"My heart is heavy. I fear for our future," said Black Kettle.

"This fella Greenwood sent two messengers a couple of weeks ago to let y'all know of this pow-wow. I reckon they didn't make it," said Porcupine.

"We have received no visitors from the agency, but we remember the words of White Antelope concerning the recent scalp dance of the Kiowa. In the morning, we will go with you to the Arkansas River," said Black Kettle. "How many gifts did Mister Greenwood bring?"

"Many wagonloads."

"It is as I feared," sighed Black Kettle. He addressed the council. "But for now, let us smoke in honor of our old friend, Porcupine, and to this new friend, Black Robe."

Black Kettle produced a long wooden pipe with a red clay bowl shaped like a tomahawk. His fringed-buckskin tobacco pouch bore a pattern of twelve blue and white beaded rectangles. The chief packed a large wad of tobacco into the bowl using a tamping stick wrapped with brown-stained, red-and-white thread. Black Kettle pulled a twig from the fire and used its burning end to light the pipe. He took a couple puffs, then handed the pipe to White Antelope.

When his turn came, Josh weakly puffed and passed the pipe on. After the pipe had been sampled by all the men, Black Kettle tapped the rim of the bowl against a rock, emptying its ashes.


Josh and Porcupine started making camp west of the outer ring of tepees. Sunflower rode over on her pony and scolded them for attempting to do such an unmanly thing. She led them to her family's lodge instead.

Sunflower introduced them to her uncle, Kicking Horse, her younger sister, Day Star, her sister-in-law Butterfly, and her brother Spotted Bear.

"Is Bear a popular name with the Indians?" whispered Josh to Porcupine.

"You best mind yer Ps and Qs. The name an Indian tells you is only his nickname. It's considered bad medicine fer him to reveal his real one."

Since Cheyenne tradition frowned upon a man speaking to an older woman who was not a relative, Sunflower did not introduce her mother. She explained to them that her aunt had died nine years prior from smallpox.

The women unsaddled the horses and erected a small tepee. Spotted Bear gave Josh a Bowie knife in a buckskin sheath decorated with a mosaic of the sun in red and orange beads. Day Star then grabbed a club and chased a dog around the outside of the family tepee in preparation for the evening meal with their honored guests.

"Shucks, this family has taken a real shine to you. It ain't every guest who gets one o' them camp pooches fer dinner. The Cheyennes consider it a real treat," said Porcupine, easing onto a buffalo hide.

"I don't think I can eat dog," said Josh, also taking a seat while making a sour face and wondering if he might throw up.

"Well, you'd better. It will be an insult if'n you don't. Besides, dog ain't all that bad, especially when yer famished."

Porcupine and Josh ate a meal of boiled dog and buffalo tongue, and visited with the men late into the night. Sunflower sat next to Josh, resting her head on his shoulder while he visited with the men. Spotted Bear gave her an annoyed look for sitting by a man without invitation, which she ignored. Once she retired for the night, Josh headed for the small tepee he had to share with a snoring mountain man.

# Chapter 4

## THE SHRINKING RESERVATION

Before sunrise Josh woke to the sounds of Sunflower filling a bucket with fresh river water and, with help from Day Star, cooking a breakfast of buffalo meat for Josh and Porcupine. After breakfast the women took down their tepee, saddled the horses, and loaded the pack mules, while Josh took in all the sights and sounds of the camp coming to life. The chiefs were preparing for their long journey to the Arkansas River. They could travel faster without the women, children, and elderly.

A warrior, who looked to be a seasoned forty years, came over to Josh and Porcupine, bringing with him a younger version of himself. He wore a loose, white cotton shirt and buckskin leggings. The younger man's hair was unbraided, and he wore a breechclout and moccasins. His back and shoulders were horribly scarred, and from his neck hung an eagle bone whistle on a leather lanyard.

Porcupine said, "This here is Sleepin' Wolf and his son Makin' Medicine. He's askin', did we see his pinto in the Kio-way camp."

"No, but you recognized it at the camp of those two buffoons the Kiowas were chasing. Remember?" said Josh.

"I sure do."

Porcupine explained to Sleeping Wolf, in a butchered-Cheyenne dialect that made the Indian visibly cringe, that although the pinto had been stolen by the Kiowas, it was last seen running toward the mountains with two white men.

Sleeping Wolf thanked him then dejectedly walked away. The young man stared at Josh for a moment then silently followed.

"What happened to that boy's back?" Josh asked.

"That there Makin' Medicine completed the notorious sun dance when he was only fourteen. He's the youngest Cheyenne ever to do it, though his pappy didn't want him to go on the warpath yet. Now that he's eighteen he'll go ridin' with the warriors anyway, if there's a need to. He's also a darn good artist. Several warriors have paid him to decorate the outside of their tepees with pictures of their buffalo hunts and coup counts."

"What is the sun dance?

"Well, on a ceremonial ground, two logs about ten feet tall are erected. On top of them is another log actin' as a crossbeam. I reckon the length of the crossbeam depends on how many warriors are gonna take part. A medicine man inserts two sharp pieces of buffalo bone into either the muscles of the chest or the back. While other men lift the warrior up, the medicine man gets on a ladder and attaches strips of sinew that are hangin' from the crossbeam to the pieces of bone. The warrior is left to dangle until the bone pieces tear through his flesh. Buffalo skulls are tied to the warrior's ankles to speed the process along. Makin' Medicine hung there fer three days until he broke free."

"I can see intelligence in his eyes," said Josh.

The conversation ended as the chiefs, who had mounted their horses, summoned the two visitors to follow. Josh said good-bye to Sunflower, longing to wrap his arms around her. He'd been informed, though, that it was improper to show affection to a woman in public. He said, "I'll look for you when the tribe reaches the fort and—"

"Let's get a move on. We're burnin' daylight," called Porcupine.

Josh climbed into the saddle, waved good-bye, and fell in with the chiefs. He missed feeling the Sharps rifle under his thigh.

A few boys also came along to drive the herd of spare ponies. Everyone had their weapons at the ready in case of a surprise encounter with the unpredictable Kiowa.

"Hey Porcupine, why are the Cheyennes and Kiowas always at war?" Josh asked.

"Because they were forced out to these parts by the white settlers.

They're two different tribes, but both competin' fer the same game, water, and grassland. When two or more groups of people want the same piece o' land, there's gonna be trouble."


Late on the fourth day they reached the bustling Fort Wise and the sprawling Arapahoe camp on the far side of the river. The chiefs wore their finest robes and donned eagle feathered bonnets. A company of cavalry galloped toward them, and Porcupine took the lead. Behind him, the six head chiefs rode proudly abreast.

Without preliminaries, a nervous lieutenant spoke orders to Porcupine. "Have those redskins in front of the agency office within thirty minutes. Everybody is waiting. Judge Greenwood wants to speak to them right away."

Porcupine squinted one eye. "Them is Cheyenne chiefs, proven warriors in battle—every last one of 'em—and if'n you want yerself horse whipped in front o' your men, call 'em redskins to their faces."

Chief Lean Bear asked Porcupine what the arrogant blue coat had said. Porcupine told him the general message and White Antelope answered on their behalf.

Porcupine turned back to the lieutenant. "I reckon the judge is gonna have to wait till mornin'. White Antelope says they're tired after their long journey and can't be thinkin' about terms of a new treaty without sleep. They'll camp by the river and be at the agency building at first light. Fair enough?" He looked sternly at the lieutenant. "It'd better be, 'cause you ain't got no choice."

The lieutenant reined his horse to the right and waved his index finger overhead in a circular motion. Without another word, the troopers galloped back to the fort. The chiefs made their camp several miles downstream.

In the morning, Porcupine led them into the fort, which consisted of a series of buildings bordering a large, square parade ground with the American flag flying from a tall pole at the center. Some plain-looking houses stood near the southwest corner. The government leased the houses to the ABCFM families who filled the jobs of terminated employees. Reverend Huelskamp had his living quarters at the Methodist church, which was located north of the housing area. Also nearby were the civilian stables, the trading post, and a saloon that the frontiersmen liked to frequent. Two-story enlisted barracks comprised the western edge of the compound.

He stopped them in front of a wide, single-story stone building with a sign that read: "Upper Arkansas Indian Agency." The chiefs dismounted, but Porcupine and Josh remained in their saddles. Staged next to the building were ten covered wagons and four buggies with well-fed horses. The brown bays hitched to the buggies all wore blinders. Judge Greenwood's entourage hurriedly set up a canopy and a large table and chairs, then summoned the Arapahoe chiefs. Rocks held down maps and papers on the table. A collection of frontiersmen, soldiers, and newspaper reporters gathered to watch the proceedings. Small cottony clouds dotted the otherwise clear sky. A gentle, warm breeze blew from the east.

When Commissioner Greenwood emerged from the building and saw only twenty-two Cheyennes, he showed surprise. "Where are the others? I specifically stated the whole tribe was to report here."

An elderly man with dark hair stood at Greenwood's side acting as interpreter and helping to alleviate any concerns of the Cheyenne. "That there is William Bent," said Porcupine to Josh. "He married into the tribe twenty-five years ago. Now he's the Cheyenne agent."

William Bent was speaking. "White Antelope says it will take twenty days for the bands to arrive here. They have many elderly and children. That is why the chiefs came alone."

"Twenty days? I leave tomorrow to meet with the Kaws," stammered Greenwood.

"They left the mornin' after I delivered yer message," said Porcupine. "Thar's no way on God's green earth them old folks and little ones could travel all the way from the Republican in so short a time."

"Confound it, man, I have a schedule to keep!" blurted Commissioner Greenwood.

An aide whispered into his ear. Nodding in agreement, he authorized a third of the treaty goods to be distributed from the wagons. With much enthusiasm, the chiefs accepted gifts of clothing, knives, scissors, blankets, sugar, coffee, and tobacco.

"The Great White Father is pleased that you have remained peaceful in the midst of hostile tribes," said the commissioner with a forced grin.

"Black Kettle says they are willing to learn how to farm and become like the white man," Agent Bent offered.

A grizzled frontiersman leaning on his Kentucky rifle shouted out, "Well they certainly drink like white men," which got the crowd laughing. He then added, "And they swear with great distinctiveness."

Arapahoe Chief Little Raven pleaded with the commissioner to allow them to occupy all the area upstream from Bent's Fort.

"Hey, Judge! If they sucker you into it, don't tell the settlers," bellowed a reporter. This got more laughs but only worried looks from the chiefs who wanted to resolve the land disputes.

Judge Greenwood spread a map on the table showing the existing Cheyenne and Arapahoe lands established by the Fort Laramie Treaty. "The new reservation will be somewhat smaller; however, I can assure you it will be somewhere on the existing lands you currently occupy."

"Where are the legal papers?" asked Chief Little Raven.

"Well, I don't have them with me now, but I'll send them out as soon as I arrive in Washington," said Judge Greenwood.

"Speaking for the Cheyennes, we will agree to nothing until all of our warriors have voted on the matter," stated Black Kettle.

"You always have to make things difficult, don't you, Black Kettle?" said the judge, whose face was settling back into its usual, dour demeanor. "I leave for the East on the morrow and will send out the necessary documents post-haste. While in Washington, I shall arrange for a formal treaty sometime this winter. Mister Bent, I believe you have an announcement."

William Bent said to the chiefs, "Even though my hair is still dark, forty years on the frontier is sufficient and retirement is now an attractive option. I have decided to reside in Westport, Missouri while overseeing my investments."

The chiefs seemed to find the news disturbing.

As the meeting adjourned, Porcupine said to the commissioner, "Now, wait one darn minute, Judge. Thar's somethin' you didn't make clear."

"What is that?" demanded Judge Greenwood now surrounded by his entourage who glared at the uncouth, outspoken mountain man.

"Where exactly were you figurin' to put this new reservation, and when?"

The commissioner fumbled with the map and said, "Well, it hasn't been settled, but the administration wants it contained between the Purgatoire River and Sandy Fork by sometime next winter. This way they will be near the fort."

"What? Why, thar ain't enough game in these parts to feed a papoose, let alone two tribes." Porcupine was hopping mad in the saddle.

Judge Greenwood's face turned red. "Mister Ogle, your mission to retrieve the Cheyennes is considered satisfactorily accomplished. If you will step inside the agency office, you will be paid for your services. Now, good day, sir."

The chiefs stoicly observed the heated exchange.

Porcupine started in again, "Of all the crooked, underhanded—"

"I said, 'Good day, sir!'" With that, Commissioner Greenwood and his companions piled into the four buggies for the first leg of their next journey. Reins were snapped and the carriages were quickly pulled from the compound.

"C'mon, mule, let's get." Porcupine tugged on the mule's lead rope. "If'n a man like that can get his self elected to Congress, then there's hope fer you yet."

Josh rode next to him. "For a man in charge of Indian Affairs, he doesn't appear to be all that concerned with their well-being."

"Now yer catchin' on."

Oscar Devenish was standing beside the dirt street, holding

his Bible and hoe. "Brother Joshua," he called out. "If you're quite through with your frontier adventure, perhaps you will be ready to start the job that brought you here."

Porcupine stared at Oscar's thick dark beard, bulging blue eyes, and Puritan-black suit and wide brimmed hat. "Who's the corn cracker?"

"That's Oscar Devenish," answered Josh in a quiet voice.

"Who?"

"You remember the guy who brought his hoe to breakfast when we first arrived?"

"Oh, yeah. How could I forget?"

"Now then, Brother Joshua," Oscar called out again. "It is essential you start a lesson plan right away, so we can convert the heathens at the earliest opportunity."

"By 'heathens,' I take it you mean the Cheyennes," said Josh, reining his horse to a halt. "It will be nearly three weeks before they get here and then I'll start working with them when I'm ready."

"Reverend Huelskamp is still expecting you," Oscar added then left in a huff.

Immediately putting Oscar out of his mind, Josh asked Porcupine, "What are you going to do now?"

"I ain't exactly sure." The mountain man scratched his beard. "It's too late to start trappin' in the mountains, so I might as well hang my hat here fer a spell. Besides, I don't want to miss the treaty signin'. Though I know it's gonna be bad."


The next day, Josh checked in with Reverend Huelskamp, who introduced him to two Methodist members just leaving the office.

"Come in, Joshua, and have a seat," said Reverend Huelskamp from behind his desk. Rain gently hit the panes of glass behind him. "I was explaining to these folks that the Lord has provided a way for the members of our mission to earn a salary. This would apply to you as well."

This news pleased Josh. "You're sure it's all right with the Board of Commissioners?"

"Of course it is. Not only will this plan help ease the financial support the board sends, which I must admit is pretty meager, but it also will help weed out the riffraff who burrow themselves into government careers. Those types pad the tribal enrollment with over-inflated numbers and charge the Interior Department accordingly. Then they purchase annuities from local contractors based on lower enrollment numbers and pocket the difference."

"Oh. Well, what would I have to do?"

"Agent Bent and I discovered that many of the tasks performed by our missionaries overlap jobs that are done by corrupt government employees. Frankly, the OIA trusts us more than they trust their own personnel. For example, the government man assigned to teach farming to the Indians was terminated last week for misappropriation of funds. He's being replaced by Brother Oscar, who has hands-on experience and is less likely to yield to temptation. You will not be paid for Bible translation, but you may be called upon to substitute teach or distribute the annuities."

Josh sat in a chair opposite the desk. "I accept. A steady income while working in the ministry would be appreciated."

"I made no mention of steady income." Reverend Huelskamp wiped his glasses with a handkerchief. "Unfortunately, I do not do the hiring. That is done by the local agent who, as you know, has now retired. Mister Bent assures me, though, as did Judge Greenwood, that his replacement will be Alfred Boone."

Josh thought for a moment. "Is this somebody I should know?"

"No, I don't suspect you would know of Alfred Boone. But I'm sure you've heard of his grandfather, Daniel, who is a mythical icon to the frontiersmen. Alfred did his share of trapping in the Rockies many years ago, but I believe he's now a businessman in Westport. In any event, the Cheyennes know him. White Antelope and Black Kettle will be glad to hear he's taking over."

The reverend continued. "Because we are taking on a great deal of responsibility from the OIA, our traditional mission work has become almost secondary. That still plays in our favor, though, since we will have a captive audience in the schools. The board has also found it must meet the medical and social needs of the Indians, so it continues to send out personnel who are cross trained in these areas. You will need to be prepared to teach children and adults alike."

Josh tugged on his white collar and cravat tie as his eyes caught sight through the window of a company of cavalry drilling in the rain. "Education is a good start, and I hope to help in that area. But what is being done to modernize the reservation?"

"What do you mean?"

"Back east you can travel onto a reservation without even realizing you have left the local county."

"Is that so?"

"The reservations not only have schools for the children, but some of the adults are being accepted into the Harvard Indian College. Wouldn't it be a great accomplishment if we could send the first Cheyenne to Harvard? Also, the reservations out there have police departments, post offices, tribal housing, saw mills, blacksmith shops, commissaries, and churches. Surely God would be pleased for us to accomplish the same here. Yet the government's just shrinking the reservation."

"Listen carefully, Joshua. The plains Indians could be as extinct as the Neanderthals by the end of the century. It's not anybody's fault; that's just the way it is. Our job is to make sure we help as many of them get to Heaven as we can before that happens. Understand?"

Startled, Josh answered, "Yes, sir."


The army assigned Josh a bedroom at the administration building. Although flat and lumpy, the bed's mattress felt luxurious after all those nights of sleeping on dirt and rocks. A vacant storeroom at the fort served as a school for the Arapahoe children where Josh worked as a teacher's aide, or sometimes substituted for a teacher.

One afternoon, while Josh changed into his work clothes, he saw an excited commotion from his bedroom window. The Cheyennes had arrived! Josh hopped onto Victoro, his horse, and rode out. The Arapahoe and Cheyenne chiefs, and soldiers were also on their way to greet the newcomers. A chaotic and joyous gathering ensued as the chiefs reunited with their families.

From the saddle, Josh looked for Sunflower. But it proved a futile task, trying to locate her in the chaotic gathering of Indians, soldiers, civilians, and horses. The dust alone obscured everything.

After dinner later, while the sun set, Josh watered his horse at the river and took in the sight of the large Arapahoe camp to the south. While deep in thought, he didn't notice that a pony and rider were heading his way.

"You want spend time with horse, not me?" Sunflower asked teasingly.

He tried unsuccessfully not to smile. He was impressed with how quickly Sunflower had picked up English words. He gazed at her, after not seeing her for so long, wanting to memorize every detail of her appearance. She wore a gray, long-sleeved, hand-me-down dress. Her raven-black hair fell in long braids. Her pretty oval face was graced by full eyebrows and a dimple in each cheek. With the exception of her thumbs, each finger was adorned with a ring.

"Where is Little Dove?" he asked.

With a few words and hand motions she communicated that she had left her daughter with her family at their lodge. Her eyes looked into his questioningly.

Josh was acutely aware that they were alone. He felt excited but awkward. "Uh, yeah. I'm glad you're here."

"In morning, we move camp." She gestured downstream.

"I guess the reservation agent wants the tribe to move away from the fort."

"I see you again?" She pointed to her eyes and then to him.

Then it dawned on Josh what she was concerned about. "If I have my way, you'll see me every day. I have big plans for helping your people, and that's what I'm going to do. Getting to see you is an added benefit." He didn't know how much of the English words she understood but hoped she caught the gist of his words and perhaps heard his heart a little, too.

They sat there, speaking a few words of English and then Cheyenne, and enjoying the silence together until after sunset. Then Sunflower excused herself to return to her family's tepee. Josh immediately felt empty without her nearness.

With the Cheyenne camp close by, Reverend Huelskamp had instructed Josh to work with them exclusively, to learn their language in the shortest time possible, and begin translating the scriptures.

After the camp was moved ten miles away from the fort, the ride there and back every day grew tiresome. Josh obtained permission from the reverend to set up his own tepee among the Cheyennes, knowing full well this meant leaving his comfortable bed at the fort.

At Bent's Trading Post, Jack Smith sold him three writing tablets, a large bottle of ink, and a pen. "Your coming here to help my people is honorable. My wife and children also stay at the camp. You will see me there," said Jack.

Josh placed the new items in a clean flour sack. "That might work to my advantage. I could use more help in winning their trust."

"If you are genuine and mean them no harm, you will gain their trust."

After reaching the settlement, Josh placed his tepee outside the camp circle at the seven o'clock position to be near the lodge of Sunflower's family. He enjoyed working at the Cheyenne camp. He could wear riding clothes or buckskins, and he didn't have to associate with Oscar Devenish. During the day, he met with several Indians who were too old for the warpath and whose wisdom the warriors sought. They sat by the river's edge while Josh explained that *Ma'heo'o* created the sun, stars, and earth, and that it was he alone who should be worshiped—not the creations. He told them that *Ma'heo'o* had sent his son, Jesus, to die for their sins and only through Jesus could they enter through the gates of Heaven.

Making Medicine attended these riverside meetings when he did not have to care for the pony herd. He posed questions even more intelligent than those of his elders. He once asked Josh, "If Creator God is all loving, why does he allow terrible things to happen?" Many of his questions were rhetorical and asked in anger. Hypocritical government bureaucrats who cheated during the week and then attended Sunday services upset Making Medicine the most.

"They lie in their treaties, they steal our land, and they kill the buffalo for sport. Is this like Jesus?" he had asked, running off before Josh could think of an answer.

Sometimes Jack Smith assisted in translating. If Josh could not understand a spoken word, he used sign language, which by then he had mastered. In the evenings, he worked on transcribing the New Testament in Cheyenne by using the Roman alphabet. He did wonder how the adults would be able to read the passages when only the children were required to attend school.

When Josh felt he had done enough work during the day, he would spend time with Sunflower and Little Dove. Little Dove ascertained the English language more quickly than her mother. Reciting the alphabet was hardly a challenge for her. Whenever Josh mangled a Cheyenne word, Sunflower politely corrected him while Little Dove giggled. Often they sat on a large rock under the sun while the river lazily swirled by them.

One autumn afternoon after class, Sunflower's brother Spotted Bear said, "Come with me, Black Robe. It is time you help provide meat for the tribe."

On a day in early November, with gray skies heavy above and snowflakes swirling in the breeze, Josh bagged a large bull elk. He still carried the old muzzle-loaded Hawken loaned to him by Porcupine. They hauled the meat back to camp. As a sign of respect, Josh gave one half to Chief White Antelope and the other half to Sunflower's family. Although he wanted to dine with Sunflower, they had to remain in separate parts of the tepee. The smiles she sent him from across the fire helped ease his frustration.

When winter hit, Josh found how hard life could be for the Indians. Over his buckskins and long underwear he wore a hairy buffalo robe and a matching hat when outdoors. Spotted Bear and Jack Smith, his half-Indian friend from the trading post, invited him along to hunt buffalo, which was easier in the winter. On horseback, the warriors routed a herd through a creek bed covered with deep snow drifts. The large animals sank from their own weight, becoming stuck. After dismounting, the warriors donned snowshoes and walked to the hapless buffalo trapped in the creek, where they easily killed them with lances.

Spotted Bear cut open the stomach of a bull and reached inside with a metal cup. When he pulled his arm out, the cup had filled with a watery, gray liquid, steaming in the cold air. He handed it to Josh, who accepted reluctantly. It smelled as foul as the open carcass; but with Spotted Bear's encouragement, Josh held his breath and took a sip. Surprisingly, it had little taste but warmed his insides and quenched his thirst. When he finished drinking from the cup, he handed it back to Spotted Bear, who refilled it and guzzled down its contents.


During one bitterly cold afternoon in February, Josh was transcribing when Sunflower entered his tepee. "You have wood for your fire?" she asked.

"Yes. Thank you, though." Josh laid down his pen.

She placed a few more branches onto the fire anyway. Josh sensed she was probing for something and figured it might take a while for her to get to the point if he didn't inquire.

"You hungry?" she asked.

"Sunflower, I am fine. What is it you want?"

Kneeling next to him but staring into the fire, she asked, "Do I not please you?"

"You please me very much. Why do you ask?"

She answered his question with a question. "Do you love me?"

Josh felt his pulse quicken and listened to the snow pelting the tepee. "Uh, of course I do. I thought you knew that already."

She still stared at the fire.

He closed his eyes. "Sunflower, I love you very much."

"Why then do you not make me your wife?"

A blizzard wind shook the tepee. "I really want to, but my support from the Board of Commissions is not sufficient for a family. Reverend Huelskamp assured me that I would be paid for what I'm already doing as soon as the new agent arrives."

"Then I pray the agent arrives soon."

Looking into her eyes, Josh slowly leaned toward Sunflower, wanting to feel her warmth. As their lips touched, the tepee's flap flew open dramatically. The cold wind slashed at the tepee and propelled swirling snowflakes all around them.

Porcupine's face appeared. "Hey there, Flapjack! I'm not interrupting anything, am I?"

"Well as a matter of fact—"

"Good, because we ain't got much time!" Porcupine stepped inside, tracking snow on the blankets. A large fur hat covered his head and small icicles hung from his beard. At the fire he removed his gloves to warm his hands. His left forearm pressed the Hawken against his body.

"Hey, Porcupine, if that thing is loaded, don't get too close to the fire." Josh was annoyed with the intrusion. "Not much time for what?"

"Pastor Huelskamp asked me to fetch you. The new agent arrived and wants to meet with all the chiefs and elders in the mornin'."

"I'll leave with the chiefs tomorrow. I'm busy right now."

"Nope. The parson wants to see you tonight. Says he spoke with old man Boone about gettin' you a proper payin' job, but he's afraid things will be too busy tomorra' when the chiefs arrive."

"Sunflower," Josh said in Cheyenne. "Your prayer was answered before you even spoke it!"

Porcupine chuckled. "Yer grasp of the Cheyenne language is comin' along, almost like you been jawin' at it yer whole life."

"Yeah, she speaks a little English and I speak a little Cheyenne, and somehow we get our meaning across."

"Looks to me like you two are communicatin' real good!" He winked at Josh and gave a friendly grin to Sunflower. Then he pulled his gloves back on. "Let's get a move on while there's still daylight."

"Will you ride in with the chiefs tomorrow?" Josh asked Sunflower.

"Yes," she answered, looking happier now.

During the ride to the fort, Josh told Porcupine about the buffalo hunt and the foul-smelling liquid Spotted Bear gave him.

"That was buffalo cider. Wish I had me some right now. When there ain't no coffee, there's nothin' better."


The next morning at the fort, a warm winter sun emerged and the snow began to melt. Members of both tribes crowded the parade ground. The chiefs wore their finest regalia. They were led into a large room with rows of wooden chairs and a table stacked with legal documents. A wooden stand, displaying a large map of an unfamiliar territory, stood behind the table. Seated at the table were two civilians and an army captain. Members of the OIA and ABCFM occupied the other seats or stood along the walls.

The officer rose from his seat. "I am Captain Elmer Otis, commanding officer here at Fort Wise. At my far right is out-going acting agent F.B. Culver. At my immediate right, I am pleased to introduce the new Indian agent, who just happens to be my father-in-law, Albert G. Boone."

The chiefs recognized Boone and nodded their approval while others applauded. Albert Boone, a short old man with a white beard, rose to his feet.

"Good morning, everyone," he said in a soft voice. "Before I go into details of the new treaty authorized by Congress, I would like to pass on a bit of news that has affected this area." With a stick he drew a circle on the map. "Those of us here are no longer on the western fringes of the Kansas Territory. We are now within the borders of the new Territory of Colorado. William Gilpin, who will be both governor of the territory and its superintendent of Indian affairs, will reside in the capitol city of Denver."

The government bureaucrats loudly clapped, while the chiefs appeared indifferent to what the land was called.

"And now for the matter at hand," said Boone. While still pointing at the map, he read from a document that described the reservation boundaries as those predicted by Judge Greenwood. It was roughly one-thirteenth the size of the original reservation, with a line down the middle. The Cheyenne half was on the left with the Arapahoe portion to the right. The Arkansas River remained the southern boundary.

Porcupine turned radish red and twisted his fur hat. "They're gonna starve them into submission, mark my words. They're gonna starve 'em," he said none too quietly.

On his other side, Reverend Huelskamp held his finger to his lips and hissed, "Shhhhh!"

Boone continued reading dryly. "In return, the United States Government promises to protect the Indians from enemies, will pay each tribe the annual sum of fifteen-thousand dollars for the next fifteen years, purchase stock and farming equipment, and build houses and warehouses not to exceed five-thousand dollars."

All the chiefs signed the treaty then solemnly filed out of the room. "They know they have no choice," whispered Josh to the reverend. "How can we modernize a reservation when it is shrinking like a spider on a frying pan?"

# Chapter 5

## A SILVER THIMBLE

When the inglorious ceremony ended, Josh changed into his buckskin clothes so he could accompany Sunflower and Little Dove on the ride back to the Cheyenne camp. Not even the brightness of the mid-day sun could lift the dejected feeling that permeated the tribe.

Moving her pony beside Josh, Sunflower asked, "You met with Agent Boone last night?"

"Agent Boone gave me a regular teaching job. Not only that, he authorized me to receive back pay since October first."

"Then we can marry?"

Josh awkwardly reached over to pat her shoulder. "Um, I guess so. If ... that is, uh ... if you'll marry me."

In Cheyenne she said something like, "Every man should learn from you how to propose marriage." Then she grinned. "Yes, Black Robe, I accept. I would laugh with joy were it not for the heaviness in my heart."

"I feel the same way. The Office of Indian Affairs shrank the reservation to the size of a postage stamp without batting an eye."

Back at the camp, many warriors loudly denounced the chiefs for selling them out for a wagonload of trinkets. Some of the immature warriors insulted Josh, but Making Medicine's father chastised them.

"Black Robe means us no harm. He has fought the Kiowa warrior White Bear, which none of you have. He has lived with us since last autumn while sharing his knowledge of the Great Spirit and learning our language."

Sunflower held onto Josh's arm in front of his tepee as the

warriors left. Making Medicine stayed behind. "Where is this Jesus you speak of? If he loves us, how can he allow us to lose everything to these white men who call themselves Christians?"

Josh didn't know how to answer.

Making Medicine stormed off.

"He is young and without understanding," said Sunflower.

"He's old enough to understand hypocrisy. Maybe someday he'll realize God alone will judge them for their sins. Forgiveness can be difficult when the injustice continues." Josh watched the angry young man in the distance.

Sunflower looked probingly into his eyes. "What about you, Black Robe? Do you forgive so easily?"

Summer's harshness turned the creeks dry. The Arkansas became a narrow stream in its wide bed. Agent Boone had ordered the Cheyennes to relocate at the Point-of-Rocks Agency forty-five miles upstream from the fort.

Joshua was thinking about these things as he descended the front steps of the mission church.

His reverie was interrupted when Porcupine trotted his horse over to him. "Hey there, Flapjack. Are you busy?"

"No, I just finished meeting with Reverend Huelskamp. Is there a problem?"

"There is, and it's fixin' to be a dandy." Porcupine frowned. "Get on yer horse. We got work to do."

Josh unhitched his horse and stepped into the saddle. "Well, hello to you, too. Where have you been?"

"I got me a raspberry seed between my teeth I gotta deal with." The mountain man contorted his mouth. "Oh, been up near the divide huntin' and trappin'. Come back to the lowland to fetch me supplies, only to hear of trouble brewin'."

"What's the trouble?"

"Let me ask *you* somethin'. How's the food situation here?"

"The drought is so bad, the buffalo have moved on and the game have gone to the meadows in the upper elevations. Agent Boone says he can't issue the annuities, because they haven't arrived yet."

"That's one heck of a whopper. I just heard that Old Man Boone is keepin' them annuities locked up until it snows again. That could be a spell. Shucks, it's so hot I saw two trees fightin' over a dog! Ain't much left of the river, so it figures all the game is gonna go where the water is. When was the last time you was at the Cheyenne camp?"

"A couple of weeks ago. Why?"

"When I rode by yesterday, it was full of angry braves puttin' on paint and totin' their weapons."

They walked together to the saloon, where they were sure to hear the latest news. A disgruntled OIA employee sat at a table drinking one glass of whiskey after another. He was a small man with a trimmed mustache, wearing a brown suit and bowler hat. Porcupine and Josh took seats across from him.

"Hey there, strangers, drinks are on me," said the little man.

"No, thanks," said Porcupine. "What's the news, friend?"

The man's speech slurred, "The news? Oh nothing. I got a letter from my wife in Cincinnati saying she's leaving me for—"

"Yeah, yeah. But what do you know about the Indians not gettin' their annuities this summer?" demanded Porcupine.

The drunken man pushed his hat back and thought for a moment. "You mean that food we keep locked in the warehouse?"

"Yer darn tootin' that's what I mean."

"Oh yeah, back in June, Mister Boone got a letter from Governor Gilpin saying not to issue the annuities till the weather turned cold."

"Why not?"

"Because the governor said the Indians would be getting pretty destitute by that time."

"They'll be destitute all right, but as sure as you'll be throwin' up tonight, those warriors will burn this fort to the ground before they'll starve to death," warned Porcupine. He stood and left the saloon, and Josh followed.

Porcupine and Josh rode over to the OIA office located at the fort's administration building. Inside, they found a bored accountant pouring over dusty ledgers piled high on a tall desk. "Hey, buster, where can I find Mister Boone?" Porcupine asked.

The snooty accountant peered over the top of his glasses and said, "Washington, D.C. If you hurry you might catch him before supper."

"Why, you little squirt, I ought to hang you from the rafters."

"It's okay, Porcupine. Let's go." Josh pulled his friend by the arm. "We'll talk to the commanding officer tomorrow."

The next morning, over a thousand Cheyenne and Arapahoe warriors on horseback surrounded Fort Wise. They did not permit anybody within the vicinity to leave. The warriors showed signs of starvation, but they were still strong enough to fight. Especially against the undersized company that remained to protect the fort.

Porcupine and Josh ran to the admin building. They found Captain Elmer Otis at his desk. The well-fed captain sported a full mustache and goatee. With his bright blue eyes, he looked at his visitors and said with a Massachusetts accent, "Gentlemen, if you must speak with me, check in with my aide first."

A corporal in a clean uniform with polished shoes also entered and said, "Sorry, sir, they ran right by me." Then, when he saw the angry look on Porcupine Pete's face, the corporal scurried back to the front office.

Porcupine returned his attention to the officer. "Chief Lean Bear is out there, and he's madder than a wet hen. He's got a mess o' warriors with him who feel the same way. If'n you don't give 'em what they want, he'll make a whole lotta trouble fer ya."

Otis jumped to his feet. "Why are they doing this? They haven't indicated anything to me about there being a problem."

"They're starving!" said Josh. "What other kind of indication do you need?"

Porcupine gave Josh a proud look. He then glared at the captain. "I reckon they intend to get their rations, or they'll cover you in honey and stake you down to a hill of fire ants. If'n I was you, I'd get out there and hear what them boys have to say."

Captain Otis only had to go as far as the front sidewalk, since the warriors rode unchallenged onto the parade ground.

"Cap'n, I'd like you to meet Chief Lean Bear," said Porcupine.

Chief Lean Bear wore a breechclout, moccasins, and a hare-bone breastplate. His forehead was painted white and a streak of black ran across his eyes and nose like a raccoon's mask. Two eagle feathers stuck out to the left from the back of his head band. He angrily shook his rifle while speaking to Captain Otis.

"What did he say?" asked the quaking captain.

Porcupine folded his arms and squinted one eye. "He says you got ten days to distribute them annuities or they'll kill everyone here and take what they want anyway."

"But my father-in-law said he was the only one who could distribute those goods," reasoned Otis.

Porcupine let out a cackle. "By golly yer right, and while yer on that anthill you can rest easy knowin' how proud he'll be of ya."

Captain Otis stared at the thousand plus warriors on the parade ground all painted and armed. "Tell him I agree to his terms. The annuities will be distributed in ten days."

"You want these cutthroats to keep you penned in here fer ten days?" asked Porcupine. "Give 'em the goods now, and they'll leave."

"I fully concur," said the captain. He ordered the soldiers to open one of the storehouses and allow the Indians to enter and take the annuities.

For the rest of the morning, the Indian women loaded the goods onto pack horses and travois while the warriors kept the soldiers from interfering. With the storehouse empty, Chief Lean Bear rode over to where the captain stood. Porcupine translated what he said. "These are the annuities promised us fer the summer. In ten days we will return fer the autumn rations."

The women with the pack horses left for their camps first. When only the mounted warriors remained, Lean Bear let out a high-pitched yelp and they galloped away from the fort, leaving Captain Elmer Otis coughing on the sidewalk in their large cloud of dust.

Josh proposed properly to Sunflower on a sunny day after church, by the river. He gave her the silver thimble he had been carrying in his pocket. "This is for you, Sunflower. I had originally given this to my wife, Michelle, instead of a ring because her family and church had a strict Puritan rule against wearing jewelry."

She held up the piece of silver to the sun and admired it. "It is very beautiful, Black Robe, but I do not want it if it will serve as an unpleasant memory."

"You will make it a pleasant memory," Josh reassured.

"Then I accept."

"I'll get you a ring when I'm able. Besides, all your fingers have rings on them already."

"I'll make room for one more."

For two days they traveled on horseback to the fort to buy a new dress. At the trading post where Jack Smith worked, Sunflower found a full-length, blue-patterned dress with a cameo brooch at the throat. Jack wrapped it in brown paper and tied it with string.

Outside the store Sunflower stood hugging the package in both arms, her gaze focused on the ground. Tears ran down her cheeks.

"What's the matter?" Josh placed his hands on her shoulders.

"I have never had new dress before," she said softly. "Black Robe is first man to care and to give gifts to me."

They found the reverend and his assistant, Walking Elk, in the office of Agent Albert Boone, who had returned from Washington. Much to Josh's disappointment, Oscar Devenish was also there. The four men were sitting around the dark mahogany desk. They glanced up as Josh and Sunflower entered.

"Good morning. How may I help you?" asked Agent Boone.

Josh nervously gripped his hat. "Actually, we were looking for the reverend." Josh put his arm around Sunflower, who held her packaged dress. "We're getting married and wanted to know if you would do us the honor of performing the ceremony."

"Well, congratulations!" said Agent Boone.

Walking Elk stood and shook Josh's hand. "Welcome to the tribe."

"Perhaps we should speak in private," said Reverend Huelskamp with a forced grin.

"If you think it's necessary," Josh said, surprised at the hesitancy in the minister's tone.

"I'll tell you why," growled Oscar, rising to his feet and gripping his hoe. "The good reverend is long overdue for a sabbatical and he will be leaving on tomorrow's stage, accompanied by the big Injun. I will be the pastor in charge here, and I do not approve of this union. Remember, the children of Israel were forbidden to intermarry with the Canaanites. The Apostle Paul told us to confront immorality in the church, and that is exactly what I intend to do."

"That was to keep the Israelites from idol worship. Don't try twisting the scriptures with me, Devenish. We're getting married whether you like it or not." Josh felt his temper rise as it always did around Oscar.

"Not on my watch! If you marry this woman, you'll be without a job," warned Oscar, his intense blue eyes bulging.

"Mister Boone, are there any conditions of my employment that state I must adhere to the demands of an outlandish zealot?" asked Josh.

"No, there aren't, Mister Frasier. Your employment with the United States Government is separate from your association with the Board of Commissioners," said Albert Boone, obviously annoyed the missionaries chose to use his office for their argument.

Oscar continued his tirade. "Brother Joshua, if you defy my God-given authority and exchange vows with this red-skinned trollop, I'll have you excommunicated!"

Sunflower ran from the office. Now enraged, Josh cocked back his fist, but Walking Elk's large hand caught it. "Turn the other cheek, Black Robe," said the soft-spoken Cheyenne missionary. "And wait for me outside."

Oscar loudly lectured the reverend and Indian agent. "Perhaps we might understand if an ungodly drunkard bedded down with a squaw for the night, but when a so-called Christian starts calling one his wife—"

"Brother Oscar, a word with you in the hall, please," said Walking Elk meekly.

"Very well," said Oscar, stepping out to the hallway. "Come, come, let's have it."

The giant Cheyenne lifted Oscar off the floor by the lapels of his jacket and pinned him to the wall. With an exacting voice he said, "Brother Joshua and the woman Sunflower will marry, and you will make no retaliations against them. If I hear you disrespect this man's wife or any other woman of my tribe, I'll throw you—naked—into a cactus patch."

Josh couldn't resist watching the incident from the partially-open front door. He snickered as he ran down the steps. Giving Sunflower a hug outside the administration building, he said, "I don't care if they do fire me. 'What God has joined together, let no man separate.' We'll find someone else to marry us."

Walking Elk came out of the building and the wooden steps creaked under his weight. His pant legs were tucked into dusty knee-high boots. Approaching the couple he said, "Don't worry about Brother Oscar. He fully understands now. Let's go to the trading post and talk with Jack about who can perform the ceremony for you."

At the post, Jack invited his guests to sit on stools around a molasses barrel and he poured cups of coffee. "By the looks on your faces, I can tell something's wrong. I hope you are not returning the dress."

Sunflower shook her head.

"These two need someone to marry them," said Walking Elk. "I'm leaving for St. Louis tomorrow with Reverend Huelskamp, and of course the Hoe Man won't do it for them. I was thinking of Father Sanchez."

Jack asked, "Josh, do you believe that only members of your church affiliation are true Christians?"

"No, of course not." Josh wondered about the strange question.

"Then you two need to go meet with Father Sanchez. He'll perform a marriage ceremony for you. Your Christian denomination and skin color doesn't matter to him, if it doesn't matter to you."

"Where is he located?" asked Josh.

"He has a small adobe church in Pueblo."

Later that afternoon, Josh met with Agent Boone alone. Although he worked unsupervised, his teaching responsibilities were vague, and he wanted clarification. He also wanted approval for leaving the reservation to get married.

Busy with paperwork, Albert Boone never looked up from his desk, even while he answered. "Yes, that's fine. And bring me a cup of coffee, please, if you're finished quarreling for the day."


Except for meal breaks, Josh, Sunflower and four other passengers bounced uncomfortably along in the stagecoach for nearly twenty-four hours. Four different teams of horses were used to cover the 113 miles to Pueblo.

The next day, Father Sanchez performed the marriage ceremony without hesitation. Josh wore his most formal black suit and Sunflower appeared amazingly beautiful in her new blue dress.

The ceremony over, they entered a dusty courtyard where the small congregation had set up a table with platters of rice, beans, chicken, tortillas, green chilies, and tamales. A musical ensemble comprised of guitar, trumpet, and violin played for the newlyweds.

"Did you make this happen?" Sunflower asked.

"No, I didn't." Josh nervously wondered how much this was going to cost him. "Say, Father—"

"It is quite all right," the priest assured him, having overheard the short conversation. "The Anglo churches often have a meal after the service with each member bringing a dish to share. We do the same, so please be our guests."

"But Sunday is tomorrow."

"Please, señor, enjoy yourself.

After lunch, the church ladies began clearing the table. With a coquetish grin, Sunflower looked up at Josh and said, "Everyone is going home. Maybe we should go to our room?"

As they began their married life together at the Cheyenne camp, Josh had a new vitality in his teaching and writing. He wrote letters to both the U.S. Senators from Missouri, and they assured him they were doing everything within their powers to see that the Plains Indians received treatment equal to that of the tribes in the East.

Josh hunted with his brother-in-law, Spotted Bear, but with the exception of an occasional jackrabbit, no game was ever seen.

In December more bad news reached the tribes. Albert Boone, who was respected among the Indians, announced his retirement from government service and was being replaced by a former army major named Samuel G. Colley. Agent Colley appointed his son Dexter as his chief assistant.

Early one February morning, Josh heard his named called. He wrapped himself in a buffalo blanket and stepped out of his tepee on the edge of camp. "That would be me." He found himself looking up at what he estimated to be a seventy-five man company of cavalry. The troops wore kepis and blue winter coats. Steam puffed from the nostrils of their tired horses. Sunflower also came out and stood behind Josh.

A First Sergeant with yellow chevrons sewn on both sleeves grinned lustfully at Sunflower and then said, "We heard tell you were a squaw man. Guess we heard right."

"Something I can do for you, Sergeant?" asked Josh.

"The name is Merrill and I have orders to bring you with us to Pueblo."

"Whose orders? I'm not in the army," said Josh nervously. Gradually, other warriors came out of their tepees to watch the conversation. Making Medicine was among them.

"Let's just say it's an urgent request from the governor," the sergeant explained. "You may not be in the army now, but you soon will be. In case you didn't know, there's a war going on, and it's moving toward this territory. A regiment called the First Colorado Volunteers has been formed in Denver and is marching south. The governor has asked that you speak with the colonel in charge."

"How does the governor know who I am?"

The sergeant only shrugged his shoulders.

Sunflower dug her nails into Josh's arm and pleaded, "My husband, please do not go with these men. No good will come of it."

"I have no choice," Josh said softly in Cheyenne. When he spotted his favorite student, he asked, "Making Medicine, would you please get Victoro from the herd and bring him here?"

Making Medicine gave the soldiers a look of contempt. Then he left to do as Josh had asked.

Josh asked the sergeant, "What do I need to bring?"

"Whatever you want, just be sure to bring your Bible."

Josh intended to bring it anyway, but still inquired. "My Bible? Why?"

"The governor's message said the regiment has its full complement of officers with the exception of a chaplain." The sergeant grinned, displaying a gold tooth.

Sunflower covered her face with her hands and wailed a lament.

Josh encircled her with his arm. "Sweetheart, I have no idea what's going on here. I'll go talk to this colonel, whoever he is, and I'll be back within a week."

"No, you will not." She broke free and returned to the tepee.

# Chapter 6

## THE FIGHTING PARSON

Josh rode with the cavalrymen at a fast pace westward. Two mule-pulled wagons followed at the rear. He had seen these men before, at the fort. They were tough in appearance, with a sense of purpose.

To the sergeant he said, "I don't like riding off and leaving my wife. How are the soldiers going to be able to protect the tribe when you're being sent to other parts of the country?"

"Guess they'll have to fend for themselves for a while. I've got my orders to escort you to the colonel, and that's what I'm going to do."

"And just who is this colonel?"

First Sergeant Frank Merrill wore a crooked kepi with a pin of two crossed sabers under a number "1". While gripping a cigar stub in his teeth, he said, "The colonel's name is James Slough. I don't know much about him except he's some lawyer from Denver."

They reached the designated meeting spot west of Pueblo that night. Josh looked over the volunteers' camp. It sprawled like the Cheyenne camp but lacked the organization. Tents big and small were pitched without any kind of pattern. Numerous campfires lit the area. Somewhere in the distance a harmonica played.

"How am I going to find this colonel?" he asked.

"Don't worry, I will not be able to sleep until I deliver you to him," said Merrill.

A sentry led them to the commanding officer's tent.

Merrill said to another sergeant, "Make camp on the other side of the river and I'll be there as soon as I drop the preacher off."

The sentry cautiously entered the tent and said, "Colonel, there's two men here to see you."

"Send them in," said a tired male voice from within.

Merrill and Josh entered. Two officers sat at a folding table. The colonel had a long shaggy brown beard and a few strands of hair that refused to leave his otherwise bald head. His blue jacket was draped on the back of his chair and he wore a white shirt with a black cravat tie. He took the paper Merrill handed him and read it over.

"Okay, Sergeant," he told Merrill. "You're dismissed. Reveille will be at six o'clock. You and your men will be going with us to Fort Union."

Merrill saluted then turned on his heels to exit the tent. The colonel continued reading the paper without acknowledging Josh. With a soft voice he addressed the other officer, a major. "John, this is the one you've been waiting for."

The officer named John set down the Bible he held and rose from his chair—all six feet, five inches, and two-hundred sixty pounds of him! His wavy brown hair was thinning and graying at the temples but his eyes appeared black as coal. With a strong voice he said, "Welcome to the First Colorado Volunteers. I'm Major Chivington. Have a seat."

Awestruck, Josh stammered a response. "You … you … you wouldn't be the Reverend John M. Chivington?"

A smile appeared on the major's bearded face. "That would be me."

Josh nervously crushed the brim of his hat while recounting a memory. "Six or seven years ago I heard you preach at a church in Missouri. There were some pro-slavery persons in the congregation who had threatened you and I recall you slamming two six-shooters down on the pulpit next to your Bible. You were determined to preach and, by golly, you did!"

The major thumped Josh on the back. "I cannot rightly say I remember you, but I do recollect that day. You're right; I put the fear of God in those southern bushwhackers. Unfortunately, it was the end of my days in Missouri. The district felt I would do less damage in Omaha."

"But you showed them," Colonel Slough said, dryly, while sifting through some papers.

"Right again," Chivington continued. "A saloon owner's entire supply of whiskey was no match for my ax. Something had to be done, not only because of what the barrels contained, but because the man had the gall to store them in an empty church."

"I haven't had much use for whiskey myself," said Josh. He wanted to go to bed as soon as possible, and decided to steer the conversation to why he was there in the first place. "So, gentlemen, what is it you require of me?"

Colonel Slough kept his eyes focused on his paperwork. Chivington ordered a cook to bring two cups of coffee from the officers' mess and then said to Josh, "Son, as you know, our country is being torn apart by civil war. President Lincoln has required all the Union states and territories to raise regiments. When the governor of Colorado asked for volunteers I was one of the first in line. Naturally, he offered me the position of regimental chaplain, but I flat-out refused."

"Why?" Josh took the cup and saucer handed to him by the cook.

"I didn't want a praying commission, I wanted a fighting commission! I love the Lord, and my country too. I helped fight the evils of slavery by assisting the Underground Railroad. And now I'm called to help slay the proponents of slavery and those who would tear apart this great country. How do you feel about that, son?"

Josh answered carefully, "I can't say God has called on me to slay anyone. But yes, slavery is a terrible evil. And if the southern states are allowed to secede, then what would stop other parts of the country from doing the same? The Confederacy must be eradicated."

Chivington said, "That's what we wanted to hear you say. Presently you're a missionary to the Cheyennes, correct?"

"Yes, that's why I was wondering—"

"A man after my own heart. I was a missionary myself to the Wyandot tribe in Kansas, by the way." Chivington pulled a letter from a leather folder. "The chaplain's position for our regiment has not yet been filled, so when the regimental office received this glowing letter from your administrator, we were eager to meet you."

"A glowing letter about me? Uh, what, may I ask, is the name of this particular administrator?"

The major picked up the letter from his desk. "It's signed by an Oscar Devenish."

"My administrator? Why, that no good—"

"The regular army requires an ordained minister," said Chivington, ignoring Josh's outburst. "But here in the volunteers the requirements are somewhat lax. All it takes is a commission from the governor—which I have for you. Do you accept the position? Those men out there have volunteered to stop a large column of Confederate troops who right now are marching up the Rio Grande. Many of them will die in the process, and they'll need a strong spiritual leader. As a chaplain you'll have no rank, but you'll be considered a staff officer and will receive one-hundred dollars a month."

Josh shook his head emphatically. "No, that doesn't fit my plans at all. Things are getting worse on the reservation, not better. All that Cheyenne land between the South Platte and the Arkansas is shrinking and will be gone like that," he snapped his fingers. "Those people need my help. That's why I came out here."

"And what do you plan to do, give them the land back?" asked the major.

"Well no, I can't do that. Wherever they live I want to help make it a self-sufficient, self-governing republic."

"Kind of a large task for one lone missionary just out of Bible school, isn't it?"

"I guess you're right." Josh sighed.

Chivington looked Josh in the eyes. "A hundred dollars a month, Joshua. Where else are you going to make that kind of money in this day and age? Think about this: the territorial leaders in Denver will be lobbying hard for statehood in a couple years. I have a reliable source who tells me that the governor is going to ask me to run for Congress. If that happens, I may be in a position to do something for your Cheyenne friends. You help me and I'll help you. I need a chaplain. If you do not volunteer, it is very likely you will be inducted into the regular army anyway. What do you say?"

Josh wrung his hands. "How long will we be gone?"

"Oh, I don't know. We're not committed for the duration of the war, if that's what you're worried about. Once the rebels have been driven out of New Mexico there should be no reason for us to remain."

Reluctantly Josh agreed. "All right Major, I volunteer. But the minute this thing is over, I'm going back to Fort Wise."

They stood and the major shook his hand until it felt numb. "Welcome to the Pike's Peakers, Chaplain Frasier. Come on, I'll show you to your quarters."

The colonel never removed his eyes from his papers or acknowledged their leaving.

It took Josh's hand five minutes to regain feeling.

At the tent next door, the major pulled the flap back and entered. A cloud of blue smoke trapped against the ceiling rolled out and upward into the cold night air. Two young officers sat at a small table with glasses of whiskey and cigars. The major gave them a disapproving look. Sternly he said, "Both of you stand up. It's a wonder how you even breathe in here. I've got someone I'd like you to meet. This is our new chaplain, Joshua Frasier. Joshua, this is Captain Edward Wynkoop and Lieutenant Silas Soule. You'll be staying here with Soule."

Captain Wynkoop stood almost as tall as the major and sported a full mustache. Shaking hands with Josh he said kindly, "'Edward' is too formal; everyone calls me Ned." His black knee-high riding boots shone like glass, setting off the red embroidery on his blue coat.

Lieutenant Soule's long cigar dangling from his teeth appeared out of place with his youthful face.

Chivington shook his head. "Look at you, Silas. You know how I feel about my officers drinking. A fine example you set for the Calvinists. I've a good mind to write your folks."

Ned grinned at Silas. "Well, I sure don't want to be in your mother's way when she comes here to drag you home by the ear. I'll say goodnight. Pleased to have met you, Chaplain. And goodnight to you, Major." He put on his kepi and a regulation blue cape with yellow liner, took a long puff of his cigar, then stepped out to go to his tent.

Chivington left soon after.

Then Silas removed his boots. "I tell you, Father—"

"Whoa. What's with this 'Father' stuff? I'm not Catholic. You can call me Joshua or Josh—either is fine."

"I think you'll like being with this outfit, Josh. The major is a natural-born leader and the men respect him."

"What about the colonel? He hardly said a word."

Silas leaned forward and whispered, "Remember, this is only a tent; keep your voice down. The colonel is the total opposite. A few years ago, he ran for governor of Kansas and lost. His law practice in Denver hasn't been too successful either. I don't know, it's like he has something to prove, and the men can't stand him."

"I never figured on joining the army," said Josh. "Do you think we'll see any action?"

"Nah, by the time we get down there, the local troops most likely will have stopped them, if the rebels are even there. I can't imagine why the Confederates would move troops from the South to the desert of New Mexico."


A month later, following two days of heavy fighting along the Santa Fe Trail, Josh found himself ascending Glorieta Mesa. It was a high and rocky piece of tableland covered with bushy piñon pines. Josh rode on a deer trail among the 490 cavalrymen who followed Major Chivington and their sombrero-wearing Mexican guide in single file. Victoro galloped at full speed to reach the level ground. Josh gripped the gelding's mane and held his head down to avoid being hit by low-hanging branches along the flat mesa. Soon the other mounted horses arrived, snorting and with sides lathered in sweat.

No one spoke. The Santa Fe Trail curved round the mesa like a bend in a horseshoe. To the east, the line held by the Colorado and New Mexico volunteers in Glorieta Pass was about to be breached. Hours before, Colonel Slough had nearly been killed by some of his own artillerymen and became totally incoherent. Major Chivington explained if they could cut directly across the base of the bend, they would return to the Santa Fe Trail and be at the Confederates' rear. As they continued west, the air turned cold and the mesa top became virtually barren. What piñons remained were squat, with patches of snow at their base.

At three o'clock, they arrived at the rim of the canyon. Their local guide, Miguel Chaves, rode over to Chivington and whispered, "You are right on top of them, Major."

Josh accompanied the major to the edge and looked down. Seven-hundred feet below them, in a dry gorge, they not only found the trail, but the entire Confederate supply train as well. A scout reported there were eighty fully-loaded wagons guarded by less than one-hundred men who all appeared to be sick or injured. Across the landscape below, adobe corrals held several hundred horses and mules in the mostly-abandoned Johnson Ranch, which had served as the Confederate camp.

Chivington ordered an attack on the supply train. Ropes were fastened together then anchored to tree trunks. As quietly as possible, the Pike's Peakers repelled down the side of the mesa. Inevitably, some rocks came loose and alarmed the Confederate guards, who scrambled to wheel around an old cannon. When they fired at Chivington's men, the shots fell short, and the Pike's Peakers easily captured the gun.

After securely tying a long rope around the branch of a cottonwood tree, Josh slipped over the rim of the mesa. He thought about his classmates at Wesleyan University. If they could only see me now! Even through his leather gloves, he felt the rope's burn as he repelled down the cliff. The second his feet hit level ground he took cover and scanned the area. Most of the Confederates had dropped their guns and were running away. Several remained behind, too incapacitated to escape. Despite their obvious lack of mobility, the major ordered they be watched at gunpoint. With bandaged limbs, they feebly raised their hands in surrender.

Fearing the main Confederate force would return, Chivington ordered a hasty reconnaissance of the canyon to locate any signs of immediate danger. Then he gave instructions to First Sergeant Merrill, the same man who had fetched him from his warm tepee on that cold morning in February. Merrill loudly passed the order to the men, "Pack those wagons side by side as tightly as they'll go. C'mon, we haven't got all day!"

The blue-clad soldiers strained to push all the wagons next to each other. Several were tipped over. After the soldiers doused the wagons in kerosene, Merrill ordered, "Put 'em to the torch, boys!" Flames leapt to the sky, incinerating tents, blankets, coffee, flour, uniforms, horse tack, and Bibles.

While the fire grew in intensity, a burning page from Matthew chapter seven landed at Josh's feet. Chivington issued another order. "Kill the livestock."

When shots resounded from the corrals, the major yelled, "Don't shoot them! We can't spare the ammunition. Use the bayonet!"

The soldiers gave Chivington several looks of revulsion. Reluctantly, they fixed bayonets to their rifle barrels and proceeded with the grisly task. While the fire raged and the shrieking neighs of terrified horses echoed off the canyon walls, Chivington held a Bible close to his chest and loudly prayed, "I thank Thee, dear Lord, for Thou hast delivered Thine enemies into mine hands."

The Confederate prisoners of the Fourth Mounted Texas Volunteers waved Josh over to the medical tent where they shook in fear. "Excuse me, sir," said an old sergeant with dirty gray hair. "From looking at your hat we assume you are a chaplain."

"Yes, I am. Is there something I can do for you?"

"We just want to know, sir, is it the policy of your unit to kill prisoners?"

Josh was taken aback. "Of course not. That's not a policy anywhere in our army."

"I don't mean to differ with you, sir, but the major there ordered the guards to shoot us if our troops returned."

Another prisoner nodded his head in agreement. "He has lost all sense of humanity and is a contemptible coward for ordering helpless prisoners shot down like dogs."

"But he's an ordained minister. He'd never do such a thing," said Josh. "Are you sure you did not misunderstand what he said?"

"Yes, sir. There is no misunderstanding," confirmed the Confederate sergeant.

"I can assure you that is not going to happen."

"If you say so, sir."

Josh turned to the soldier in charge of the four guards. "Corporal, is it true, that the major gave you orders to shoot these prisoners if their troops came back?"

The corporal lowered his eyes. "Yes, sir, that's what he said to do."

Josh looked at the prisoners then the guards again. "You do realize that's an illegal order and that you can be court-martialed for obeying it?"

"Yes, sir, but we also realize we could be shot in their place for failing to obey an order in the face of the enemy."

Josh tried to make sense of this predicament, but couldn't. "I thought we were supposed to be the good guys."

The prisoners wept as they listened to the terrified screaming of their horses and mules. Over five-hundred animals had been killed in less than thirty minutes. Josh suddenly worried about his own horse still on the mesa. "Sorry, but I must take my leave."

He passed the burning wagons, passed the bloody adobe corrals, and what a relief to find Victoro standing on the mesa's rim. A detail of men, sent by Merrill, climbed the ropes to bring their horses down into the canyon.

Gunshots and cannon fire from the battle echoed through the canyon. Since the soldiers still had their weapons at the ready, he pulled out his heavy Dragoon .44 from its holster. He had just passed a large piñon when, in his peripheral vision, he caught a glimpse of someone sneaking behind him. While turning on his heels, he leveled the revolver and cocked it. A wounded Confederate tried to aim his Enfield rifle. Both guns fired at once.

The rifle shot went high, but Josh's bullet hit the soldier in the middle of his chest, leaving a small black powder burn. Shock gripped them both. The Confederate, wearing a tattered butternut uniform, dropped his rifle and slumped to the ground with his back against the tree trunk. His blue eyes showed fear as he spoke. "I'm sorry, sir. I didn't know you were a Chaplain."

"Never mind. Try not to move." Josh thought the dying soldier looked very young. "We don't have much time, so I must ask: do you know the Lord Jesus?"

"Yes, sir, I do. I was praying to him when you startled me. I tried running away with the others, but couldn't keep up. I'm in an awful way. Would you do something for me, sir?" he gasped.

"Yes, what is it?"

"Inside my rucksack is a letter to my folks. Would you see that it gets delivered to them after the war?" He spoke with effort.

"I promise I'll try. Where can they be reached?"

"The Reverend and Missus Samuel Hislop of the First Baptist Church in Fort Stockton, Texas." The soldier's voice was weakening to a faint whisper. "If you would be willing to write, tell them I love them, but please don't mention …" He could speak no more.

Josh prayed over the enemy soldier, who died before the Amen.

He forgot to ask the boy's name. Looking at the blue sky, he shouted, "Why am I here? This is not what I sought out to do!" He lifted the Enfield and wondered, *How did a British rifle get into the hands of a Confederate soldier in New Mexico?* With a heavy heart, he shouldered the rifle and rucksack, gripped a rope, and climbed to the top of the mesa, tossing the Enfield over the cliff.

His beloved Victoro lay on his left side with a gaping bullet hole in his right shoulder. The chestnut horse lifted his head and vainly attempted to get on his feet. "That boy's shot didn't miss after all," muttered Josh. He stroked the side of Victoro's neck until he saw the detail of cavalrymen climbing into their saddles to depart. Despairingly, he withdrew his revolver and placed its muzzle between the eyes of the stricken horse and fired. Gun smoke formed a cloud over the motionless horse.

The next morning, after an all-night roundabout ride to the east, the cavalry reached the Santa Fe Trail at the recently abandoned Kozlowski's Ranch. A despondent Colonel Slough made his headquarters at the single-story ranch house. Far to the east, the forested land became desert.

The ruins of the Pecos Pueblo Mission lay a mile north of the ranch headquarters. Dismounting the army horse, Josh removed the saddle and gave the animal a thorough brushing across its sweaty back. Then he carried his bedroll into one of the collapsed buildings. In actuality, the room was nothing more than a ninety-degree section of adobe bricks about four feet high. While eating a simple breakfast of hardtack and canteen water, he leaned over into the corner, exhausted.

After the men rested, Colonel Slough called his officers to the ranch-house parlor. Josh wished he had been allowed more time to sleep.

Awkwardly, Slough said, "Gentlemen, it is with great remorse and reluctance that I must announce the resignation of my commission. Unfortunately, I have urgent matters I must attend to in Denver. Therefore, I am bestowing the rank of full colonel to Major

Chivington who will also take over as commanding officer."

Most of the officers applauded. But Josh noticed that Lieutenant Colonel Tappan stood silent in the background. Even though his was the higher rank, it was Chivington who was appointed as the new commanding officer. While the others spoke highly of Chivington, Tappan kept a jaundiced eye on him.

"Thank you, Colonel Slough. You shall be greatly missed," said Chivington while he shook hands and accepted the shoulder boards with silver eagles. To the officers he said, "To fill my former position, with the promotion to major, I have chosen Edward Wynkoop of Company A."

Ned Wynkoop stood speechless at the surprise announcement. He shook hands with the three senior officers and accepted the gold oak leaf shoulder boards. "Thank you, sirs," was all he could manage.

As Chivington took over command of the house, the officers, with the exception of Sam Tappan, gathered in a large tent. With cigars and glasses of brandy, they congratulated each other on promotions and victories. Josh drank coffee and passed on the cigars. Eventually, Ned told them the real reason for Colonel Slough's sudden departure. "When Colonel Canby heard about our victory, he was more upset that Colonel Slough had disobeyed his orders to remain at Fort Union than he was glad about us winning."

"Just sour grapes," said Silas, already refilling his glass. "No doubt he wanted to become a hero for the locals and he can't abide knowing that a regiment from Colorado saved his bacon."

"Colonel Slough had a tidy collection of reprimanding dispatches from Canby. He probably felt it wise to resign rather than face a possible court martial upon arrival in Albuquerque." Ned puffed on a long cigar and leaned against a table.

An artillery captain sarcastically added, "Yeah, and you can't press your luck too often with those cannon balls either."

All of them roared with laughter while Ned feigned disgust.

"Wait a minute, what's this about Albuquerque?" Josh asked.

"We leave tomorrow before sunrise to join forces with Canby. Once we're linked, we'll finish off what's left of Sibley's Confederate Army," said Ned, picking lint off his uniform.

Inside an officer's tent, Silas sat on the edge of his cot, brushing polish onto one of his boots. "I know the major—uh, I mean the new colonel—can be more than a little obsessive, but ordering prisoners to be shot is a tough pill to swallow. It's nothing you would ever catch me doing. No offense, Josh, but I don't need any religion to tell me what's right or wrong."

"Okay, then answer me this, Silas: where will you go when you die?"

"I don't know. Nowhere I guess. I was reared in a strict Calvinist community in Bath, Maine; I know the answer I'm supposed to give. Sorry, but I'm an incurable agnostic."

"Well then, it would be quite a tragedy for me if I were to see you shot down. So take extra care when we meet with those Texans."

"Jesus was a good man, but when it comes to protecting my life, I put my faith in ol' Sam Colt." Silas patted his holstered revolver.

"Well, look at it this way. Sam Colt has been dead for ... what? two months now?"

"Yeah?"

"Jesus walked out of the tomb on the third day."

# Chapter 7

## STIRRING THE HORNET'S NEST

In early October the War Department finally released the Pike's Peakers from their duties. Jubilantly the men marched through the desert and over the mountains. Even the intense Colonel Chivington appeared lighthearted and spoke excitedly of the future. "My information was correct, Joshua; the new governor sent me a letter asking that I run for Congress. This would be on the condition, of course, that the people vote for statehood. With this victory I could get elected to Congress. Hopefully, there will be another victory between now and then to ensure I make it to Washington. The new governor is also from Ohio, and he has solid business sense to help Colorado become a leading economic power."

"You would be a great help in implementing changes to the Cheyenne reservation. I hope you don't stop pounding the pulpit. Your sermons don't exactly allow a person to doze off," Josh kidded.

The large parson sat rigid in his saddle and looked straight ahead as he spoke. "Seek ye first the kingdom of God, and all these things shall be added unto you. Always put God first, son, always put God first!"

Josh couldn't keep a grin off his face as they made camp on the Arkansas River. Sunflower and Little Dove were only half a day's ride away, and he felt he would burst from excitement. He'd been gone nearly a year.

In the morning, Josh pulled on his buckskins and packed his things. As he strapped his saddle onto his new horse, Charger, Chivington came walking up briskly. "Good morning, Joshua. You are no doubt anxious to get back to your wife."

"Yes, sir, I am." Josh stepped into the stirrup and hoisted himself onto the saddle.

"What are your plans now?"

"I guess I should finish what I came out here to do in the first place. Before all this started I was making pretty good progress teaching English to the Cheyennes and showing them how to read."

"The war may be over for us, but there are still plenty of hard times ahead. Governor Evans and I are determined to make this territory fit for settlement. Major Wynkoop and Lieutenant Soule here are going to help us do it. Becoming a state won't be easy." Chivington gripped his Bible as he spoke. "There's something else I think you should know. When we return to Denver, I shall be appointed commanding colonel for the territory's military district. I could use an intelligent man of God like you as my aide. Your pay would remain the same."

"Colonel, I just might take your offer some day. But right now I want to get back to my teaching position, if it's still there."

Chivington narrowed his eyes. "Well, you're still considered to be a chaplain in the reserves and are subject to recall. And as long as you don't resign your position, you may keep that horse."

"Thank you, Colonel. I'll be at the Cheyenne camp if you need me." Josh reined Charger to the right and they galloped downstream.


Josh was first spotted by camp dogs that barked at his arrival. A noticeably smaller Cheyenne camp was located across from the new OIA agency building south of the road. Even the dog population had dwindled.

From his in-laws' tepee, Sunflower ran out and threw her arms around him in a warm embrace. In response, he brought his lips to hers and kept them there until the other women in camp began to laugh.

Little Dove approached timidly. He knelt and hugged her. "Look what I made, Father," she said in Cheyenne, handing him a necklace of blue beads. Then she repeated her words, this time in English.

"That's terrific, sweetie. You've made so much progress," said Josh in Cheyenne. Standing, he asked Sunflower, "Where is everybody?"

"The people go hungry. The agent and his son charge high prices for our rations. The men leave the reservation in search of game. Most of the women remain here, but many go with their husbands to the hunting camps."

Josh closed his eyes and took a deep breath. "I had hoped I would not find the situation like this. In the morning I'll speak with Jack Smith at the trading post. I hoped we could spend some time together before I had to deal with things. The new agent, Sam Colley, is he really selling the rations?"

"Yes, but not always for money; sometimes in trade. His wife uses our annuity flour to bake pies to sell to the soldiers at the fort. ... Black Robe, my family has no food!"

"Where is Spotted Bear?"

"He is out hunting with the others and has been gone many days."

"Where are the annuities kept?"

"Mostly in warehouses at the fort, but the trading post here has some. They sell to anyone with money to buy them."

Josh decided to go to the agency trading post and buy enough groceries to sustain his in-laws until he could figure out what had gone wrong. The injustice compelled him to analyze the situation, and a crazy idea popped into his head. He asked Sunflower's nephew, Black Hoof, to bring a packhorse and two riding ponies. Then he told Black Hoof's mother, Butterfly, to inform the other women in the camp that they would be able to get some of their monthly rations at the post. It didn't take long for word to get around and soon about thirty women with baskets assembled at the camp circle.

"Ladies, let's go shopping," said Josh, feeling determined.

"Dear husband, you cannot feed the whole camp," said Sunflower in bewilderment.

"I'm only making sure they get what already belongs to them."

Josh led the women to the trading post which had been hastily constructed of logs and mud and was leaning to one side. Josh pulled out his army carbine and went through the front door, with Black Hoof and Sunflower following. Behind a crude wooden counter stood two men. The first was a middle-aged bald man with a ring of uncombed gray hair who wore a sweat-stained undershirt. His body odor made a buffalo chip fire smell downright delightful. "That's the man our people call Skunk. He is not very hospitable," Sunflower whispered to Josh.

Next to Skunk stood a red-haired younger man dressed in a mail-order suit who had recently had a fresh haircut and shave. "And that's Agent Colley's son, Dexter. His tongue is forked like his father's."

"Yeah, I remember him."

"Listen, Chaplain, you're welcome to shop here, but those two Injuns need to wait outside. They know the rules," barked Skunk through his tobacco layered teeth.

"One of those Injuns you're referring to happens to be my wife."

"Your wife? You're funnin' me, ain't you?" Skunk laughed.

"Mister, I'm not in the mood to hear that talk right now," warned Josh.

Except for the guns and whiskey, every box and bag in the store was marked *U.S. Govt. OIA*. Casually Josh spoke to Black Hoof in English. "Tell the women to come inside and collect all the goods they can carry."

"You're out of your mind, preacher," yelled Skunk, reaching for a double-barreled shotgun mounted on the wall behind him.

Josh raised the carbine to hip level and pointed it at the two men. "I've just finished a forced march through New Mexico and back, and I'm feeling a little cranky. So let's make this as quick as possible."

Skunk lost interest in the shotgun.

The Cheyenne women hurried in and emptied the store. When Sunflower opened a package of beef, she covered her mouth to keep from vomiting. "Black Robe, this meat is crawling with maggots."

"Crawling? It looks more like they're swimming. Is this meat being sold to the Indians as well?" Josh demanded.

"Occasionally we get some that wasn't salted in time. It happens," said Skunk.

Black Hoof examined all the packages of meat on a table. "Uncle, none of this is fit to eat."

"Where's the beef you sell to the government employees and the travelers?" Josh demanded.

Skunk jerked his thumb over his shoulder and said, "Out back in the ice house."

"Black Robe, the bacon is fine," said Sunflower.

Josh kept his eyes on Skunk. "Good, we'll take it."

Dexter pointed at Josh while his face turned redder than his hair. "I know who you are. You're that Methodist teacher who thinks he can fix the reservation!"

"That's right."

"Consider yourself fired," yelled Dexter. "My pa is the agent here now. When he hears that you robbed a reservation trading post he will notify the U.S. Marshal, that I promise you!"

"You read my mind, Dexter," said Josh pointing the gun at him. "I am no longer a teacher working for the Office of Indian Affairs. As of today I am the aide to the Commander of the Military District who answers directly to Governor Evans. Perhaps the marshal would be interested in your misappropriation of government funds and under-the-table cash transactions."

The two men behind the counter looked skeptical. Finally Dexter said, "All right, mister, take all the Injun feed you want. If you're content with not bothering the marshal, then so am I. Just don't let me ever see you again."

"You know, for a man who is at the wrong end of a rifle barrel, you still got a lot of bark, don't you?" said Josh.

This seemed to take the starch out of the cocky Dexter. This time he kept quiet.

That evening, despite the dark times they found themselves in, a festive mood prevailed throughout the Cheyenne camp. For the first time in months, the women cooked large servings of bacon and beans. Sugar sprinkled fry bread and hot coffee were served for dessert.

After eating his fill, Josh eased back against a pile of buffalo hides and watched the children play. Sunflower knelt beside him for a moment to whisper, "Even though you and my mother are forbidden to speak to each other according to our customs, I want you to know she is very grateful for what you did."

Josh smiled at Sunflower in acknowledgment of what she said, though he knew it already. While supervising her daughters in cooking the meal, Josh's mother-in-law, Hummingbird, had smiled at him and nodded her thanks. She was only forty-eight, but her weathered face and gray hair made her look much older.

Early the next morning, Josh rode to the army post, which had been renamed Fort Lyon. The shrunken Arapahoe camp remained across the river. Near the church, he saw a new schoolhouse with a few Indian children inside. "So Oscar Devenish forged ahead with the school while I was gone," he muttered to himself.

At Bent's Trading Post his friend Jack Smith described how things had deteriorated since the Colley family took charge. "Nothing in the treaty has taken effect, and the reservation boundaries are only lines on a map. None of the allotted acres to the chiefs and warriors have been awarded because nobody has been enrolled yet. Sam and Dexter Colley aren't interested in enrolling the Indians, because then they can exaggerate the numbers. Since my people cannot get their annuities, they hunt buffalo from here to the South Platte River like before. The warriors can feed themselves on the prairie, but often the elderly, the women, and the children go hungry."

"That settles it." Josh set his tin cup on top of the barrel. "I will go to Denver where I can hope to make some real changes."

"What do you mean?" asked Jack.

Josh paced the floor in frustration. "This whole thing is getting out of hand. I had this vision of an ideal reservation with a thriving Christian community. First the government reneges on the land promised to them, and now a corrupt agent is lining his pockets at their expense."

Jack gave Josh a quizzical look. "Does this surprise you? It seems you have much to learn about the real way a reservation operates."

Josh rubbed the back of his neck. "You're not surprised? You mean you find this type of corruption acceptable?"

"How can you ask that? Listen to what I say: My father told me a long time ago that there is the way things should be and there is the way things are."

"Well that's not good enough," Josh shouted then immediately lowered his voice. "I'm sorry. I'm not angry with you. You see, the colonel offered me a full time job as a chaplain and I'm going to take it until this whole thing is resolved."

Looking across the street, Jack said, "Dexter Colley is over there with two known drifters who are bad news. That pinto belongs to Sleeping Wolf."

Josh saw the immaculately dressed Dexter speaking in a hushed voice to two men wearing tattered, grimy clothes. One wore a derby and the other had his hair in a low ponytail below an English riding cap. The two men held the reins of a fine pinto and a palomino. Dexter handed a gold piece to the taller man with the ponytail.

The man's greedy eyes lit up and he spoke with a high-pitched voice. "Come on, Joe, let's get a bottle!"

Josh thought they looked familiar, but paid them no heed.

"Where are you going now?" Sunflower asked as she watched Josh packing his clothes again.

"I've got to get to Denver right away."

"You have just returned. For more than two days you ride to the fort and back. Now you tell me you go to Denver?" A tear was welling in Sunflower's eye.

Josh pressed his fingertips against his temples. "The corruption here is unbelievable. These so-called caretakers of the Cheyennes will starve them to pad their own bank accounts. I need to get to Denver and let Colonel Chivington and Governor Evans know what's happening here."

"You think they don't know? Black Robe, your concern for my people is good. But rushing off to Denver will not fix the problem. You said God wanted you to build a school on the reservation, but that was done by the Hoe Man while you were absent. You wanted to translate the Bible into the Cheyenne language, but what have you done except write one book of the Bible in your notebook?"

"Not much." She was right, and this made Josh want to sulk. "The schoolhouse built by Oscar is only for the Arapahoe children at the fort. A lot more needs to be done than just building a school, but first I want to get this mess resolved."

"I need a husband, and Little Dove needs a father. Can not these other things wait until after winter?"

Josh stopped his packing and took her in his arms. "I guess you're right, as usual. I suppose I could wait until after Christmas."

"Good. My mother's lodge is preparing special feast for you."

"A feast for me? Why?"

"Because you fed my family the day you returned. The camp knows your brave deed against the younger Colley. My mother spoke with Chief Lean Bear and Uncle Kicking Horse. They agree you should be accepted as a member of our lodge. By tradition, you would present a large elk to my mother. But she is happy and satisfied with the bacon and beans and flour you provide. My nephew, Black Hoof, brought back a buck. We'll cook that for the feast. He is becoming a skilled hunter."

Josh went to the river where he bathed, shaved, and put on

clean clothes. Black Hoof formally invited Josh into his grandfather's tepee. Josh made his way to the rear of the tent, where Kicking Horse, who sat on a buffalo robe, invited Josh to sit at his left. At his right sat Chief Lean Bear.

Hummingbird took a large portion of hot venison from the fire and gave it to her brother on a wooden plate. Kicking Horse stood and presented the meat to the four major points of the compass by extending the platter of meat in his arms while facing north, then east, then south, and then west. After he returned to his seat, Hummingbird, without making eye contact, gave a portion of meat to Josh. When all the men had been served, they began eating.

Lean Bear spoke. "Black Robe, we are aware that you have angered some of your people in order to feed your in-law's lodge, and we will do what we can to help you. We want peace with the government and hope you will speak with their chiefs on our behalf. I would speak with the Great White Father if I could."

"I will do what I can," promised Josh.

After the meal, Kicking Horse nodded his head toward Hummingbird, who brought to Josh a robe of dark reds and purples. She had made the exquisite piece of work herself. She laid it on the buffalo hide next to Josh. With a pair of tongs, she took a glowing coal from the fire and set it on the bare ground in front of her son-in-law. She then placed sweet grass on the coal. As previously instructed by his wife, Josh put on the robe and stood over the coal, so the smoke filled the inside of the garment. Afterwards, he thanked only Kicking Horse, then he exited the tepee being careful not to walk between anyone and the fire. He hadn't been so moved—and so nervous—since that awful day at Glorieta Pass when he had witnessed so much death and destruction.

That night Josh and Sunflower lay together in their bed of rabbit-fur blankets. Sunflower said, "Now you may speak to my mother, but only if she speaks to you first. And you must never address her by her name. You may also enter my family's tepee, but only if Uncle Kicking Horse gives his permission."

"I hope I can remember all these rules!" He said, then momentarily forgot everything else as he kissed her.

Josh fished for brown trout on the Arkansas River as the sun came up. His tension eased a bit as he watched his fly-lure drift in the current and listened to the water running over the rocks.

A movement on the far bank startled him. It was a Cheyenne warrior in full regalia minus the war paint. On his back sat a quiver of painted arrows. To Josh's relief, it was Jack Smith on horseback. Josh had never seen him wearing anything but white-men's clothes before.

As Jack dismounted and walked his horse across the stream, Josh called, "Thanks a lot, Jack, you nearly scared ten years off my life. How long have you been watching me?"

"Not long. Sunflower told me I would find you here."

"Did you bring a pole?"

"I prefer to fish by having my wife and daughter drag a willow net along a shallow bottom while I give them instructions. Besides, there is no time for fishing, Joshua. There's plenty of trouble about, and it's looking for you," said Jack.

Josh's heart sank. "Now what?"

While his horse drank from the river, Jack explained. "You upset powerful people that day at the trading post. Unfortunately, my father is on friendly terms with Sam Colley and his son. Perhaps too friendly."

"You mean your father also knowingly cheats the Indians? How can he, when your mother and you are both tribal members?"

"He does what he must to stay alive in these uncertain times. However, that is not what I came to tell you. Last night at the fort's saloon there was some loud talk. It all came from those two bottom feeders we saw. Their names are Joe Blackburn and Nate Talbot. They drank much whiskey. Do you know them?"

Josh thought for a moment. "I've heard the names and seen

their faces more than once, but I can't say I know them."

"They know you. The more they drank, the more they talked. They used to hunt scalps in Mexico when there was bounty on the Apaches. Those two cowards found it easier to scalp a friendly Indian than a hostile one. The local gobernador learned what they were doing and chased them back to the States. They did time in Kansas for robbing a stage and came here when they got out of jail. They also may have worked as low wage 'contractors.' Until recently, they were content with claim jumping, cattle rustling, and horse stealing. Two days ago they became contractors again. Someone is willing to pay them a hundred dollars for your scalp."

"Dexter?" Josh asked nervously.

"Most likely."

"Wait a minute; you said that pinto belongs to Sleeping Wolf. Now I remember where I've seen those two before. Porcupine and I came across them on our way to the Republican River. Except they didn't steal that pinto from Sleeping Wolf, they stole it from the Kiowas who were hot on their trail."

"Thieves chasing thieves. Sleeping Wolf only wants his prized gelding back. Anyway, my friend, watch out for those two."

"I'll do my best."

Jack strung an arrow onto his bow and shot into the water near Josh's feet. Jumping back, Josh saw a trout pinned to the sandy stream bed. "Enjoy your breakfast," Jack called as he rode away.

Josh set down his fishing pole. Fire-roasted trout did sound good. But the tension had returned.

# Chapter 8

## THE SMOKY HILL

Chivington sat comfortably in his plush leather chair. "I'm glad you're working for me, Joshua."

"Well, Colonel, it's good to be back in Denver," fibbed Josh as he fidgeted in his seat.

"What else is on your mind?" the colonel asked shrewdly.

"Well, sir, even though I am concerned for the spiritual well-being of the regiment, that was not my primary reason for returning this winter." Josh wiped sweaty palms on his trousers.

"Go on."

"Do you remember me speaking about modernizing the reservation?"

"Yes I do, and you can certainly be more effective working with the governor and me than teaching at some Indian schoolhouse. Don't forget, though, the war is still being fought, and everything else is lower priority."

"I understand. This war is such an inconvenience."

"The regiment has been renamed the First Colorado Cavalry. In fact, the whole territorial militia has become cavalry, because it's more effective at Indian fighting."

"Indian fighting? What Indians are we fighting, sir?"

"At this point it is only a precaution. The First is headquartered at Fort Lyon and is now under the command of Lieutenant Colonel Tappan. Most of them are here to protect the capitol. A second regiment has been raised, but the regular army is using it in Kansas to chase down Confederate guerillas."

Later that afternoon at a meeting in the governor's office,

Chivington's staff officers discussed the usual Indian problems and the incompetence of the Office of Indian Affairs. With some trepidation Josh spoke up, "It's my understanding that in the past the OIA has sent delegations of chiefs from various tribes to Washington to meet with the President and his cabinet. Afterwards, there is always a dithery peace, albeit a temporary one."

The other officers balked. Nevertheless, Governor Evans replied, "That may not be a bad idea. At least while they're gone the warriors will return to the reservation and we'll have time to think.'

"Governor, the Cheyennes want to return to the reservation, but they're starving. Agent Colley and his son are selling the annuities as if they came from their personal inventory. Replace Colley with an honest agent, and the Indians will be content to live peaceably on the reservation. It's that simple!" pleaded Josh.

Governor Evans rolled a cigar on his fingertips and glanced at the colonel. "I hate to differ with you, Chaplain, but it is not that simple. Agents are replaced by the Secretary of the Interior with approval from the President. Right now President Lincoln is so preoccupied with the war, it is difficult to get him to address other domestic issues. However, a trip to Washington for the chiefs is feasible. I'll contact Secretary Usher. Meanwhile, if you could return to Fort Lyon and pick three chiefs to represent the Cheyenne tribe, that would be a tremendous help."

"Yes, sir, I'll get right on it." Josh tried not to show his excitement at the opportunity to see his family and friends again.

When the meeting dismissed, Chivington said to Josh, "That's a pretty good idea of yours. Be careful on your trip."

Their footsteps echoed down the long, dark corridor as Josh told the colonel about the contract killers Dexter Colley had hired. A letter from Jack reported that the two lowlifes were rumored to be in Denver. Was he being followed? Reluctantly he asked, "Sir, do you think you could provide an escort for me?"

Chivington shook his head. "I'm sorry, son, but I need every man I've got here in the capitol. Did you know a couple months ago some Cheyennes rode into town displaying scalps? You'll be all right; keep your Bible in one hand and your gun in the other. I've preached more than one sermon that way. You would be amazed how few people doze off in their pews."

Not exactly what I was asking about.

As quickly as he could, Josh changed into his riding clothes, said a prayer, and left for the stables. He asked the Lord to resolve the situation regarding the two hired killers. He knew he would be safe on the road leading out of town which had a lot of traffic; however, the further south he went, the more desolate the road.

Around sundown it began to get cold, but not enough to warrant staying at some stage-line hotel. Besides, he was running short of cash and those hotels were always more expensive then the ones in town. He found an out-of-the-way spot under some cottonwoods along Cherry Creek.

After building a fire, he heated pork-and-beans for dinner and opened his Bible. He read from Psalm 59 silently then out loud. "Deliver me from mine enemies, O my God: defend me from those that rise up against me. Deliver me from the workers of iniquity, and save me from bloody men."

A branch snapped.

Except for the firelight in his immediate area, there was total darkness. Josh heard an excited high-pitched voice, but couldn't make out the words. A familiar but unfriendly voice then said, "Shut up, he'll hear us!"

Josh already had his bedroll laid out by the fire, so he stuffed his heavy coat into it and put his hat on the pillow. After grabbing his carbine, he hid behind a log in the dark. He whispered a prayer of protection for his horse.

Several long minutes passed, and Josh could see the horse looking off to his right. Bullets from a sudden fusillade of gunfire shredded the bedroll and hat. Charger neighed and tried to back away, but the lead rope kept him tethered to a tree. When the shooting stopped, Blackburn and Talbot jumped into the firelight carrying the advantageous Henry repeating rifles.

"I got him, Nate! He's deader than Julius Caesar!"

"My bullet hit him first, otherwise he would've moved on you."

"Ah, shut up! Check his teeth for gold before you carve him."

Blackburn started to reload his rifle while Talbot pulled out his knife then loudly swore. "He ain't here, Joe!"

"What?"

Josh stepped into the light with the carbine pointed at them. "You fellows looking for someone?"

The two outlaws dropped their weapons and reached for the sky, fear in their eyes.

"Sorry, Chaplain, we thought you were somebody else," said Talbot.

"How did you know I was a chaplain? I'm not wearing a uniform."

Blackburn cursed at his partner. "Stupid!"

"Go ahead and shuck those gun belts," ordered Josh.

The two men complied then raised their hands back in the air.

Josh concentrated on keeping his composure. Besides his conscience, there was nothing to stop him from firing, but he savvied that such an act would be murder. He tried to sound as threatening as he could. "You boys may be dumber than a box of rocks, but you're smart enough to know if I see you again I won't be so forgiving. The way I see it, you owe me for a bedroll, a coat, and a hat. Be on your way and leave the money at Bent's Trading Post."

Talbot cautiously said, "Thank you, sir, but we'll be needing those Henries, and the Colts too. Is it all right to take them back now?"

"Ah, shut up!" spat Blackburn, smacking his friend on the back of the head. Then to Josh he said, "Thank you, sir, but if you want to keep them guns they'll more than cover the cost of your hat and blanket."

"They're stolen."

"We'll leave the money at the trading post then."

"Where are your horses?" asked Josh.

"They're tied downstream about a hundred yards," said Blackburn. "Why?"

"Heck, I know you have no intentions of paying me back, but I am going to slow you down some. Leave one of your horses." Josh held the muzzle of the carbine an inch from Blackburn's chest.

Sweat ran from under Blackburn's derby and down his razor-stubble face. "We'll leave the palomino."

"How come it has to be my horse?" protested Talbot.

"I told you to shut up! We'll be going now," said Blackburn. He and Talbot then carefully moved back into the dark and ran off.

Josh stayed behind them a hundred feet to make sure they left the horse and to listen to any information they might divulge.

In the darkness, Talbot smacked head-on into a tree. He cursed loudly. When they reached their horses, he whined, "Now what are we going to do?"

"Give me a minute to think," said Blackburn.

"Little Colley said that chaplain would be no trouble at all. I ain't never had a preacher get the drop on me before. We should go pay him another visit."

"Oh, we'll pay him another visit, all right, when we collect that hundred dollars, but first we got to find us another scalp. Remember how we done it in Sonora?"

"I sure do," answered Talbot, perking up.


Josh rode into the Cheyenne camp with the palomino in tow. Black Hoof, Sunflower's nephew, took the horse's lead and said, "Jack Smith says the men who have Sleeping Wolf's pinto also had a palomino with a new saddle. This looks like the one he spoke of. How did you get it, Uncle?"

*Of course! Those were the guys with the stolen pinto! Why didn't I think to ask them about the pinto?* thought Josh ruefully. Well, it had been dark.

"It's a long story for another time, Black Hoof."

"This mare has not been cared for and has suffered abuse." Black Hoof looked over the palomino. "Maybe this is why the Great Spirit wanted you to take *her,*" he said generously.

Only then did Josh notice the fresh scars and exposed skin on the horse's right side. "You could be right. In fact, I'm glad I got her instead. If you bring her back to health, you may ride her as much as you wish."

"I will take care of her, Uncle."

At Fort Lyon, Josh met with Agent Colley, his son Dexter, and Lieutenant Colonel Samuel Tappan. During the New Mexico campaign, Tappan had been courteous to Josh, but had never engaged him in conversation. Content to be a loner, he shunned the nightly gatherings of the officers, whereas Silas had always been one drink ahead of everyone else.

Since Sam Tappan detested the Colley Family, Josh decided to tell him about Missus Colley's pie enterprise at the fort. Sure enough, he put an end to it until she could provide proof of purchase for the ingredients she used.

However, sitting in front of the commanding officer's desk, Josh felt awkward. He sensed Tappan had the best interest of the Indians in mind, but he seemed cool and distant. Tappan sat in his chair holding a piece of paper with Chivington's hastily scrawled orders. He looked Josh over for a minute before sternly asking, "Why are you here?"

Josh leaned forward. "Uh, the governor and Colonel—"

"I can read. I want to know why you, Joshua Frasier, are in this regiment."

"Well, sir, I am the chaplain, and I was hoping to help make some dramatic improvements—"

"On the reservation. That's all I heard you talk about when we were in New Mexico. It was as if you didn't even realize there was a war being fought."

"I'm afraid I don't follow you, sir," stammered Josh.

"I want the same thing you do, but first things first. Do you read me?"

"Yes, sir, I think so."

"I don't think you do." Tappan rose from his chair. "Not everyone in this territory is looking out for the welfare of the Cheyennes. Including those fat cats you've been rubbing elbows with. They'll tell you whatever it is you want to hear, so long as you don't interfere with their political ambitions. I'm not going to spell it out for you, because I've got my own career to think about."

"What about sending three chiefs to Washington?"

"I couldn't care less. The purpose for them going isn't so they can meet with the President; it's to impress upon them that they cannot win a war against the United States. ... But I'll approve whichever three you choose, so the governor can get this thing started."

Josh worked with the First Regiment's detachment at Fort Lyon throughout the spring. In May, a great feast was held inside the big lodge of the Cheyenne camp for Chiefs Lean Bear, Standing-in-Water, and War Bonnet when they returned. They told stories about meeting President Lincoln, going to P.T. Barnum's museum in New York City, and having their photographs taken by Mathew Brady. Lean Bear stood and proudly showed the peace medal around his neck and a document signed by the President declaring him peaceable.

"Your face looks much happier than it did when it was covered with paint that day at the fort," laughed Josh.

"Yes, too bad I was not allowed to wear it for the camera," jested Lean Bear.

About one-third of the regiment remained at Fort Lyon, giving

Josh plenty to do, so he didn't have to rush back to Denver. He held Sunday services at the fort's chapel, prayed for sick soldiers in the infirmary, and raised money for the less fortunate Cheyenne and Arapahoe families. Much to his disappointment, though, no one from the government arrived to help them become self-sufficient.

Sam and Dexter Colley watched the distribution of the annuities, which were now monthly, and Josh watched the Colleys.

Dexter walked up to where Josh sat on the top rail of a corral and declared, "There's no need for you to be here, you know."

Josh kept cool. "Yeah, well, every time I'm not here the Indian complaints of being cheated increase."

A few weeks later, the Cheyennes gradually left the reservation for their summer buffalo hunt. Only a few lodges remained at the reservation camp. At the fort, Josh found Samuel Tappan cleaning out his office.

"Excuse me, sir, but where are you going?"

"The colonel is relieving me of command because I sent First Regiment troops to Fort Larned to help them with the Kiowa problem. I wish you luck."

In July, the colonel summoned Josh back to Denver. When Josh arrived, a guard ushered him into Governor Evans's office where Chivington also waited. They sat in overstuffed leather chairs surrounded by walls lined with books. For once, the prima donna Chivington remained silent while the governor spoke.

"Chaplain, are you aware of the great Sioux uprising that occurred in Minnesota last year?"

"Yes, a missionary couple who befriended my late wife and me were killed there," said Josh looking over at Chivington.

The governor continued. "I'm sorry to hear that. We've learned that in May, the Cheyenne chiefs, including Black Kettle and White Antelope, met with representatives of the Sioux tribe about seventy-five miles north of here. The Sioux and Cheyenne have been nominal allies at best, so this sudden meeting of their leaders is disconcerting. We believe that the Cheyenne and Arapahoe, with backing from the Sioux, are planning to drive all Americans out of the territory."

"So what can I do for you?" asked Josh.

Governor Evans continued. "Chaplain, last month we met with several Arapahoe chiefs here at the capitol building and I warned them with all sincerity that if they make war with us, it will be a war of their extermination. I instructed them to return to their camps and spread the word. Of course nobody wants a war of eradication, especially Colonel Chivington and myself."

"I absolutely agree," said Chivington with concern in his dark eyes.

"The colonel has informed me that you are married to a Cheyenne woman, which means you are held in high esteem by that tribe. We would like you to take a wagon full of the usual annuity goods and locate the main Cheyenne hunting camp. Try to convince them that making peace is in their best interest."

Missing the hint of threat in the governor's words and bewildered at that odd request, Josh asked, "I'm sure they would love that, but where exactly am I to find this hunting camp?"

"Come now, Joshua," said Chivington with a touch of anger, "you should know by now that those Indians always have their summer buffalo hunt along the Smokey Hill or Republican Rivers."

"That's a little vague, wouldn't you say?"

"Find the headwaters of the Smokey Hill and follow it downstream. Lieutenant Colonel Tappan recommended you highly for this assignment," said Chivington.

"He did?"

"That's right. He also highly approved of the chiefs you selected to go to Washington and says he didn't influence you in the least. Unfortunately, I found it necessary to reassign him."

Governor Evans spoke with a cigar clinched in his teeth. "Tell the Cheyennes to meet us where the Cherry Fork flows into the Arickaree. Agent Sam Colley has tried to persuade the Indians camped around Fort Lyon to ride north to meet with us, but they claim their ponies are too weak to make the journey. Sounds like a bald-faced lie to me. What do you think, Chaplain?"

Josh stood, put on his hat, and said, "Well, if there's anyone who would know a bald-faced lie, it's Sam Colley."


Josh left the city with twin muleskinners, Zeke and Zed, the annuity wagon, and four mule teams. Zeke and Zed were a couple of well-fed farm boys with full beards and dressed in matching denim overalls. The brothers took care of the wagon and mules while Josh rode ahead on Charger. Four days later, Josh located the hunting camp just across the Kansas line on the Smokey Hill River.

The warriors received Josh coolly. It didn't matter that they were related by marriage; he still worked for the army. Josh let them take the sacks of flour, sugar, coffee, and tobacco from the wagon. The Cheyenne women prepared a meal and Chief Lean Bear invited Josh to eat with them. Zeke and Zed had to fend for themselves. Josh was delighted they had had success hunting buffalo so no camp dogs would be butchered for use in the cooking pot. While the chiefs passed a pipe around an outdoor campfire, Josh told them where Governor Evans wished to meet them.

Lean Bear still wore the peace medal given to him by President Lincoln. He had not seen Josh since that feast in Kicking Horse's lodge. Finally he said, "Black Robe, tell the white chief we have no need to speak with him. There are plenty of buffalo here and for the first time since we signed the treaty, our bellies are full."

Josh wondered why the governor would interfere, since the Cheyennes seemed content on this remote section of prairie. While he pondered this, the chiefs and lead warriors held discussion among themselves.

Then Lean Bear addressed Josh. "Return and tell the white chief we will meet him at the place he has chosen, two moons from now, the last week of September."

Two months later, Josh led the governor, Sam Colley, and the Sioux agent, who the governor simply introduced as, "Mister Lorey," to the designated meeting spot. They only found four lodges and the occupants informed them the main camp had yet to arrive. Josh told the men and their escort of ten soldiers to wait there while he went in search of the Cheyennes. He felt he had taken on the role of his friend, Porcupine Pete. Fully dressed in buckskins and with a rifle across his saddle, he rode twenty-five miles up Beaver Creek, but saw no sign of Indians. Frustrated, he headed back toward the Smoky Hill River. A couple days later he found plenty of unshod tracks and fresh pony droppings.

Crossing back into Kansas, Josh found the Cheyenne camp at the exact location where it had been in July. Now it had expanded from 150 lodges to 240 and included the Dog Soldiers warrior society. A group of warriors on horseback quickly surrounded him with rifles and loaded bows, but Making Medicine spoke, "Don't harm him, he is a friend to our people. He is married to the woman Sunflower of Kicking Horse's lodge."

The warriors left without a word and galloped across the river. Making Medicine stayed and rode with Josh to the camp. On the way, out of the blue, Making Medicine asked, "Black Robe, I have learned much English and have been reading a Bible given to me by the Hoe Man. Why does Jesus say we are to forgive others who have wronged us even if they have not asked for it?"

Josh had been thinking about how to get the Cheyennes to the governor's location, and Making Medicine's question caught him off guard. "Huh? Well, uh, when we sin we transgress against the true living God who is pure and righteous. Nothing men do to us is as offensive as our sins are to God. We deserve death and eternal hell. Yet Jesus died that death for us. His forgiveness is an undeserved gift. Therefore, should we not be willing to forgive others as well, whether the offender asks for it or not?"

The young man's long, black hair blew back from his face as they rode into the wind. "I see your point. But how can my people forgive those who take away our land and lie about wanting to help us?"

They pulled up to Lean Bear's tepee, where several sub-chiefs had gathered. "Making Medicine, we'll discuss this further at another time. Right now I need to speak with the chief," said Josh.

Making Medicine gave Josh a disappointed look and then galloped his horse back across the river to rejoin the other warriors.

During that night's council in the big lodge, Josh asked Lean Bear, "Why did you not go to the Arickaree as promised?"

Lean Bear leveled a stern look at Josh. "Our camp has been ravished with whooping cough and diarrhea. Since we last saw you, thirty-five of our children have died. Even Black Kettle is here but is too sick to see you. Besides, why should we leave when there are plenty of buffalo? Why return to the reservation where there is no game?"

Josh thought for a moment then spoke. "That makes sense, but you need to understand; I'm only inquiring on behalf of Governor Evans."

At the mention of the governor's name, Lean Bear became angry. "Here is something else you can tell the white chief. The whole treaty at Fort Wise was a lie!" He imitated a forked tongue with his index fingers. "White Antelope told us he did not sign it; those who did were tricked. We did not surrender the headwaters of the Republican or the Smoky Hill. The whites may build their railroads across our land, but they must not dwell there. Also, we learned that a Cheyenne was shot by an Osage at Fort Larned. Why does the white man's government spurn us by siding with our enemy?"

"I haven't heard anything about it. Lean Bear, I don't know what to say."

"Then do your talking with the white chief. Tell him we will not meet him at the Arickaree and we will not return to the reservation." Lean Bear spoke forcefully. He then smashed the clay bowl of his peace pipe against a stone.

Josh returned to his tepee at the reservation camp. Nearby, at Point of Rocks, a new agency building was being constructed along with a blacksmith shop and a warehouse. Sunflower told him about the rumors of the Sioux uniting with the Cheyennes, Arapahoes, Kiowas, and Comanches for an offensive against the Americans in the spring. In the meantime, they were to gather supplies and acquire guns and ammunition. Josh felt the rumors were validated when he learned three different wagon trains had arrived at the fort totally empty, raided by Indians.

At an officers' meeting with Agent Sam Colley present, Josh met the fort's new commanding officer, Major Scott J. Anthony, whose square beard complemented his formal dress uniform complete with sword and tasseled crimson sash.

The officers discussed the lack of food and the possibility of war with the Indians. Josh learned that Chief Little Raven and two-thousand starving Arapahoes had returned to Fort Lyon.

"There aren't any buffalo around here for two-hundred miles," said Colley. "They're committing depredations from sheer starvation."

*No thanks to you*, Josh thought.

At the head of the large conference table the new commanding officer tapped his notepad with a pen. "The Cheyenne and Arapahoe tribes are in a destitute condition and we will be obligated to feed them." A sinister look crossed his face. "Or we can let them starve to death, which would be a much easier way of disposing of them."

Back at his tepee, Josh had just removed his boots when Sunflower ran in, crying hysterically. He jumped to his feet and put his arms around her. "What is it?"

She tried to explain but was too distraught to make sense.

"Calm down and tell me again. I won't let anyone hurt you."

In a choked voice, taking large gasps of air, she said, "Day Star just saw ... her husband murdered ... in the clearing ... by the corn field."

"I thought he was at the hunting camp."

"He did not announce his return. He came back to surprise my sister."

"Did she see who killed him?"

"Two white men rode from the clearing. They were dressed in dirty clothes. One was on a pinto and the other was on a gray horse."

"Oh, dear God!" Josh stepped back from her.

"They even took his scalp!" She sobbed.

# Chapter 9

## THE PEACEFUL INDIAN

Ten days later Josh, Sunflower and her sister Day Star were waiting at the trading post with Indian Agent Sam Colley when U.S. Marshal Alex Hunt rode up. The marshal dismounted his black gelding and slapped the dirt off his black suit with a pair of riding gloves. His six-foot, two-inch frame was topped with a head of shaggy gray hair and a trimmed mustache. His white shirt opened at the collar and he wore a blue neckerchief like an ascot. Around his waist was strapped a brown gun belt with a Model '62 Navy Colt.

Agent Colley stepped forward and extended his hand. "Welcome to the Point-of-Rocks Agency, Marshal. I'm Sam Colley and this is Joshua Frasier, the chaplain who sent you the wire." Colley's voice had become raspy, and the chin and sideburns of his short red beard had turned gray.

The marshal studied Colley's open hand for a second before reluctantly shaking it. To Josh he gave a nod.

"I thought we could meet in my office across the way," said Colley.

Marshal Hunt only responded with, "It was a long ride."

"Came all the way from Denver, did you?" asked Colley rhetorically. "We have a kitchen here. I'll have the cook prepare you something. Maybe some of her famous pumpkin pie?"

"No ... thanks." Hunt stared at everyone and everything around him. "Where can I get something to cut the dust?"

That request bewildered Josh, but Colley tilted his head toward the trading post entrance. "Of course. Right this way."

The marshal shouldered his saddlebags and took his Henry out of its scabbard, and followed the nervous-looking Sam Colley, who signaled Josh to accompany them.

Inside, they found Skunk wiping egg yolk off a fork with his sweat-stained undershirt. Colley and Hunt joined Major Scott Anthony and Dexter Colley at a small table near the bar, and these last two were introduced. Josh stood to the side with his wife and sister-in-law.

Skunk asked, "Can I get you something, Marshal?"

"A bottle of that stuff you've got under the bar. And a clean glass if this place has one," said Hunt doubtfully. Then, giving his attention to Anthony, who still wore formal attire, he said without preamble, "I understand you run this reservation like a prison camp."

Anthony cleared his throat. "Well, sir, that's not exactly the way I see it. The savages have to understand that I am the commanding officer of Fort Lyon, not Chief Little Raven. That silver-tongued devil may run the Arapahoe camp, but he isn't in charge of this post." As the major spoke, he avoided eye contact with the marshal.

Hunt stared hard at the expressionless Anthony for an awkward moment. "Is Susan your sister? The one I've been reading about in the papers?"

"No, sir, she is my cousin."

Hunt lit the unused half of a cigar. "How did a worm like you crawl into that family, anyway?"

Anthony remained silent, though Josh noticed tension lines in his face.

Hunt addressed Colley. "Who is the witness?"

*Now he is getting down to business.* Josh reached his arm around Day Star who was standing between him and Sunflower. He cleared his throat and spoke up. "My wife's sister is the witness."

Hunt looked up to where Josh stood with the women. "So you're the one who wired for me to come?"

"Yes, sir," replied Josh.

"Which one is your sister-in-law? I need to speak with her."

With a hand on her shoulder, Josh encouraged Day Star to step forward, and Hunt motioned for her to take a seat across from him at the table.

"Her name is Day Star," said Josh, pulling out a chair for her. "It was her husband who was murdered, and she saw the whole thing."

"Can you interpret?"

"I sure can." Josh pulled up a chair beside his sister-in-law and another for his wife. The women sat stiffly, uncomfortable with the situation.

"Okay, start talking."

At that moment, Skunk came to the table and brought the bottle Hunt had ordered. "Is there anything else I can do for you?" asked Skunk.

Hunt poured himself a glass of whiskey. "Yeah, I want you to grab a bar of soap, go ten miles downstream … and jump in." All eyes looked downward at the table.

Then, breaking the awkward silence, Josh encouraged Day Star to tell her story. With his interpretation, she described the terrible afternoon she witnessed her husband shot down in a clearing. She had remained hidden in the nearby woods while two white men went to work on her husband with knives. Afterward, they rode off on a gray horse and a pinto.

"Joseph Blackburn and Nathan Talbot."

"Wait a minute, Marshal, you mean you know who they are?" Josh asked.

Hunt emptied his glass then refilled it. "Yeah. I've got enough complaints about them to fill a wagon crate. Did she see in which direction they left?"

"She says it looked like they were heading toward the agency. At that point she ran for help."

"So they removed the victim's scalp and allegedly rode toward the agency compound. … Why did they do that? … Anybody here ever seen those two?"

Everyone except Josh shook their heads. Josh explained. "I had a run-in with them a while back on the road from Denver but haven't seen them since."

Dexter pulled out a handkerchief and wiped his forehead.

Marshal Hunt asked him, "Are you feeling too hot?"

"Oh, no, sir."

"Then why are you sweating in this cold room?" He turned to Josh. "Tell me about your run-in with Talbot and Blackburn."

Josh told how they had tried to sneak up and kill him. "They also mentioned something about being hired."

The marshal stood, tossed a silver dollar on the table, and grabbed his rifle and saddlebags. "That should be enough to get them put away for a while. I'll meet with Judge Harding and swear out a warrant."

"Marshal, I'd like to speak with you alone outside, if I may," said Josh.

"Come on, then."

As Josh and the marshal left together, Josh turned to see Dexter watching them and sweat pouring off him like a beat mule.

Marshal Hunt threw his saddlebags back onto his horse. "What's on your mind, Chaplain?"

"There's something I couldn't tell you inside. I have reason to believe it was Dexter Colley who hired those two men to kill me. And I think he knows more about the murder of Young Deer than he's letting on."

Hunt stepped into a stirrup and pulled himself into the saddle. "You're probably right. I'll make a note of it in my affidavit."

"Aren't you going to question him?"

"Listen, son. You don't get to be an Indian agent like his father did unless you've got a lot of political clout in Washington. Arresting Blackburn and Talbot won't be a problem, but I'm not detaining any Colley until I speak with the judge."

That night in his and Sunflower's tepee, Josh sat on a buffalo-hide blanket, holding his open Bible and feeling depressed.

"What's the matter?" Sunflower asked.

"I don't understand how I got involved in this mess. Sometimes I think this war will never end and the Cheyennes will always remain a nomadic tribe of hunters and gatherers. Not long ago, I told people here about God's love and I tried helping them to understand the Bible. My words are like water that cannot penetrate a rock. The Cheyennes will never accept what I say as long as my people continue to cheat them."

Sunflower cupped her hands about his face. "Remember the parable Jesus taught about the sowing of seeds? Some of the seeds were eaten by birds and others were choked by weeds. Yet some, a few perhaps, landed on fertile soil. All you see are the seeds that have landed on the stony places. You do not yet see the fruit of what has been planted in good soil. Maybe only one stalk of corn will grow, but it will produce an abundance of additional seeds. God's work will come to fruition according to his time, not yours, dear husband."

In early April 1864, Josh was summoned by the colonel back to Denver. He was greeted at the militia headquarters by his friend from the Glorieta Pass campaign, Silas Soule, who had been promoted to captain. Silas briefed Josh on recent events.

"Well, the peace lasted a little while after those chiefs came back from Washington, but it's over now. A couple head of cattle were stolen near Fremont's Orchard and two cowboys were killed. A Cheyenne bow was found. I don't know if you've ever met Major Downy, but the colonel had him take a company to follow the South Platte and kill the Cheyennes responsible."

"I don't know him. Where is he now?"

"Fort Sanborn."

"Are any of his troops part of the First Regiment?"

"They're all part of the First."

"Then that's where I need to go."

"Hold on there, buddy." Silas leaned forward. "If the old man summoned you from Fort Lyon, then you better report to him before going anywhere else."

Inside Chivington's office, the colonel said, "Joshua, forget about going to Fort Sanborn. Downy is only chasing some rogue warriors. I have something else in mind."

"What would that be, sir?"

"The ICB is going to try to track down an entire herd of stolen cattle. More than likely they were taken by the Cheyennes to feed their families on the reservation. I have a feeling there is an alliance between all the plains Indians to drive us white people out of this territory. If the ICB makes contact with the Cheyennes, they will need an interpreter."

"What's the ICB, sir?"

"The Independent Colorado Battery. Report downtown to Lieutenant Eayre and tell him I am sending you as his interpreter. He's a fine artillery officer, but still a bit green and over confident. Therefore, I am also sending along Sergeant Major Hawley and a detachment of cavalry in case Eayre gets lost."

"An artillery unit? Sir, don't you think that is a bit cumbersome for chasing a few Indians?"

"Maybe, but there's not enough cavalry available. The enlistments for most of those cannon cockers expire soon, and they've done nothing so far except drill."

Josh rose to leave, then stopped at the door and said, "At least the Sergeant Major is coming along. He's tougher than hardtack. When we were in New Mexico I thought he was going to kill those Navajo scouts when they threatened to leave us in the desert. Good day, sir!"

Lieutenant George Eayre's connecting eyebrows, full beard and baggy eyes gave his face a severe, somber aspect. He informed Josh that 175 head of cattle had been stolen from a government contractor by a band of Cheyenne.

"Are you certain they're Cheyenne?" Josh wanted to know.

"Apparently that is what the contractor told the colonel and that is what he has passed on to me. You will have to tolerate me, Chaplain, for I am not a particularly religious man and I see no need for an interpreter. My orders were to punish the offenders, not to converse with them. Now, if you will excuse me, I must get this expedition underway."

Eighty men of the cavalry company, along with two twelve-pounder howitzers and ten heavy wagons, rode thirty miles to the southeast before camping.

The group was led by Sergeant Major Chuck Hawley, a solid, raw-boned man who stood at six feet, two inches and sported a thick, gray horseshoe mustache. He wore a ten-gallon Stetson. He warmly shook hands with Josh and said with a western drawl, "You have a different look from most chaplains I've known."

Josh grinned, recalling what he knew about Chuck Hawley that was different from most army officers he had known. When they were in New Mexico together, the sergeant major had chosen to ride with the regiment's Navajo trackers.

Now the two men watched the soldiers make camp. Josh said, "You know, Sergeant Major, sometimes the army doesn't make sense to me. Sending an artillery battery after Indian cattle rustlers? The men are mounted. Why not use them as cavalry and leave the guns behind?"

With a strain of frustration in his voice, Hawley answered, "I've been in the army for twenty-two years and not a day has gone by where everything made sense. I heard that these guys would only agree to enlist if they could be in the artillery and they're not real artillery unless they drag those cockamamie cannons along."

Josh nodded. "I'm also extremely concerned about the plight of the Cheyennes. I'm the type who likes to know of bad news the minute it happens—or before."

"What makes you think there will be bad news?" asked Hawley as they led their horses to the picket rope.

"From what I understand, the Indian rustlers we're looking for are Cheyenne. I think I told you before, I'm married to a Cheyenne."

"Yeah, you told me. That doesn't necessarily mean the ones we're after are from your wife's band. You have my word that I'll do what I can to keep things from getting out of hand."

The column of horses advanced slowly through the grassy slopes of the prairie. A week later, they crossed the ridge of hills that separates the South Platte Valley from the Arkansas Valley. When they reached the headwaters of the Big Sandy they made camp just in time, before a spring blizzard roared in. At sunrise the snow began turning to slush. Back in their saddles, the soldiers followed the creek for twenty miles until Hawley cut a trail.

Josh and Eayre followed him. Eayre asked, "What did you find, Sergeant Major?"

"Take a look for yourself, Lieutenant. Cattle tracks as wide as a road."

The tracks ran in a straight line to the northwest. "How many head would you say?"

"A hundred, easily," answered Hawley. He then pointed to something else. "You see those U-shaped hoof prints on the outer edges? Those are from horses without shoes. The only horses you'll find around here that haven't been shoed are Indian ponies. I'd say these are the ones we're after."

Josh added, "These tracks are not heading toward the reservation as the colonel predicted. In fact, they appear to be doubling back from where we just came."

Eayre was agitated. "That's right. Maybe if we had shifted due east we could have found this trail a lot sooner."

Hawley scowled at the upstart officer. "I'm not a mind reader, Lieutenant. I didn't exactly hear you giving orders to change directions."

Josh was tired, hungry, and anxious, but knew better than to complain, since everyone was in the same condition.

Nettlesome mud clung to horses' legs and soldiers' boots. The slush and animal hooves had turned the trail to mud, so the artillerymen tried to keep their wagons on the grass. Two days later, as they approached the Republican River, a scout galloped over to Eayre. "Sir, there's an Indian camp in a small defile about a mile ahead."

Eayre halted the line of horses then said to Hawley, "Send two of your troopers into that encampment to ask about the stolen cattle."

Ten minutes later the troopers returned at a full gallop. The horses skidded to a stop sending muddy grass and rocks in Eayre's direction. "Lieutenant, we've been spotted," one trooper exclaimed. "Squaws mounted on ponies are fleeing to the hills, and a band of warriors is headed this way!"

Several soldiers checked to ensure their revolvers were loaded. The mud and terrain made advancing with the wagons difficult. On a hill fifty yards from Eayre's position, a Cheyenne warrior appeared on foot. "Over there, shoot him!" ordered an artillery sergeant named Fribbley.

"Wait! Don't do that! He's not armed," said Josh.

"The chaplain is right. Take the redskin as a prisoner," ordered Eayre. "We need him to talk."

Two artillerymen rode to the hill. When they came near, the warrior produced a rifle that had been lying at his feet and shot one soldier through the belly. The wounded man fell to the ground and died. The other soldier fired his revolver, but the warrior ran off. Eayre cursed and shot Josh an angry look.

"I told you to shoot him," said Sergeant Fribbley, shaking his head and riding away.

Josh didn't recognize the Indian warrior. To no one in particular he said, "I'm sorry. I didn't see his gun."

"Don't second guess yourself," said Hawley. "But if we had

captured him, he could have told us where the cattle are."

The soldiers formed a protective shield to the front, while the exhausted mules labored to pull the transports with their mud-caked wheels across the soggy ground. The warriors never attacked.

"It was just a diversion so their families could escape," said Hawley.

"Sergeant Major, let's have a look at that village," said Eayre.

With their rifles at the ready, the column entered the abandoned village. Inside the tepees they found immense quantities of dried beef and pemmican. They also discovered undressed buffalo robes, cooking utensils, gunpowder, lead, and beads. To the north was a trail strewn with discarded robes, blankets, dried meats, and lodge poles

As evening approached, it became overcast and the temperature dropped. Two scouts returned from the Republican River with nine-teen head of cattle.

Hawley showed Eayre and Josh the "Irwin & Jackman" brand on the animals. "These are definitely from the stolen herd."

"This camp was too small to have more than that," said Josh. "Now that we found them, will we return to Denver?"

"You're just along for the ride, Chaplain," said Eayre. "In the morning we'll continue looking for the rest of the herd. Nineteen is a far cry from a hundred seventy-five."

"You better back off from me, Eayre," warned Josh. "Don't let this uniform fool you into thinking I'll keep putting up with your mouth."

"Right now I need you two sirs to stay focused on the problem at hand. You can settle your differences later," barked the Sergeant Major.

Broken lodge poles cluttered the camp. Fire pits still smoldered and from a short tree hung dog bones, black feathers, and decorated medicine bags. The bones acted as lonely-sounding wind chimes in the cold breeze.

One artilleryman still in his saddle said, "Hey, Lieutenant, this place is downright creepy! Do we have to stay here tonight?"

"I don't like it here any more than you do, Davis, but we've got nowhere else to go," snapped Eayre. Addressing the rest of the men, he said, "We're in no condition to begin pursuit, so we'll bivouac here. Tomorrow we'll see what we can find."

Early the next morning, the scouts found fresh tracks leading east. These tracks merged with others coming from the southwest until a discernable trail formed. Eventually it followed the south bank of the Smoky Hill River.

Their first night after crossing into Kansas, they could hear Cheyenne drums and high-pitched chanting. Hawley ordered all campfires extinguished. In the morning, they continued down the trail with guns at the ready. Josh's heart raced.

At 9:15, the expedition halted their horses when they spotted a large contingent of armed Cheyenne warriors cresting a hill to their right. The soldiers turned and aimed their rifles eagerly in that direction.

"Nobody do anything stupid," Hawley warned.

"I don't want them to shoot me down as they did Billy!" one soldier called.

"Sir, one of those Injuns is riding forward with a piece of paper in his hand," said a private.

Josh recognized Chief Lean Bear. "I know him! And he's not armed. Let me speak to him."

"Stay out of this," barked Eayre.

"I already warned you once, Lieutenant."

"Shut up!"

Lean Bear wore the peace medal he had received in Washington. He guided his horse down the face of the hill, while the warriors remained at the crest.

"Let him approach," Eayre instructed.

"It's a trick! Remember what happened last time," said Sergeant Fribbley. "Let me handle this, Lieutenant. The colonel gave orders to kill all hostiles."

"He is not hostile!" shouted Josh. "That's a signed document by the President declaring him peaceable."

Eayre cursed. "I told you—"

"Peaceable, my butt," roared Fribbley. "No disrespect, Chaplain, but you already got one of our men killed."

"The lieutenant told you to let the Indian approach, Sergeant," scolded Hawley.

"This doesn't concern you, Hawley," said Fribbley. Sunlight highlighted the red stubble covering his chubby face.

"That's Sergeant Major Hawley to you, and this most certainly does concern me."

"That's enough," shouted Eayre sternly, reining his horse to the right. "Sergeant Fribbley, come over here and explain your plan."

After Sergeant Fribbley quietly spoke with him, the lieutenant signaled Lean Bear to come toward him. Fribbley kept well to the right. In broken English, Lean Bear pleaded, "I have a letter from the Great White Father saying I am a peaceful Indian."

Fribbley sneered, raised his right arm while extending his index finger, and said, "What's that? Sorry, nobody here speaks gibberish." He then dropped his arm as a signal.

"Lean Bear, watch out!" shouted Josh.

Rifle fire knocked Chief Lean Bear backwards off his pony.

"Second squad, make sure he doesn't get up," ordered Fribbley.

Five artillerymen galloped over to the dead chief and emptied their revolvers into his chest. The ribbon suspending the medal was severed and Lean Bear's peace document signed by Abraham Lincoln blew across the short prairie grass.

# Chapter 10

## THE AVENGING ANGEL

The instant Lean Bear hit the ground, artillerymen promptly unhitched the two twelve pounders and rotated them to the left. They rammed a self-contained projectile of powder and canister shot down the barrel of each gun.

With blood-chilling war cries, Indian warriors—two hundred abreast—charged the columns of soldiers. A few fired rifles while others leveled their lances.

Without hesitation, Lieutenant Eayre maneuvered his horse to the rear of the cannons. "Sergeant, are these guns ready?"

"Yes, sir!"

"Fire!"

When the gunners yanked their lanyards, the cannons acted as giant shotguns and belched fire. Fifty-four grape-sized pellets triggered the muzzles to make a metallic ring. Spouts of dirt spewed upward from the ground as the iron balls tore through the line of Cheyenne warriors. Ponies tumbled forward.

At the front of the militia's columns the cavalry troopers unsheathed their sabers, as Sergeant Major Hawley tried to decide where his men were needed most. The mounted artillerymen drew their M1860 revolvers and frantically shot at the warriors who continued to charge. The soldiers with revolvers screwed on the detachable stocks for better accuracy. The gun crews reloaded the cannons.

The Cheyennes shifted to their left and exploited the mile and a half gap between the main body of artillerymen and their supply wagons. Hawley's cavalry charged to the rear and scattered the warriors, but not before four of the wagon drivers were killed.

His command to advance the wagons was drowned out by another discharging of the cannons. The order to bring the wagons forward wasn't necessary, though. Rifle bullets splintered the wooden sides of the wagons, and teamsters snapped their reins, driving the mules to a high-speed gallop.

This time the volleys by the big guns were ineffective. Eayre had them hitched to the caissons. When the entire unit was assembled again, they moved southeast along a rocky trail leading to the Pawnee River. From that point there was no orderly formation. The mounted soldiers continued to keep the warriors at a distance with an exchange of small-arms fire.

Josh had never prayed so urgently in his life. Seven hours and thirty miles later, they were finally within the fort's firing range and a detachment of Kansas cavalry chased off the warriors then escorted the ICB to Fort Larned.

Similar to Fort Lyon, this post had no protective walls, and it sat on a stretch of prairie flat as a table top. It was situated in a bend of the river and across from it on the north bank were about one-hundred Kiowa tepees.

Inside the fort's compound the men dismounted. Josh felt his knees wobble and had to hold the saddle horn to steady himself. His hands shook as he lifted his canteen for a drink. Several Kiowa warriors stood about the compound watching the soldiers.

Hawley startled Josh by slapping him on the back. "Wow, that was about as fun as falling through ice!"

"Yeah, some fun," Josh replied dryly and returned the cork to his canteen. "Why are the Kiowas here?"

"Their agency is located here. That big warrior over yonder with the yellow handprint on his shoulder sure is giving you a hard stare. Are you two acquainted?"

Josh looked around, but couldn't see the Indian because of the dust raised by the horses and mules.

Still in the saddle, Lieutenant Eayre rode over. "Splendid, Sergeant Major! The men performed superbly."

"Yes, sir. I guess this ends our search for the missing cattle," said Sergeant Major Hawley.

The lieutenant ignored his comment and instead beckoned an exhausted artilleryman over to him. "Corporal, I want you to wire a message to Colonel Chivington in Denver informing him that we were attacked by four-hundred Cheyenne warriors. We killed twenty-five of them plus three chiefs. Four of our men were lost, but the rest of us are now safe at Fort Larned. We will remain here awaiting his orders to return to Denver."

"That's a lie!" cried Josh, fed up with the upstart officer.

"I was not addressing you, Chaplain."

"That was a fight you started with the Cheyennes who were only half that number. It was more like ten warriors killed with only one chief. Need I remind you that that particular chief was an acquaintance of President Lincoln?"

"Even presidents make mistakes."


On a warm June day, a freight wagon rolled into Denver containing the four bodies of the Hungate family who had all been brutally murdered and scalped. Inside a shed on Larimer Street, the bodies were placed in a wooden box with the girls between their parents. News of the tragedy spread fast and it seemed that everyone in town filed past to get a glimpse of the corpses. The thirst for revenge increased.

When Governor Evans arrived, people demanded to know what he purposed to do about the Cheyennes. An angry man shouted, "Hey Governor, the Good Book says, 'An eye for an eye and a tooth for a tooth,' so do your Christian duty."

"How about a bounty for scalps?" asked another man.

And over the din was heard the worn-out cliché, "The only good Indian is a dead Indian!"

Josh folded his arms and released a sigh of disgust as he witnessed the crowd work itself into a frenzy. Loudly he said, "The

Good Book also says in Deuteronomy, '*Vengeance is mine*, saith the Lord.'"

"Save it, preacher!" someone yelled.

Governor Evans stood in the back of the emptied freight wagon. He raised his hand to hush the crowd. When it was quiet enough, he spoke. "I can assure you that those responsible will be brought to justice."

The crowd sounded skeptical. "In a pig's eye they will! Those red-skinned killers will just slink back onto the reservation like nothing happened," yelled a businessman with a ruffled shirt and string tie.

A toothless mountain man wearing a badger-skin hat rummaged through the Indian artifacts at the governor's feet. He picked up the feathered end of a broken arrow, brought it close to his wrinkled face, and eyed it carefully.

"Hey Badger, what you got there, Black Kettle's ration card?" asked a loud-mouthed miner.

"Nope, because this ain't Cheyenne." Badger had everyone's attention, including that of Governor Evans.

The crowd groaned as slight relief washed over Josh.

"Terrific, Mister Andersen. Then who did do it, do you think?" asked the governor.

"Well, it weren't the Quakers. And this arrow is too plain lookin' to be Cheyenne. This here has to be Arapahoe." Badger asked a witness next to him, "They was headin' north, you say?" Not waiting for the man's answer, Badger continued. "Most likely goin' to the Green River country where their main camp is. They didn't come from the reservation, if'n that's what yer thinkin'." His raised eyebrow reached up into his tattered hat. "Question is, why would Arapahoes be doin' the dirty work fer Cheyennes?"

"Because they're all in it together, that's why," said one loud-mouth. "Cheyenne, Arapahoe, Kiowa, Comanche, Sioux—they're all trying to kill as many honest folks in the territory as they can. Why is the army here in town marching in circles instead of hunting down those red-skinned murderers?"

The angry crowd echoed his sentiments.

The governor's face turned red. "I can assure you, a military reprisal will be launched the minute Colonel Chivington arrives."

Inside a large conference room at the capitol building, former Cheyenne agent William Bent met with Governor Evans, Colonel Chivington, Josh, and several staff officers. Josh felt the tension could be cut with a knife.

At the head of the table, the governor spoke first. "Mister Bent, we appreciate you coming out of retirement to help us in this crisis. As you know, the Cheyennes without provocation tried to attack an expedition the colonel sent out in search of stolen cattle. One of their chiefs was killed by soldiers defending themselves and they have used that as an excuse to murder innocent civilians. Furthermore, we understand you have been contacted by Chief Black Kettle."

Bent, who seemed to be trying unsuccessfully to find a comfortable position in his chair, said, "That is true, though Black Kettle's version of what happened near the Smoky Hill is somewhat different than yours."

Josh nodded his agreement and felt the tension increase.

Bent continued, "He acknowledges that some renegade bands of his tribe have committed atrocities—warriors who were young and hot-headed and refused to listen to the elders. Many atrocities have been committed by their enemies, the Kiowas, yet the white men still blame the Cheyennes. I would have gone directly to the army authorities, but they are at the far end of Kansas. Maybe it is best I deal with the army commanders here. The Cheyennes are not concerned with who is right or wrong; they only want peace."

Chivington spoke up and his voice easily carried across the room. "I am not authorized to make peace treaties with the Indians! You can tell them I am on the warpath."

"Colonel, you're a man of God. You know a peaceful solution is always better than a path to war," Bent reasoned. "Going to war against the Cheyennes would be very dangerous. Think of the settlers along the Arkansas. You don't have enough troops to protect all of them."

"Then with the help of almighty God, the settlers will have to defend themselves," thundered Chivington. By the looks on faces, these words startled everyone in the room. "Black Kettle started this war, but you can be sure I shall end it!"

William Bent slowly rose from his chair and softly announced, "The good King Solomon wrote in Proverbs 23, 'Speak not into the ears of a fool: for he will despise the wisdom of your words.' It is obvious, Colonel, you haven't the slightest understanding of what is happening here. Therefore, I shall heed the wise king's advice and no longer speak with you on the matter." He left the room.

Josh snickered under his breath.

"Is something funny, Joshua?" demanded the colonel.

"No, sir."

Governor Evans slammed his fist down on the table. "Colonel, get that third regiment recruited now!"

Chivington huffed a sigh. "Sir, we've been trying to do that, but the men in town aren't showing much interest. All the decent ones have already fulfilled their military obligations."

"Colonel, right now we aren't concerned about decency," said the governor. "I don't care how many rocks you have to overturn. Get that regiment manned and activated. We cannot fulfill our political ambitions until this Indian problem is eliminated once and for all."

Josh rubbed the back of his neck. "A third regiment? Are you serious? For a few renegade warriors?"

"Just in case there are more than a few, Chaplain. Just in case."


When Josh finally made it home to his family on the reservation, Sunflower expressed her fears. "What is going to happen to us,

Black Robe? A new white chief has taken over the fort and he seems concerned with our welfare. Yet he says all Cheyennes off the reservation are considered hostile, so the warriors can no longer bring us meat."

"Who is the new commanding officer?"

"I don't know his name, but he seems very distressed."

Josh didn't want to spend this precious time together talking about political affairs. He waved Little Dove over to where he sat. He thought of the two murdered girls he had seen and started to choke up. When his daughter stood in front of him, he managed to ask, "You had a birthday last week, didn't you?"

The little girl nodded.

"How old are you now?"

"Six."

"Did I give you your present yet?"

"Not yet." She looked hopeful.

"Gee, I thought I did. Maybe it's in here." Josh reached into a saddlebag. He pulled out a rectangular box wrapped in pink paper. Little Dove tore into the package and, when she saw the rag doll with yellow-yarn hair, her face broke into a big smile. She reached her little arms around Josh's neck and gave him a tight hug.

The next day, Josh rode to Fort Lyon and was glad to discover that Major Ned Wynkoop had recently replaced the obsequious Scott Anthony. His friend, Silas Soule, had taken over as the fort's second-in-command. The three friends sat around Ned's office sharing stories about their time together at Glorieta Pass and drinking coffee despite the July heat.

Ned gave a briefing of what had been left to him by the departing Major Anthony. "This fort looks more like a dump than an army post. Thanks to Anthony, the troops are as malnourished as the Indians. While he was enforcing petty regulations on the men, renegade Indians and Confederate guerillas in the area were running rampant. And the Second Regiment is still in Kansas chasing down rebel bushwhackers. I sent a request to Chivington for additional troops and rations. He agreed to send food at least."

Ned wore his highly-shined riding boots. With his feet propped on the desk and staring into his cup he said, "I've managed to keep an uneasy peace with the Cheyennes still on the reservation. But with all these other enemies about, the colonel still refuses to send the bulk of the First to our aid. I've also heard talk that he's seeking permission from General Curtis to take the First on an offensive into Texas. Confound it! How thin can one regiment be stretched?"

"I don't think that's going to happen," said Josh. "The governor wants him to start recruiting another regiment."

"What did he say?" asked Silas.

"Not a whole lot. It's what they both want, but I've heard that General Curtis doesn't think another regiment for the war's duration is practical. However, he would be in favor of a hundred-day regiment."

"What man worth his salt is going to quit his job for a hundred days of enlistment?" asked Ned.

"Those fellows who aren't already working," guessed Silas.

"I'll tell you who: drifters and lowlifes looking to earn some fast money." Ned answered his own question. "There will be judges getting stuffed envelopes from backers of the governor who, when sentencing convicts, will give them the option to serve a year in jail or a hundred days in the army."

The other two couldn't argue his point. Josh then told his friends what else had been going on in the capitol. "The legislators are trying to fulfill the requirements for statehood. Right now as we speak, a constitutional convention is underway as to when to vote on the issue. Those same legislators want Chivington to be our representative in the U.S. House, with Evans continuing as governor and Henry Teller in the Senate."


Back on the Cheyenne reservation, Sunflower gave Josh a handbill with Governor Evans's new proclamation. "What does this mean?" she asked.

Josh read over the handbill then explained, "It states that all Cheyennes must return to their reservation or be considered hostile. It's nothing but a written notice of a policy that has already been set in place. The governor has no choice but to make war on the Dog Soldiers and other warrior societies who are causing all the problems. He only wants to make sure that none of the friendly Indians get caught in the crossfire."

Sunflower began carefully braiding Little Dove's hair. "These pieces of paper were handed out to those of us already here. What about those peaceful Cheyennes who are camped off the reservation because they cannot get their annuities?"

"You're right. I'll talk to Jack and ask what is being done to reach the others."

"Probably nothing." Tears welled in Sunflower's eyes. "They're not supposed to be off the reservation, remember? This reverend you speak so highly of, who is chief of the blue coats, thinks a Cheyenne is hostile simply for leaving the reservation in search of food."

"That's not true," said Josh slightly irritated. "He doesn't want the peaceful Indians to get hurt because of the bad ones. Colonel Chivington wants what is best for everyone in the territory, which is also what Governor Evans wants. I admit, though, their political ambitions worry me."

"Husband, I fear the compliments they give you are only a veil to hide their true intentions."

"Are you saying I should leave my job? How would I support us?"

"Did you ask Creator God's guidance before leaving your previous position? Did you seek his permission? Go take a look at what the Hoe Man is doing. Schools are being built and crops planted. But there is no love in him. It would not be that way if you had remained there and fulfilled what God had called you to do. You have said you want to share the gospel with my people and modernize the reservation like the ones in the East."

Feeling cornered, Josh changed tactics. "How can I help your people when they continue to steal cattle then lie about it? Your people haven't even entered the Iron Age yet. Heck, they don't even know how to use a wheel." Seeing the look of hurt in her eyes, he added softly, "I'm sorry, I didn't mean that."

"Yes you did," she replied in a quiet voice.

Sunflower stepped out of the tepee, and as the flap was opened, the twilight briefly cast an eerie light inside. Josh motioned Little Dove over and said, "Your mother is right. Let's pray now for guidance."

Two weeks later, Silas visited Josh in his office and briefed him on the proclamation and the outfitting of the new regiment. As it turned out, Sunflower's fears were not unfounded.

"By the time the Indians off the reservation heard of the governor's proclamation about the fate of the Cheyennes, it was already rescinded," said Silas.

"But why?" Josh wanted to know.

"The governor received funding from Secretary of War Stanton for a third regiment, so he has sent out a second proclamation. In this one he authorizes the citizens of the territory to capture or kill any hostile Indians they encounter. He says it is their patriotic duty to do so. There are a couple problems with this. First of all, the governor doesn't tell them how to distinguish between a hostile Indian and a friendly one. Second, nobody has told the Indians about the nullification of the first proclamation."

"This is getting out of hand," Josh thought out loud.

Silas stood gazing out the window. "It gets worse. I've seen some of the men who are joining this new regiment the governor is putting together. Ned was right; he's scraping the bottom of the barrel."

Company A of the new Colorado Third Volunteer Regiment rode into Fort Lyon on a hot August afternoon. Josh noticed by their appearance they were not the professional soldiers found in the First. They wore standard blue uniforms but had personal necker-chiefs and carried unauthorized knives and pistols. Some appeared to be laughing at some joke while others looked brooding and troubled.

After they stabled their horses, a private entered Josh's chaplain's office and asked, "May I speak with you, sir?"

"Sure, I'm Chaplain Frasier. Have a seat," said Josh.

The young cavalryman sat on the other side of the plain desk. "I'm Private Andrew Buckham. I'm not a professional soldier, just an out-of-work stable hand. I figured riding for the army for a hundred days was better than not working at all."

Josh nodded. "What can I do for you?"

The soldier hesitated a moment, folding and unfolding his hands, before speaking. "Sir, I'm not sure if I should be telling you this, but I feel it needs to be said."

Josh braced himself for something serious. "Go on."

"Well, sir, we left Denver with five Confederate prisoners to bring here for trial. If you take a look out the window, you'll see that we don't have any prisoners."

Recalling Glorieta Mesa, Josh sat back with a sickened feeling and asked, "Where are they?"

"About ten miles south of Franktown. On the fourth day out, Captain Cree stopped the column and ordered Sergeant Williamson to select a firing squad and dispose of the prisoners. I got picked. When we were off the road a ways, the sergeant had us line up with our rifles and point them at the prisoners. The poor fellows were still in chains and begging for their lives. When Sergeant Williamson gave the order to fire, none of us did. He threatened all of us with a court martial, but we still refused."

"Then what happened?" asked Josh.

Private Buckham rubbed his white knuckles. "Sergeant Williamson killed four of them with his revolver and Sergeant Shaw killed the other. Nothing was said about it for the rest of the trip, nor was there any further mention of a court martial."

"Did Captain Cree or Sergeant Williamson speak of this incident with anyone outside of your company?"

"Yes, sir. As we passed through the reservation we were met by a patrol from the First Regiment. I couldn't hear the whole conversation, but Captain Cree bragged about it to the lieutenant in charge of the patrol. I thought the lieutenant looked kind of sick when he heard about it."

Josh glanced out his window through the thin white curtains and saw an agitated sergeant with a red beard glaring at the door of Josh's office. "Without moving the curtains, I want you to look outside and tell me if that is Sergeant Williamson."

"It is, sir."

"Buckham, would you like me to pray for you concerning the upcoming campaign against the hostile Indians?"

Buckham looked a bit confused for a moment, then he answered, "Yes, sir. I would like that."

Josh stood and placed his hands on the man's shoulders. "The Bible is very clear about the effectiveness of prayer with the laying on of hands." After he prayed for the soldier, they walked out of the office onto the parade ground.

Sergeant Williamson started to say something to Buckham, but stopped.

"Is Private Buckham under your command, Sergeant?" Josh asked.

"Yes, sir, he is." Williamson looked from Josh to Buckham and back to Josh, as if not sure who to look at.

"He was in my office receiving prayer for protection against hostile Indians. How about you, Sergeant? Would you like me to pray for you as well?"

"No, sir, that's quite all right."

"Private Buckham is a fine soldier." Josh looked the sergeant directly in the eyes. "I would hate to see anything happen to him."

"I'll see to it nothing does," said Williamson as if reading Josh's implied message. He saluted and walked with Buckham to the stables.

When a patrol came in, Josh approached a distraught-looking officer. "Good afternoon, Lieutenant. You didn't happen to have a conversation with Captain Cree of the Third Regiment, did you?"

"Yes, I did. How did you know?" asked the man, who introduced himself as Lieutenant Cramer.

Josh deflected the question with one of his own, "Did you two discuss missing prisoners?"

"Yes, we did. How did you know?" Lieutenant Cramer repeated.

"I was just going in to speak with Major Wynkoop. Come with me." Josh led the way to Ned Wynkoop's office. Ned looked swamped with paperwork but smiled at Josh. He set down his pen and asked an orderly to bring in coffee. "Take a seat, gentlemen," he said to Josh and Lieutenant Cramer.

After Josh related Private Buckham's story, Ned sat back in his chair and rubbed his temples. "How about you, Lieutenant? Is your story along the same lines?"

"Yes, sir, it is. Except the captain didn't mention anything about a mutiny amongst the firing squad," said Cramer.

"This Captain Cree hasn't even reported to me yet with his orders," said Ned while cleaning his fingernails with a letter opener. "Did he say why the prisoners were to be shot, and who authorized him to do so?"

"He did," said Cramer. "Apparently the prisoners were not regular Confederate soldiers. They were in civilian clothes and were supposed to be recruiting in the territory for the Southern cause. But I guess they found robbing stagecoaches more profitable. They were captured by a civilian posse and turned over to Marshal Hunt. Since the U.S. Attorney is currently back East, Colonel Chivington persuaded Hunt to turn the prisoners over to his care so they could go before a military tribunal. Company A was bringing reinforcements to the fort, so the colonel had Cree transfer the prisoners—with a certain understanding."

"With what understanding?" Ned was turning red in the face.

"That they were not to make it to Fort Lyon alive."

"Who gave Cree the order to make sure this happened?"

"Colonel Chivington told him to make sure the prisoners attempted an escape and that he was to have them shot in the process," said Cramer.

Josh reacted in disbelief. "Why? There's no doubt the tribunal would have found them guilty, so why not let them pronounce sentence?"

Cramer said, "The colonel wired General Curtis, asking permission to execute the prisoners if a guilty verdict was rendered. He couldn't get an answer because the general was in the field. His adjutant told Chivington that permission could not be given."

"Cree told you all this when you met him?" asked Ned, his voice rising.

"He told me during the ride back to the fort that this was normal policy. He seemed to consider the whole thing an amusing incident."

Ned looked at Josh. "Seems like our dear Colonel Chivington has promoted himself to Avenging Angel."


Josh rode through Denver tired and covered with dust. The last ten miles with Marshal Alex Hunt had been quiet. The marshal said little, but he didn't seem to mind having Josh tag along. Josh wanted to ask about the investigation into Young Deer's murder, but the only thing Hunt appeared to be interested in was his silver flask.

Josh felt his pulse surge when they rode past an alley where a large group of men stood in a circle shouting and cheering. Just then Josh caught a glimpse of two familiar figures. "Marshal, that's them!"

"That's who?"

"The two guys we're looking for—Blackburn and Talbot."

"Well, Padre, it looks like we're making some progress on your case. Stay behind me and I'll take them to the sheriff's office, if they don't get themselves killed first."

Hunt and Josh maneuvered their horses behind the pair as they crossed the busy street. They could hear Blackburn and Talbot speaking to one another in complete unawareness that their crime spree was about to come to a halt.

"Why did you bet all our money on that Rhode Island Red? That puny rooster was scrawnier than my sister's canary," whined Talbot.

"Well, he still could've beat you," snapped Blackburn. "Come on, let's get to the hotel before that landlady locks us out."

"Some hotel it is! Sharing one big room with a bunch of other ex-cons and sleeping on the floor."

"Well, it's better than sleeping on the sidewalk, which is where we'll be if we don't get some money by tomorrow."

"How we gonna do that?"

"I'm not sure yet. I need to go to the saloon and think it over." Blackburn looked both ways but didn't see the horse that came from behind and knocked him over. Irate, he grabbed his crumpled derby and sat up. He cursed the rider but held his tongue when he saw the badge attached to the big, Stetson-hatted man looking down at him.

"Start walking your butt to the jailhouse, Blackburn," ordered Hunt while pointing down the street. "You too, Talbot!"

Talbot helped Blackburn to his feet and they nervously walked to the sheriff's office in front of their escorts. "What did we do, Alex? We ain't done nothin'. You gotta tell us what we're charged with," whined Talbot.

"I don't have to explain nothing to you, Talbot," said the marshal, glaring at him with cold blue eyes.

Arapahoe County Sheriff Richard Sopris sat at his roll-top desk sipping coffee through his white mustache. His belly sagged over his belt buckle. The walls of the office were bare except for a calendar and a fully-stocked gun rack. At a side table a deputy poured himself a cup of coffee, while another deputy swept the floor with a broom.

Joshua and Hunt came in with Blackburn and Talbot. Hunt greeted Sopris. "Howdy, Richard."

Sopris gave the prisoners a hard stare and then said to Hunt, "Howdy, yourself. What are you doing with those two road apples? I'd like to tar-and-feather their worthless hides just for being in my county."

"I'd appreciate it if you held them until I can bring them before Judge Harding," said Marshal Hunt. "There's a federal warrant on them for killing a Cheyenne on the reservation. The Indian's wife witnessed the whole thing."

"That's a lie! Ain't nobody else was in that clearing!" Talbot protested loudly.

"Ah, shut up!" Blackburn jabbed the point of his boot into Talbot's shin.

Talbot doubled over in pain.

Sopris jumped out of his chair, grabbed Blackburn from behind, and threw him against a brick wall. Both prisoners wailed like children.

Josh was disgusted. These self-absorbed prisoners didn't bat an eye when they caused pain to their victims, but they whined and cried about their own predicaments.

"J.W., Lester, take these two upstairs and lock them up for the federal court. Make sure you search them for weapons and don't be too gentle about it," ordered Sopris.

The two burly deputies grabbed the prisoners by the legs and dragged them like sacks of laundry up the stairs to the jail. While Talbot's head bounced off each step, his voice turned staccato. "We killed one Cheyenne is all! Word's out there's a colonel looking for men to do much more than that. Just wait and see how many get killed then!"

# Chapter 11

## UPPING THE STAKES

S ounds like things have gone from bad to worse," said Ned Wynkoop. "I just received a telegram from Fort Larned that says a band of Cheyenne Dog Soldiers attacked a settlement along the Little Blue River, killing fifteen people. They kidnapped a Missus Lucinda Ewbanks, her two small children and a nephew, and a seventeen-year-old girl named Laura Roper, a neighbor who had been visiting when the attack occurred."

He took a deep breath then continued. "It pains me to say this, but we are now at war with the Indians, and I feel there are no alternatives. Any male Indian over the age of sixteen not found at one of the forts designated by Governor Evans will be shot."

"That's the kind of coldhearted thing the devious Major Anthony would say," protested Josh, who was feeling the strain of constantly traveling between Denver and Fort Lyon.

"I didn't create this situation, Joshua; I'm dealing with it," snapped Ned. "Besides, the colonel has told all fort commanders to issue similar orders. You're married into the Cheyenne tribe, so if you have any concern for their welfare, make sure they do not leave the fort."

The new Point-of-Rocks agency, forty-five miles upstream, nailed its doors shut and the staff moved downstream to Fort Lyon. In compliance with the governor's mandate, the main Cheyenne camp relocated to the fort as well, leaving the agency grounds forsaken.

In early September, a Cheyenne messenger named One Eye was ushered into Major Ned Wynkoop's office by two soldiers. One Eye produced a letter addressed to Agent Sam Colley, who had made a profit on the rations meant for the Indians. In this letter, Black Kettle stated he knew of Cheyenne prisoners held in Denver, and he now had white prisoners of his own to exchange for them.

Major Ned Wynkoop called for Josh, who hurried over, bringing Silas with him. They were surprised by the look of anger in the major's face. He told them, "Black Kettle is holding the children from the Blue River raid. I need you to interpret, Josh."

"When I first met Black Kettle and the other chiefs they seemed so noble and wise, but now they're being incredibly stupid," muttered Josh in disgust.

"Keep those thoughts to yourself and stick to interpreting," Ned replied. Then he called in his staff to be witnesses to the conversation with One Eye, instructing a clerk to take notes.

"Black Kettle states that the Cheyennes have three war parties on the prairie and the Arapahoes have two. They will make peace with the government provided there is also peace with the Sioux, Kiowa, and Comanche."

"At the headwaters of the Smokey Hill River, there are about two-thousand Cheyenne and Arapahoe warriors," said One Eye. "The Sioux have forty lodges, which includes women and children in addition to warriors. You are to send a delegation there to work out a solution for an exchange of prisoners."

Josh translated for One Eye then commented, "Sounds like a trap."

"They could crush us like grapes," Silas added.

Ned stared at One Eye for a long, tense minute. He then pointed his letter opener at the Cheyenne. "All right, I'll go. However, until that happens, you and your traveling companions will come along as our prisoners. If the warriors show any signs of aggression toward my men, you'll be dead before the first arrow reaches us. Agreed?"

One Eye returned his gaze solemnly. "I have faith in my people. It is not the Cheyenne who breaks his word."

Two days later, Ned, Silas and Josh led a company of 127 troopers to the northeast. Accompanying them were the three Cheyenne prisoners, One Eye and his wife, and Min-im-mie. From under his wide-brimmed hat, Josh kept an eye out for hostile warriors. Josh had had to tighten the belt of his uniform. He hadn't shaved and wondered what Sunflower would think of his whisker-stubbled face.

On the fourth day, while they camped, Ned summoned the prisoner Min-im-mie. "Go and tell the tribe we are here to discuss their letter concerning the white hostages."

His only reply an austere glance at the major, Min-im-mie mounted his pony and rode toward the Cheyenne camp.

Ned led the company in the same direction. The next day they followed the North Fork of the Smoky Hill. The shallow water rippled peacefully, but everyone remained on edge. They rounded a bend, and the sight before them made Josh's blood run cold.

Across their path, and on both sides of the river, eight-hundred mounted warriors with painted faces and an assortment of weapons waited for them. Upon seeing the soldiers they let out a chilling war cry and shook their rifles over their heads.

Ned instinctively drew his revolver and pointed it at One Eye's head.

"Lord Jesus, help us," prayed Josh out loud. Then to the soldiers around him he said, "Nobody do anything foolish."

The wagon train formed into a defensive circle. The cavalrymen integrated into four ranks abreast. They had practiced the maneuver hundreds of times. But the move only seemed to further agitate the warriors.

When they came within two-hundred yards of the warriors, Ned ordered the cavalry to halt. Turning to One Eye he shouted over the din of Indian war cries. "Go tell them we are here for the hostages. And remember, I still have your wife."

The outnumbered soldiers anxiously watched One Eye on horseback ascend a low hill and vanish amongst the warriors. Ten minutes later, One Eye returned and said to Ned, "Black Kettle has agreed to meet with you in council tomorrow."

The cavalry retraced its steps for eight miles, to put distance between them and the Cheyennes, then made camp near a dry creek bed. However, a large group of warriors followed them and taunted them with persistent war cries throughout the night. Nobody slept.

At nine o'clock the next morning, Black Kettle and the principal chiefs rode in. Forming a half circle, they sat on the ground in front of Ned's tent. Ned and Silas, along with two lieutenants, and Josh as interpreter, also sat on the ground. Despite the blue sky and puffy white clouds, it was windy and an occasional dust devil twisted its way through the camp.

The Cheyennes looked at Josh with recognition but little warmth.

Ned pulled out the letter given to him by One Eye and read it to the group. When he had finished, he showed it to the chiefs and asked, "Were all of you present when this was written?"

Each of them confirmed that he was.

Ned then told the Indians, "I will not make you any promises I cannot guarantee. I am only a small chief and cannot finalize treaties. But releasing the hostages to me will show your good intent to make peace with your white neighbor. If you do this, I promise I will speak on your behalf to the greater authorities." He then read them the proclamation issued by Governor Evans.

"What about our people being held in Denver?" asked Black Kettle.

"I am not aware of Cheyenne or Arapahoe prisoners as stated in this letter. If you release the hostages I will speak to the big chiefs in Denver about any prisoners they may be holding. Every officer here will support me on that initiative," said Ned.

The chiefs listed a series of grievances, while a company clerk took notes. Black Kettle remained silent. The others spoke and sat with a dignified posture and a slight smile. Then Black Kettle stood and wrapped his whole body in a blanket. At last he spoke, "It was I who had the letter written and I am pleased that it resulted in Tall Chief arriving here. We all want peace, but there are bad white men and bad Indians who keep pushing us to the brink of war. The whites, though, are to be blamed for this latest war. I think giving up the white prisoners would benefit my people; however, other chiefs believe your attempt at peace is not enough. They will only return the prisoners when they receive an assurance of peace."

Ned also stood and adjusted his kepi. "As I said, I am in no position to guarantee peace. Nevertheless, I implore you to consider my proposition. Discuss it among yourselves. We will be camped twelve miles upstream for two days. I shall expect your answer by then."

Black Kettle said, "We will come, but some of the prisoners are with the Sioux. It may take more than two days to bring them to you. Even if the chiefs here reject your recommendation, you may return to the fort unmolested, since you came in good faith."

Five hours later, the council adjourned and the soldiers moved to a different campsite.

"Why do we have to keep moving?" asked Josh, pulling the saddle from his horse.

"If they should decide to attack us, we'll be that much closer to Fort Lyon," said Ned who was already in the saddle.

"Major, those braves *will* attack us. I suggest we keep on riding back to the fort," said a gray-haired sergeant.

"Negative. Black Kettle said he would be here within two days, so this is where we're staying," said Ned.

On the second day, the men were about to eat their midday meal when a scout rode into the camp and reported to Ned. "Major, some Indians are approaching from the north with a white woman."

The soldiers took cover behind rocks and some of their wagons, with their guns at the ready. Ned attached the stock to his .44 Dragoon and looked across the river. Chief Left Hand and two Arapahoe warriors came into view. They brought a young female hostage in a dirty, torn dress. Her blonde hair was tangled and unwashed. Dark bruises covered her swollen face. Her hands were bound in front and a thin rope around her neck served as a leash, with one warrior holding the other end. Cautiously the group approached, riding their ponies across the shallow river.

Josh felt his face flush. He spat. "Those contemptible savages!" He cocked his carbine and held it at the ready.

"We can kill all three of them redskin devils, Major; just give us the word," shouted a trooper who aimed his rifle at the trio.

"Any of you who fires without my permission will be shot without benefit of a court martial," Ned sternly warned. "That goes for you too, Joshua."

The Arapahoes with the girl entered the camp and stopped. "That has to be Laura Roper, the neighbor girl who was kidnapped by the Cheyenne Dog Soldiers," said Josh.

"Cut her loose," ordered Ned.

The warrior looked over at Left Hand, who nodded his head once. Laura lifted her wrists while the warrior cut the sinew straps with a bone-handle knife. Two cavalrymen helped Laura off the pony and escorted her to the medical tent.

With Josh interpreting, Ned said, "Left Hand, you and the warriors will remain with us until the other hostages are returned."

Later that afternoon, the same scout reported to Ned, "You're going to want to see this, Major. The Cheyennes have brought the kidnapped children."

Ned and Josh rode out to meet Black Kettle and the other principal chiefs who had three white children in tow. There were two eight-year-old boys and a girl who was four.

"Where are Missus Ewbanks and her baby?" Josh asked from his saddle.

Black Kettle said, "I have not yet been able to locate them."

The children appeared as soulless beings with crazed eyes. Back at the camp, Laura said to the soldiers, "The little girl is Isabel Ewbanks. The poor dear watched the warriors kill her father."

"Come on, Major, how much more proof do you need?" asked the gray-haired sergeant. "Let's hang these redskins and be done with it."

Ned squared his shoulders and took a deep breath, trying to control his temper. He then faced the sergeant. "How about those warriors? Do you think they would mind if we just hanged their chiefs and meandered back to Fort Lyon?"

The chiefs stood ill-at-ease in the center of the army camp with the soldiers glaring at them.

Finally the major said to Black Kettle, "We will travel with you to Denver tomorrow. While there, I'll arrange for all of you chiefs to meet with Governor Evans. Is that agreeable?"

"It is," answered Black Kettle.


In front of the governor's mansion, quite a spread had been laid: pans of baked potatoes, baked beans, corn bread, pies, and bar-bequed beef adorned eight long tables. Most of the prominent citizens of Denver were in attendance. Posted signs read, "Colorado Statehood," "Evans for Senate," and "Chivington for Congress." Members of the stockmen's association, who donated the beef, stood about in their suits, riding boots, and ten-gallon hats, discussing politics. Though soldiers stood guard around the property, a festive mood presided. It was a comfortable afternoon at seventy-one degrees with some high clouds and a pleasant breeze.

Josh hadn't expected to find this crowd when he arrived. Tired and saddle sore from the long ride, he wasn't prepared to be jovial. A servant escorted him past the socialites and cattlemen, and introduced him at the governor's private table on the large veranda.

Chivington, the governor, and two other men sat at the table eating thick steaks. With a cigar clinched in his teeth, Governor

Evans rose from his spot at the head of the table and shook hands with Josh. "Chaplain, I would like you to meet the other senate hopeful, Henry Teller, and this is our primary sponsor among the stockmen, T. Wright Mendenhall."

Josh shook hands with the men. Mendenhall had the firmest grip. The cattleman also wore the biggest hat at the table.

"I'm pleased to meet you, gentlemen," said Josh. "Governor, I am ready to report on my trip with Major Wynkoop. The long story short is that Black Kettle wants to meet with you."

"I am aware he is in town, but that can wait. Please help yourself to some of this delicious food," said the governor. "We'll talk business when Marshal Hunt arrives."

Josh sat next to the colonel and ate a generous portion of barbequed brisket and beans. He couldn't remember the last time he had food that was so tasty and so plentiful. About halfway through a large piece of apple pie, he noticed the others watching him.

"Slow down, Joshua. There's more than enough here for everyone," Chivington teased.

"I wish more folks enjoyed my beef the way you do," Mendenhall drawled then wiped his mouth with a linen napkin.

When Marshal Hunt arrived, he took a seat at the far end of the table. He shot a brief, agitated glare at the governor.

"May I offer you a steak or some brisket?" asked Governor Evans.

Hunt looked over at the liquor stand. "No, thanks. But I'll take some of that bourbon."

Chivington shook his head disapprovingly then drank from his glass of lemonade.

"A glass of bourbon for the marshal," Evans instructed the server. Then he said, "Marshal, as you know, this country is at war, and Colorado has been affected. War is a terrible thing."

"I found that out in Mexico," said Hunt, sipping the bourbon.

The governor continued. "The war back east has drawn all federal troops out of the territory, and the Indian tribes are taking full advantage of the situation. We have been tasked with building our local militia for protection. So far we've been successful in raising two full regiments; however, one of those has been inducted into federal service and the other is vastly overburdened. The War Department has authorized us to raise a third regiment of hundred-day volunteers. Our problem is the hundred-day clock has already started, yet the regiment is still grossly undermanned."

"The Cheyennes are not undermanned. They continue to kill settlers and have now resorted to kidnapping," said Henry Teller, whose dark hair was combed straight back without a part.

"They've killed several of our ranch hands and are rustling cattle to the point it's becoming an epidemic. And I don't have to tell you what an economic disaster that can cause," said T. Wright Mendenhall.

"That's because the Indian agent is stealing their annuities," protested Josh. "The settlers keep goading the warriors into a fight, and then when they do fight back, the settlers go crying to the army for protection."

"Hold your tongue, Joshua," ordered Chivington. "You'll get your chance."

Josh took a deep breath and clenched his fists under the table.

"What does all this have to do with me?" asked Hunt.

"We need more men," said Governor Evans bluntly. "Our recruiters have resorted to visiting saloons and transient hotels, but they still haven't filled their quota. We've even taken some prisoners off the hands of Sheriff Sopris."

"Sounds like you've got yourself a crackerjack unit," said Hunt.

Chivington picked up a piece of paper and stared at the marshal. "Are you acquainted with Edward Lavally and William Winget?"

"Not that I would want people to know it—but yes, I am." Hunt took another sip and glared back at the colonel. "Were they part of that crew you got from the sheriff?"

"Sheriff Sopris steered us to the hotel where they were

registered," said Chivington. "And they in turn steered us to you."

"Is that a fact?"

"It is." Chivington's eyes darkened. "They told us you've got two prisoners that you transferred from the county jail to the federal prison."

Josh started to stand and voice his objection, but the colonel put a firm hand on his shoulder and pushed him back down into the chair.

"The two lowlifes you're referring to are Joe Blackburn and Nate Talbot, and no, you can't have them," stated the marshal.

"Why not?" demanded Chivington pounding his fist on the table.

"Because I spent the better part of a year tracking them down, that's why not," said Hunt. "I also recollect what happened the last time I turned prisoners over to you."

Chivington hissed, "That was an entirely different matter."

"Marshal, we understand the two prisoners in question were arrested for killing a Cheyenne," said Evans.

"That's right," Hunt confirmed.

"Well, Marshal, that's exactly the type of men we're looking for," said Governor Evans. "We need men who are willing to fight the Cheyennes."

"I didn't say they were arrested for fighting Cheyennes. They were arrested for killing a man in cold blood. There's a difference." Hunt checked his pocket watch.

"Unfortunately, Marshal, the task before us requires the use of some cold-blooded killers," said Chivington.

"Well, you would be the one to know," retorted Hunt. "But only Judge Harding can release them."

"I'm afraid you're wrong there, Marshal." Evans leaned back in his chair and blew three smoke rings. "As governor I have the authority to pardon prisoners within the territory. Naturally, I wanted Judge Harding to drop the charges, but he said it is customary to inform the arresting officer first. You might say this was merely a courtesy call.

Now, are you sure you won't have something to eat?"

Marshal Hunt slammed his glass down and rose from his chair. "If you want those two cutthroats that bad, then perhaps you deserve them. Keep in mind that putting blue uniforms on those animals won't make them soldiers. Pigs in silk pajamas are still pigs." He left without saying good-bye and ignored all greetings from the party goers he passed.

Josh watched him go then exclaimed, "Gentlemen, have you all gone crazy? Those two men tried to kill me!"

"Joshua, you've nothing to fear. You are the chaplain for the First Regiment and these men will be assigned to the Third. They will be ordered not to have any contact with you; and if they do, I will have them hanged," said Chivington.

Josh excused himself from the table and left the party.


The seven principal chiefs of the Cheyenne and Arapahoe tribes met with Governor Evans and Colonel Chivington at Fort Weld, located two miles north of Denver. Josh was asked to interpret.

"I must admit, Chaplain, I'm reluctant to meet with the chiefs for fear of appearing defeated," said the governor. What if they get the idea that I'm asking for negotiations as a result of their atrocities? After my repeated requests, the War Department has finally financed and equipped the Third Regiment. The Colorado Third Volunteers have been raised to kill Cheyennes, not to parlay with them. How is it going to look in Washington if I inform Secretary Stanton that the regiment wasn't needed after all?"

"Sir, not every Cheyenne is at war with the government," reasoned Josh. "Black Kettle and the other chiefs are here with the express desire to end the hostilities."

"All right, I'll meet with them," said Governor Evans, "provided they formally surrender to the United States Government."

Inside the large meeting room sat Cheyenne chiefs Black Kettle, White Antelope, and Bull Bear, and Arapahoe Chiefs Neva,

Bosse, Heap-of-Buffalo, and Na-Ta-Nee. Also present were Dexter Colley, Ned, Silas, several other officers, and a few Denver businessmen.

Black Kettle spoke about the confusion over the governor's proclamation that had sent them on the warpath. He also claimed that even though he secured the release of four hostages, Lucinda Ewbanks and her infant remained far to the north with the Sioux.

The governor made little effort to find a peaceful solution. He looked harshly at Black Kettle and said, "You have gone into an alliance with the Sioux who were at war with us. I brought you many presents when you were camped on the Smoky Hill. In turn, you sent messengers to say that you wanted nothing to do with me. Your people then went away and smoked the war pipe with our enemies."

The chiefs gave each other a puzzled look.

Josh paused in his translating and quietly spoke to the governor, "Sir, there is no such thing as a war pipe. They smoke for peace, not war."

"Oh, confound it, they know what I'm talking about!"

"Yes, sir."

Governor Evans continued his diatribe. "It is utterly out of the question for you to be at peace with us while living with our enemies and being on friendly terms with them. The only way you can show your friendship with us is to make some kind of arrangement with the army."

"We will return with Tall Chief to Fort Lyon. Then we will return to our village and take word back to our young men," said Black Kettle.

"How can we be protected from the soldiers on the plains?" asked White Antelope.

"You must make that arrangement with Colonel Chivington," answered the governor.

"I fear these new soldiers who have gone out may kill some of my people while I am here," said White Antelope.

"There is a great danger of that," said Evans.

Colonel Chivington sat silently with folded arms. Finally he spoke. "I am not a big war chief, but all the soldiers in this part of the country are at my command. The warriors are nearer to Major Wynkoop than anyone else, and they can go to him when they are ready for peace."

When they adjourned, the chiefs seemed satisfied and shook hands with everyone there. The chiefs consented to having their picture taken, but Governor Evans and Colonel Chivington declined to take part.

On the fifth of November, Ned and Josh were talking in the commander's office when a smug-looking Major Scott Anthony stepped in and presented a folder, placing it on Ned's desk.

Ned looked over the folder. "This doesn't make any sense," he said. "After all I have done to make this treaty possible—"

"What is it?" Josh wanted to know.

With dejection in his voice, Ned said, "I've been relieved of duty with orders to report to Fort Riley. Anthony here will be in charge."

Anthony folded his arms, smirking. "Word got back to General Curtis that it is the Indians who are running Fort Lyon. Looks to me that is exactly what's going on. I'm going to do everything within my power to get their camps far away from the fort. In the meantime, starting tomorrow morning, I'll shoot any redskin I see on this post without a proper military escort." Turning to Josh he said, "And that includes your in-laws, Chaplain. I don't want to see that squaw of yours unless she's within three feet of you."

"That marshal was right; you are a worm," said Josh between clenched teeth, making an effort to stay calm.

The officers studied a map of the area that was tacked to one of the office walls. Anthony said to Josh, "Chaplain, the Arapahoes will be moving thirty miles due east of here, hoping to find sufficient game to get through the winter. We need a spot on the reservation to send the Cheyennes. You've been married into their tribe now for, what? three or four years? Where do you recommend they go?"

Josh looked closer at the map and pointed to a blue, curved line that marked the east boundary of the reservation. "I think this spot forty miles to the northeast would be ideal. The maps label this stream as the Big Sandy, but everyone around here knows it as Sand Creek."

# Chapter 12

## THAT DAY BY THE CREEK

The Cheyenne camp was packed and ready for traveling. Josh rode with Major Anthony to where the chiefs sat on their ponies, waiting. Stopping in front of Black Kettle, Anthony asked, "Are you clear on where you are to set up the village?"

"Yes, but what guarantee have we that the soldiers will not attack us for leaving the fort?" Black Kettle wanted to know.

"Do you still have the American flag Judge Greenwood gave you?" asked Anthony.

"I do."

"Fly it from a tall lodge pole in front of your tepee. Underneath it, attach this fabric as a flag of truce." Anthony pulled out a white bed sheet from his saddlebag. "If you fly them together I guarantee you that any soldiers on the warpath will know you are peaceable."

Black Kettle took the truce flag and handed it to a warrior. He looked at Josh and then at Anthony. "I will do as you say. When can we expect our rations to be delivered?"

"Just as soon as I clear everything with Agent Colley. I will send a wagonload; but remember, I expect that wagon to be filled with buffalo hides for the return trip."

"If we are not forced to move again, we will find plenty of buffalo." Black Kettle nodded to Josh then heeled his pony forward.

Sand Creek gently snaked its way southward through the prairie. A cluster of sand hills forced the creek to run due east for two miles before resuming its course to the Arkansas River. During that time of year, ice crusted over much of the narrow stream. Black Kettle's camp of a hundred lodges was in the bend where the creek changed directions. Their herd of ponies grazed two miles east of the new Cheyenne camp.

As Josh rode in with Jack Smith to deliver the wagon of annuity goods, he thought the camp looked relaxed. Children played near the water and the women went about their numerous chores. Several buffalo hides had been stacked outside a large tepee to be exchanged for the delivered goods, but most of the warriors were gone. Josh figured they had returned to the herd on the Smoky Hill River.

Josh received permission from Sunflower's uncle to sleep in their lodge. He was only going to be there for one night and Kicking Horse wanted news of the army's intentions. Later, while snuggled with Sunflower under a buffalo blanket, Josh watched Little Dove sleeping soundly in the glow of the fire's coals. In her arms she held the rag doll he had given her.

"Once again, we are here so far away from you at the fort. How are we ever going to be together again?" Sunflower whispered.

Josh didn't know what to answer. "You've endured so much; but when this war is over, we'll live a normal life. As normal as we can make it."

In the early-morning darkness of November 29, 1864, Josh got up and put on his uniform, expecting to return to the fort that day. First, he needed to go to the tepee by the buffalo hides where his saddle and other tack were stored. His enlisted assistant, Private David Louderback, was sleeping there and probably needed to be awakened.

When he reached the stack of foul-smelling hides at the eastern edge of the camp, he saw his nephew, dressed in buckskins and a robe, riding the palomino mare in the early light.

"Where are you off to, Black Hoof?"

"To the herd," said Black Hoof. "Grandfather asked me to bring him his swiftest pony—"

Several shots rang out, coming from where the herd of ponies was pastured.

"What's that shooting?" Josh looked up in time to see Black Hoof topple off the back of the palomino. The horse then bolted from the camp.

Before Josh could check on the boy, a shock wave from an exploding shell knocked him to the ground and he saw two women and an old man tossed into the air. As another explosion showered dirt over Josh, he covered his ringing ears and cried, "Sunflower!"

Josh crawled into the storage lodge, keeping his head down. Bullets whined, zipping through the lodge skins.

Louderback, a tall husky farm boy, was trying to lie flat behind his saddle on the grass floor. With a bewildered and frightened expression, he said, "Excuse me, sir, but could you tell those Indians to adjust their fire in another direction?"

"Indians don't have artillery, Louderback!" Josh shouted. "Most of the shooting seems to be coming from the other side of the creek. I'm going to try and make my way over there and see what's going on."

"I'll stay here and make sure nobody takes our stuff."

"Yeah, you do that." Josh dug through his saddlebags and pulled out a pair of binoculars. He then scrambled outside and crawled on his stomach through brown grass and patches of snow toward the creek. Wedged between the camp and the pony herd to the east was a company of cavalry, the rising sun to their backs. The cavalrymen were firing indiscriminately toward the tepees.

More bullets were freely flying from the detestable Third Regiment directly across the creek. They were dismounted and kneeling as they excitedly fired their Burnside carbines. Most weren't even taking aim.

From behind a decaying log, Josh tried to assess what was taking place. With the binoculars he looked east and then west and saw large numbers of soldiers in both directions. He was not a military strategist, but he could see that some units had overlapped. Members of the First Regiment were lying on their bellies as the Hundred Day Volunteers fired overhead. They took casualties from the blocking force to the east, who in turn received "friendly" fire from the Third. Cavalrymen of the First, under the command of Silas Soule, were not shooting, but looked to be in danger of being killed by their own men. Major Anthony and Silas were arguing about something.

As women and children ran out of the lodges looking for a place to hide, Anthony hollered, "Kill them! Kill them all!"

Josh couldn't hear what Silas was saying, but he must have told his company to disregard the order, for that is what they were doing.

Anthony, who appeared to be enraged, issued another order that only resulted in mingling the regiments even more.

It would be foolish to keep standing there and make himself a stationary target, so Josh sprinted back to the tepee where his tack was stored. He took cover behind a pile of firewood next to the buffalo skins with Louderback.

"What did you find out, sir?" Louderback asked.

"Those are our troops from Fort Lyon, but they won't stop shooting long enough for me to identify myself." He felt he was in a bad dream from which he couldn't wake. Withering gunfire nearly turned the wood pile into kindling.

Louderback tied a white handkerchief to the end of a stick and handed it to Josh. "Here, sir, they're less likely to shoot an officer."

"Don't be so sure," said Josh taking the stick. He stood cautiously and walked back toward the creek. The firing to their front halted when Josh raised the handkerchief. As he got close, someone yelled out, "Hey, that guy's a squaw man!" The shooting resumed, and Josh dove behind the same decaying log as before.

A private from Silas's company saw Josh's predicament. He jumped on his horse and took off for the camp. The well-meaning soldier took a bullet through the back, fell to the ground and died on the bank not far from Josh.

A member of the Third held a smoking carbine and said, "If there's one thing I hate as much as a squaw man, it's a friend of a squaw man. Pass me that bottle, Will."

Josh retreated back to Louderback's cover behind the woodpile.

As the howitzers found their range, the shelling intensified. Shrapnel and lead balls shredded the lodge skins, and many caught fire.

"We'll never get out alive if we stay here. Let's start moving to the front of the camp so we can keep those lodges between us and the creek," said Josh.

Louderback's green eyes widened. "How do you know they won't shoot at us when we get to the front of the camp?"

"I don't. Maybe there's another company over there that isn't as trigger happy as these Neanderthals. Come on!"

Cautiously but quickly they made their way westward through the camp. Plenty of bullets still passed overhead, but at least none were directly aimed at them. They stopped when they saw Black Kettle's tepee.

"Look at that, will ya?" said Louderback.

"Yeah, maybe that will get them to cease fire."

Black Kettle had raised the large American flag with the white flag of peace on a long lodge pole. Now, over eighty frightened women, children, and elderly men huddled around the flagpole. But the cannon and rifle fire continued.

Approximately fifty yards away, and just beyond the creek, sat the bulk of the Third Regiment on their horses. From his saddle, Colonel Chivington calmly observed the huddled Indians through his binoculars.

The tribe's most respected chief, White Antelope, ran to the middle of the creek bed and folded his arms across his chest indicating they did not want to fight.

Chief Standing-In-Water ran out to stop his friend. Ironically, he wore the peace medal awarded to him in Washington, D.C. Several bullets cut him down.

Josh spotted the two murderers Governor Evans had pardoned. Talbot put his hand on Blackburn's shoulder and said, "Look, that's old White Antelope standing in the creek."

Blackburn still wore his tattered derby. He took careful aim with his carbine, fired, and then said, "You mean that *was* old White Antelope." They both laughed.

The bullet struck White Antelope square in the chest. Coughing up blood, he fell back through the ice of the shallow water.

Talbot ran over and started to cut away the dead chief's buckskin trousers. "You know what I'm gonna do? I'm gonna get me a new tobacco pouch!"

"Oh Nathan, you are bad. Hee hee, you are bad," chuckled Blackburn. "After his scalp, I'm gonna get his ears and hide them in the captain's office, so I'll know when he's talking about me."

A bursting shell killed several people around the flagpole. When Black Kettle's lodge burst into flames, the Indians inside ran out in all directions. Black Kettle carried his wounded wife. Pandemonium reigned throughout the camp. People ran into each other and small children wandered dazed and aimless, crying for their parents.

Much to his dismay, Josh heard a bugler play "Charge." The remounted Third Regiment took off with their swallow-tail American flag fluttering overhead. Each company carried a similarly-shaped red and white guidon. The Hundred Day Volunteers thundered through the camp shooting down every living creature they encountered, be it man, woman, child, or dog. The First Regiment, obeying Captain Soule's order, refused to participate.

Josh had gotten separated from Louderback during the maelstrom. By now, several tepees burned out of control, and he became disoriented by the heat and choking smoke. The atrocities he witnessed exceeded any nightmare he ever had. Arms, legs, and heads littered the ground, and a dismounted cavalryman tossed an infant onto the sharpened ends of some lodge poles.

After the Third Regiment charged through the camp, the Volunteers rode about and shot at targets of opportunity. They gunned down numerous women and children whose hands were raised in surrender. Dozens of troopers now dismounted with unsheathed knives in order to continue their dirty work at close quarters.

Josh's personal safety had improved now that so many other cavalrymen were on foot while collecting their gruesome souvenirs. Horror and shock muddled his senses. He heard his sister-in-law Butterfly scream and saw her running with her clothes on fire. A cavalryman galloped behind her with a raised saber. Spotted Bear emerged from a defensive pit and shot the trooper with his rifle. The wounded rider jerked back on the reins, and with the horse neighing in fright, both fell backwards and crashed through a tepee.

Another trooper skid his horse to a stop and fanned his revolver. Spotted Bear's body twisted to the right as the bullets passed through it. A kneeling trooper took aim with his carbine and calmly shot Butterfly through the back. Her burning clothes marked the ground where she had fallen by the water's edge.

The Third Volunteers scalped and removed body parts from the dead Indians for trophies. Regimental adjutant Major Hal Sayr tried to scalp a severely wounded girl for the silver ornaments in her hair while she begged to be killed.

"Let her go!" Josh screamed, pointing his pistol at Sayr's face.

"What's the matter with you, Chaplain? Let's send this little she-devil to hell where she belongs." But Sayr stepped away from the girl.

Josh holstered his weapon and lifted the girl into his arms. She bled profusely from her head and left side. Unable to speak, she looked at him with frightened, tear-filled eyes. "This girl is no more than fourteen, and you've got the gall to ask what's wrong with *me*? No, Major; what's wrong with you?"

Sayr drew his sidearm without pointing it at anyone, and yelled, "That scalp belongs to me! Put her down. That's an order!"

"Just try and take her from me," Josh threatened.

Sayr ran off to find other victims.

Josh pleaded with the soldiers around him. "Stop! Please, stop!" But his voice was drowned out by the gunshots, bugle calls, screaming women, crying babies, and raging fires. "Dear God, make them stop!" he cried out in desperation. When he saw that the girl in his arms had died, he gently placed her on the ground.

Josh ran from the camp when he saw an artillery caisson moving along the north bank. He jumped on it. A feeling of dread descended upon him as he thought about Sunflower and Little Dove. If they weren't already dead, they would be hopelessly running toward the open prairie. When he arrived at Chivington's location, he got off the caisson and staggered down to the creek. He splashed the blood from the water and took a drink, hoping it would taste like fresh mountain water without a metallic, salty taste.

Standing to his feet he indignantly yelled, "Colonel! Have you gone completely insane? Is it not enough you let these maniacs kill the women—but the children too? I saw three of those Volunteers shooting at a little toddler like it was a competition to see whose bullet would make him drop!"

Chivington glanced coolly at Josh. "Nits makes lice," he said.

Josh saw members of the Third Regiment's Company B on top of a high embankment working their knives like they were field dressing a deer. Blackburn cut away something grotesque and Talbot could not stop laughing.

"Lord, forgive me, but I do hate those men terribly," Josh muttered. Below the embankment, the few remaining warriors had made a futile defense by digging shallow rifle pits. They were all dead now, their bloody heads showing where their scalps used to be.

Nearby, he found the bodies of Sunflower's sister and uncle.

Day Star, pretty as ever, lay on her back with her eyes open, as if staring at something in the sky.

By three o'clock that afternoon, the companies under Anthony's direct command returned after pursuing several Indians who had escaped to the east. An unscathed tepee held the "prisoners," which for the moment consisted of three small children and an infant. Jack Smith emerged from the smoke with raised arms and a gun to his back. Major Sayr held the gun in his right hand and a scalp with silver ornaments in his left.

As much as Josh wanted to help his friend, he was desperate to find Sunflower. He'd inquire about Jack later. He watched the men of Company B ride from the embankment to the front of the camp.

The Hundred Day Volunteers wore captured war bonnets or other souvenirs and mockingly reenacted a scalp dance with the dead at their feet. An officer asked Josh to identify a body, thinking it was Black Kettle. Exasperated, Josh said, "That's not him. It's One Eye." He recalled that day when One Eye had said, "It is not the Cheyenne who breaks his word."

Josh ran toward the area where he had seen Company B using their knives but was stopped by a civilian scout, his face pale. With a choked voice he said, "Joshua, you don't want to go up there."

Ignoring the advice, Josh sprinted the rest of the way. On the backside of the elevated embankment were forty dead and mutilated bodies near the entrance of a shallow dugout. He located Sunflower by her red robe and saw that her fingers and rings had been removed. On the edge of the embankment was the crumpled body of Little Dove. Her face was missing. He identified her by the rag doll in her left hand. "This isn't real. I just kissed them good-bye this morning."

As he sobbed, his attention was drawn to Black Kettle's American flag, which had caught fire. Around the flag pole, with whiskey bottles in hand, the Hundred Day Volunteers continued their victory dance.

Numbly Josh staggered back to the camp. "God, sometimes I wonder if you really exist. How could you allow this?" he cried.

Next to the supply wagons, Company B looked over their looted items. Josh reached his breaking point when he saw Blackburn holding the silver thimble he had given Sunflower on their wedding day. Blackburn's eyes widened when he found himself looking down the barrel of Josh's .44 and heard the cylinder rotate.

Josh held out his free hand, palm up. "That's mine."

Blackburn gave him the thimble without any questions.

"I should have killed you two when I had the chance," Josh said.

Blackburn and Talbot exchanged a grin. "That's right, you did have a chance," said Blackburn. "But you can't do it now, because there are too many witnesses."

Josh holstered his gun and turned to leave.

"Looky there, he's scared of us," taunted Talbot who flapped his elbows while strutting like a chicken. "Bawk, bawk, bawk, bawk."

With lightning speed, Josh grabbed a shovel from a supply wagon and swung it like a baseball bat, smashing Blackburn's nose. Reversing his swing, he hit Talbot in the mouth. The shovel's spade rang like a bell. Both men fell backwards onto the ground. Josh tossed the shovel onto Talbot's chest and walked away.


Jack Smith was shoved into a lodge. Several men from the Third Regiment stood around the tepee and discussed what they should do with Jack.

"Let's hang the dirty half-breed," one man shouted.

A sergeant hollered over to Chivington, "Excuse me, sir, but we found that half-breed scout, Jack Smith, coming out of a tepee. What should we do with him?"

"Sergeant, do you remember my order not to take any prisoners?" Chivington asked.

"Yes, sir, I do."

"Then what is it you don't understand?"

"Nothing, sir. I understand perfectly."

Tired and disgusted as he was, Josh walked over to Chivington and asked, "Colonel, why is Jack Smith being held prisoner? He is a federal employee who does work for the army as a tracker."

Chivington sat on a portable chair and took a long drink from his canteen. "The person you're referring to was found in the company of the Cheyennes and only surrendered when confronted by our men."

"Of course he was in the Cheyennes' company. Major Anthony requested we bring food to the camp in exchange for buffalo hides." Josh hoped Chivington would show fairness and let Jack go.

Private Louderback walked over from the prisoners' lodge looking frustrated.

A gunshot sounded.

Louderback spun around. He glared at the lodge. "They shot Jack Smith! It's a shame to kill a man like that without letting him have his say."

Chivington smirked.

A sergeant yelled, "Get back to your company or you'll be shot too, Private."

"Louderback, thanks for helping me these past couple of days. Now you should return to your company," said Josh.

"Yes, sir," said Louderback through clinched teeth and giving Chivington a hateful stare. He shuffled off, shaking his head and mumbling under his breath.

Chivington turned his attention to Josh. "Well, I guess the matter concerning Mister Jack Smith is now a moot point."

Josh kept silent.

"We'll be leaving shortly so we can attack the Arapahoes in the morning."

Before Josh could respond, he found himself suddenly yanked backwards and thrown to the ground. While trying to get air back into his lungs, the bloody-faced Blackburn sat on his belly, holding a knife to his throat.

Hysterically, Blackburn screamed, "I got the dirty Injun lover now. Look what he did to my nose. I'm gonna kill him and get his scalp so the whole family will be together again."

"Blackburn, what's going on here?" demanded Major Sayr.

"Major, this man is one of them, and he tried to kill me."

"Get him to his feet," said Sayr. "I don't doubt your word, Private. This man also pointed a gun at me while I disarmed an enemy combatant."

Blackburn and another member of the Third forced Josh to stand.

The colonel acted as if he had not seen a thing and calmly strolled over to his horse.

With blood lust in his eyes, Blackburn called, "Colonel—sir—just give us the okay and we'll shoot this Injun lover just like he was a rabid dog."

Other members of Company B echoed his sentiments.

"Dear God, is this how it all ends? I thought you brought me here for something better," Josh prayed out loud.

Talbot painfully stood and spat out a bloody tooth. "That's right, say your prayers, boy, because you're all mine."

The normally-calm Lieutenant Colonel Tappan galloped to the scene and pointed his Colt .44 at Sayr. "Major, you order this mob of yours to stay away from this man or I'll splatter your head like a ripe melon."

"He was found in the company of the enemy," whined Sayr, stomping his foot like a child.

Lieutenant Joseph Cramer had his Company G gallop into the camp and face off with the group of Hundred Day Volunteers. "Give us the word, sir, and we'll make sure he receives his award posthumously," said Cramer, also aiming his pistol at Sayr.

"Lieutenant, do you know to whom you are pointing that weapon? I am the most respected surveyor in Denver," said an aggravated Sayr.

"Enough!" shouted Tappan. "Right now you're nothing but an

overpaid civil engineer with one foot in the grave. If you don't order your men to return to the other side of the creek, I'll open fire on you and the rest of this rabble."

Sayr bit his lip when he heard the loud metallic sound of cocking pistols and carbines. With frightened eyes, Sayr and Company B glanced at the gun barrels pointed in their direction.

"Well, I'll be dipped in manure and rolled in sugar if they ain't serious,' said Blackburn, holding his broken nose.

Trying his best to muster some courage, Sayr said, "All right, boys, we've had enough fun for today. Holster your hardware and fall back to the other bank."

Company B did as instructed, leaving behind Josh under the protection of Cramer's guns.

"Thank you, Lord," sobbed Josh.

Tappan reined his horse toward Chivington's and cursed. "Why didn't you do something? Are you the commanding officer or not?"

"How dare you use that language when addressing me," Chivington growled.

Tappan shouted another curse at Chivington, then the two senior officers turned the air blue and their faces red exchanging profanities.

When Tappan rode over to Company G and had them holster their weapons, Chivington hollered, "Yes, I am in charge and don't any of you forget it!"

With legs like rubber, Josh approached Chivington. "With your permission, sir, I would like to remain behind and bury my wife."

"That's out of the question. It will be far too dangerous to leave you here alone. If the warriors return, you will not be spared."

"Just a minute ago you were going to let those men kill me, but now you're worried about my safety?"

Chivington was agitated. "All right, fine. Tonight we'll be camped fifteen miles downstream. Do what you have to do and then hightail it to that location. Get a fresh mount from the quartermaster."

In the late afternoon, the cavalry assembled in four long ranks with the raging infernos at their backs. Colonel Chivington stood in his stirrups surveying the men with pride, beaming from ear to ear. Raising his voice, he said, "Today, you men of the First and Third Colorado Cavalries have taught the Cheyennes that actions have consequences. They can no longer commit acts of murder, kidnapping, and rape, then beg for peace. More importantly, many years from now your grandsons will ask, 'What did you do in the Great Cheyenne War of '64?' You can hold your head high and say, 'I fought at Sand Creek.' May history never forget what we did here this day!"

A loud cheer erupted from the ranks. Hats were tossed high in the air. A bugle sounded. Then the cavalrymen maneuvered their horses into columns and left the massacre site.

Josh returned to the spot where the group of forty had been killed. Charred tepee frames were silhouetted against the setting sun. Whiffs of smoke from the lodge poles were carried on a gentle breeze. With tears running down his face, Josh dug two graves. He placed Sunflower in one and Little Dove in the other. Furiously he shoveled the sandy dirt over their bodies. He could not so easily fill the gaps left in his heart. Dropping to his knees, he pounded his fists on the ground and let out a heartrending cry. He remained until the tears no longer fell.

The prairie was silent, as it had been for centuries.

# Chapter 13

## THE BUFFALO HUNTERS

Josh sat on his bed studying a hand-drawn map of what was supposed to be the future reservation with its post offices, shops, and churches. The images only served to mock him. He felt that, if they could leap off the paper, they would laugh in his face for his naivety. He tore it into bits and threw the pieces onto the floor. "God, you sent me to minister to these people and to help bring them out of the Stone Age only to have them wiped out? My wife was brutally murdered and disfigured! Is that why you brought me here? Throughout the Bible, you say you hate those who shed innocent blood. Will you allow these murderers to go unpunished?"

Josh stepped outside into the cold breeze blowing across the parade ground. The bright sun shone in a cloudless sky, but tiny needles of frozen air pricked his face. He had just descended the front steps, with hands plunged deep in the pockets of his heavy, blue coat, when a man bundled in black clothes stepped in front of him. The man's nose and cheeks were red from the cold and his dark beard was blown to the side. In his right hand was a hoe.

"Brother Oscar, is there something I can do for you?" he asked wearily.

"Yes," began Oscar loudly. He then softened his voice. "I am—that is, all of us at the mission were—saddened when we learned about the death of your wife and those of her band. We were also greatly distressed for your own safety and are relieved to see you have returned."

Josh was dumbfounded, unable to speak.

Oscar continued, his righteous anger evident in his voice. "Major Anthony is like the serpent of Eden. You can be assured I gave him a piece of my mind that night before the cavalry rode from here. I also laid into that false prophet Chivington who calls himself a Methodist preacher. Fear not, Brother Joshua, the blood of your wife and daughter shall be avenged. Chivington and Anthony will wet their britches come Judgment Day!"

The Hundred Day Volunteers spent Christmas Eve reveling in the saloons of Denver. That same night, Colonel Chivington held a Christmas party for the officers at the Masons' Hall. Josh did not want to attend, but he agreed to go after several requests from Silas Soule.

The two friends sat together at a round table in the large hall decorated with green and red streamers and a tall fir tree with silver tinsel and an abundance of colorfully-wrapped packages beneath it. Instead of enjoying the festive ambiance, though, Josh sat glaring at the colonel and hardly touched his food. Silas drank a lot of brandy.

"You want a drink?" Silas asked with a slightly slurred voice.

"No, I don't want a drink. I want justice."

"It's Christmas, Joshua. The courts are closed."

Josh wasn't amused.

Silas continued, "Okay, you want justice? Here's my gift to you: Hal Sayr is due to go to the outhouse any minute now. When he returns, he will have a broken nose."

Josh knew it was the liquor talking. "Don't do anything stupid, Silas. You'll only get yourself in trouble."

"I'm already in trouble. The colonel and his henchmen want to kill me," chuckled Silas who then drained another glass.

"Why?"

"Because General Curtis wants Chivington to explain why I did not order my company to charge through the Cheyenne camp."

Three days later, Josh bought a newspaper and saw an article about the Colonel. He felt a ray of hope as he read a reprinted dispatch from Washington, D.C.:

> *The affair at Fort Lyon, Colorado in which Colonel Chivington destroyed a large Indian village and all its inhabitants, is to be made the subject of a congressional investigation. Letters received from high officials in Colorado say that the Indians were killed even after they surrendered, and that a large portion of them were women and children.*

Shortly after the new year of 1865 began, Josh received a wire from Major Ned Wynkoop ordering him to Fort Lyon per instructions from the military district's commanding general. When Josh arrived, Ned took him inside an office at the administration building and explained what was happening.

"I let General Curtis read the letter you sent me regarding the events of November twenty-ninth. When he heard Congress would be investigating a massacre within his district, he ordered me here to take statements from the men who had been at Sand Creek. Joshua, I must admit, I'm going to enjoy watching the downfall of Colonel Chivington. Here's what I've accumulated so far." Ned showed Josh his report and the attached affidavits he would be sending to district headquarters.

"This is very incriminating evidence," said Josh. "They all seem to corroborate each other that women and children were killed."

"Here's something else I found out: Chivington's commission had expired two months before the massacre. If the army had caught this error, he would not have been in charge of any troops, let alone command the entire territorial militia."

A week later, Josh saw Major Anthony, dressed in nice civilian clothes, gallop away from the fort. He went to Ned and asked, "What was that all about?"

"I guess he heard Colonel Chivington is no longer in the army, and he figured he would be the scapegoat." Ned was holding Anthony's resignation letter with ink still wet. "He's not out of the woods yet, though."

"How so?"

"A special committee within the U.S. House of Representatives has subpoenaed him, as well as Dexter and Agent Sam Colley, and some other officers from here at Fort Lyon. I'll have to give Sam Colley some credit. No doubt he made his fortune by cheating the Indians, but when he heard about the massacre, he became incensed and wrote a letter to Senator Doolittle of Wisconsin. Doolittle contacted Colorado Chief Justice Benjamin Hall. These were the 'high officials' mentioned in the newspapers. The senator also notified Army Chief of Staff General Halleck. Governor Evans is visiting Washington as we speak. Little does he know that he, too, is about to be dragged before the committee. I know it's hard to believe, but this whole investigation was launched by Sam Colley."

"I guess that shows that God can soften a man's heart."


The House committee made a special trip to Denver to question the Reverend Chivington at the capitol building. Josh sat in the crowded chamber each day, hoping that some kind of justice would be served. Chivington dressed as the simple country preacher of his past, looking smart in his black suit and string tie over a white shirt. In his testimony, he declared that Major Anthony had led him to believe the Indians were hostile. He also claimed there were only a few women and children among the dead. Although he maintained an air of innocence during the questioning, he seemed nervous and continuously drank glasses of water to replenish the sweat that poured down his face.

At the conclusion of the inquiry, the committee chairman read his prepared remarks:

*As to Colonel Chivington, this committee can hardly find fitting terms to describe his conduct. Wearing the uniform of the United States, which should be the emblem of justice and humanity; holding the important position of commander of a military district, and therefore having the honor of the government to that extent in his keeping; he deliberately planned and executed a foul and dastardly massacre which would have disgraced the most savage among those who were the victims of his cruelty.*

The chairman had similar words for Governor Evans. In the end, all the committee could do was condemn what happened. Chivington's term had expired before the massacre and he left the army a month before the investigation began, so he could not be prosecuted for any crimes. Josh's heart sank.

Nevertheless, a commission of three senior army officers set out to determine who was to blame. Josh was called to testify. He had seen too many atrocities on that awful day to mention them all. He often paused to collect his thoughts, so he could talk about what was relevant to the case, and to leave out the rest, such as his memories of Sunflower, which kept pressing to the forefront of his mind. During cross-examination, he saw the true Reverend Chivington, whose face became red as blood and his eyes black as ink. Josh wished the reverend understood that the Bible was a message of salvation, not a book for fanatics to hide behind and use as justification for wholesale slaughter. Gone was the friendly minister turned army officer who warmly welcomed him as a new chaplain three years prior.

On the front steps of the capitol building, Josh found Ned Wynkoop smoking his pipe. Josh told him, "Since the committee told me I would not be recalled, I stayed for Silas's testimony."

"Did Chivington and his lawyer give him a hard time?" asked Ned.

"It was brutal, and he has to be back Monday morning for another session. I have a question of my own maybe you can answer."

"What's that?"

"How come Silas's refusal to take part in the massacre was never mentioned?"

"The defense doesn't want to address his disobedience of the order, because the order itself was unlawful. Chivington would have been within his rights to order Silas to charge the warriors in the rifle pits, but he could not lawfully order him to kill women and children."

"Why didn't the commission mention it, then?" Josh asked. "They read your report."

Ned sighed. "They don't want word to get out that there was a complete breakdown of discipline on the battlefield."

On a Sunday evening after church, Josh walked home with Silas and his wife, Hersa. They had invited him for pie and coffee.

"I'm glad you accepted the reverend's invitation to be a guest speaker tonight. That was a fine message you delivered," said Silas, dressed in a new blue suit and wide-brimmed slouch hat.

"If that's what it takes to get you into church, I'll keep accepting those offers." Josh grinned. "Especially if there is coffee and dessert afterwards."

Just then three shots came from the direction of the blacksmith shop across the street. In the surrounding houses, lanterns were lit and the sound of barking dogs pierced the air.

"Go into the house!" Silas told his wife. He ran to the shop and grabbed his favorite Navy .36 from its holster under his jacket.

Josh followed close behind. "What are you doing, Silas? You're an army provost-marshal, not a city marshal."

"I want to know who is firing gunshots so close to my house."

A tall man stepped out from the shadows of the blacksmith shop, looking at them with menacing, cold-gray eyes, a razor-stubble face, and a nasty scar across his left cheek. He carefully aimed a large revolver at Silas. From eight feet away, Silas raised his gun. Both men fired at once. The stranger cursed in pain, dropped his gun, and clutched his shattered right arm. At the same time, Silas silently fell, his bleeding face a testament to where the fatal bullet landed.

"Silas!" yelled Josh who ran over to assist his friend.

"Hold it right there, mister." Blackburn emerged from the shadows, pointing his .44 at Josh.

With arms raised, Josh lowered his head, hoping the brim of his hat would conceal his face. Fortunately, the gas streetlights weren't on yet.

The wounded stranger sat on the ground. With pain in his voice he said, "Help me to my horse, Talbot. Come on, we ain't got all night!"

Talbot stepped out from a doorway with his revolver in hand. "To tell you the truth, Squire, you don't look like you're in any shape to be riding."

"What does that mean?" Squire demanded.

"What he means is that you will just slow us down," answered Blackburn. "You earned your share of the money by taking out that witness, but I guess Lady Luck has walked out on you. Sorry, friend, but you're a goner and we'll need your horse for this fancy-looking dude who will be our shield."

Squire cursed a torrent of colorful words. "You double-crossing gutter rats! When I catch you, I'll cut your hearts out! You hear me?"

Talbot bellowed a loud ha-ha. "The only thing you'll be doing is taking that cakewalk at the end of Judge Harding's rope. And as for Cap'n Soule, I don't think he'll be testifying at that hearing tomorrow."

With his pistol still aimed at Josh, Blackburn ordered him to get onto Squire's Appaloosa. "Give us any trouble and I'll bore a hole in you the size of a train tunnel," he threatened. When they were mounted, Blackburn grabbed the Appaloosa's reins and they galloped out of town.

Both scared and confused, Josh quietly prayed, "Dear Lord, what else must I endure? I just want to live a peaceful, solitary life." When the city lights were left behind, he thought about this newest tragedy, and lamented, "Silas, why did you have to die putting your faith in Sam Colt's revolver instead of Christ? Just going to church doesn't save you."

After four hours of hard riding, they pulled off the trail into a cluster of trees. Only a crescent moon provided light as Josh's hands were bound and he was tied uncomfortably to a tree trunk. For him, it was a sleepless night.

In the morning, Talbot said, "I could sure use a cup of coffee right now. Guess I should build a fire."

"Nah, we ain't got time for that. Have a swig of this," said Blackburn handing over a bottle. "We gotta keep movin'."

"I like a good drink of whiskey as much as any man, but not for breakfast," said Talbot, taking a sip anyway. "I wonder why no posse came after us."

"Because I told Squire that we would be making our escape to California. No doubt that's what he's telling the law. While the posse rides in that direction, we'll be heading for St. Louis."

"You know, Joe, you're smart enough to be one of them professors. When we get to St. Louis you should apply to be one," said Talbot.

"I'll do that just as soon as the saloon closes."

Talbot freed Josh from the tree trunk, and a sinister smile of recognition broke across his ugly face. He removed Josh's hat for a better look, then cried out, "Well, look what the cat drug in! Hee, hee, Joe, get a look at this one. Don't he look familiar?"

Blackburn stopped fiddling with his saddle and came over to where Josh was slumped against the tree. A look of shock registered on his face. "I'll be dog-goned if he ain't the nutty chaplain who tried to kill us. You're crazier than an outhouse rat, preacher, you know that?"

Josh kept silent, but defiantly met Blackburn's gaze.

Talbot pulled out his gun. "I was spitting teeth for three days. You handled that shovel just like my first wife did."

"And my nose." Blackburn putting a hand to his face. "It never did heal right. Every time I sneeze it whistles."

Josh did his best to keep a brave face, but felt certain he was about to experience a painful and terrifying death.

"I say we do unto others what they have done unto us. Let's break his nose, knock out a few teeth, then shoot him in the knees and leave him here for the Cheyennes," said Talbot, cocking his revolver. "There ain't no posse after us, so we don't need him no more."

"Wait a minute. He might still be useful. He's been living with the Cheyennes, right? We could use him as a guide," reasoned Blackburn. "How about it, preacher man? You guide us safely through Cheyenne country and we'll release you when we get to Missouri."

With a dry throat, Josh croaked, "How do I know you won't kill me at the end of the trail when you no longer have need of me?"

Blackburn put his hands on his gun belt. "It don't look like you have much choice. You either agree to guide us or we'll do like Nate said and leave you here in less than mint condition. So what's it gonna be?"

Josh saw the logic. "I guess I'm going back to Missouri with you."

"Fine. Now, which route are we gonna to take?" Blackburn asked.

Josh thought for a moment. "Following the Arkansas downstream would be the easiest."

"We're a pretty fair piece from the Arkansas, wouldn't you say?" asked Blackburn suspiciously. To Talbot he said, "Everyone knows that bottomland is swarming with hostiles. Sounds like a trick to me. We'll head to the Arikaree."

"Whatever you say."

They followed the Arikaree River for three days without seeing another person. Their food—army hardtack and beef jerky—had run out after the first day, and both Blackburn and Talbot failed miserably at hunting. Game crisscrossed their trail, yet they all continued to starve. Josh offered to shoot a buck, but they didn't trust him with one of their rifles.

One morning, Talbot rose early and scouted the area. He returned to camp just as Blackburn was throwing back the blanket of his bedroll.

"Hey, Joe, remember when you told me to keep an eye out for buffalo hunters so we can trade some of our items?" asked Talbot.

Blackburn put on his derby and rubbed his eyes. "Yeah, I remember. So what?"

"There's a group of 'em about five miles downstream."

"Buffalo hunters, huh? How many?"

Talbot scratched his head. "I don't know, five, six … maybe twenty."

"Strange to have that many hunting together," observed Josh.

"I don't care how strange it is; I'm famished," said Talbot.

"They won't be able to see us in these cottonwoods. Let's get the merchandise on display and ride out to meet them," said Blackburn, quickly dressing.

Blackburn and Talbot each had six scalps strung like fish draped across their horses' manes. Out of their saddlebags came two decorated robes, which were laid across their saddle pommels. Josh felt his temper rise and it took every bit of willpower not to cry out when he saw Blackburn put on a necklace made from Sunflower's rings. He knew his best chance to escape would be when they all met with the hunters.

"If these fellas trade us some buffalo hides for this stuff we can sell them when we get to St. Louis," said Blackburn.

Talbot let out a whoop. "I'm gonna buy me a bottle of the finest whiskey in town!"

Josh was told to ride point so Blackburn could keep an eye on him. With Talbot to the left of Josh and Blackburn to his right, they rounded an outcrop of rocks and came to a sudden halt. A hundred yards in front of them were thirty heavily-armed Cheyenne warriors with painted faces. Seven of them wore buffalo-head bonnets with the horns intact.

As the warriors rode forward, Blackburn turned to Talbot. "You moron! Did you not bother to find out what kind of buffalo hunters they were?"

One warrior wore an upright eagle feather attached to a hairpiece made of yellow porcupine quills with black tips. His face was artistically painted red with a black triangle on each cheek. An eagle bone whistle hung by a lanyard around his neck. The gray horse he rode had a black circle painted on each leg. Although he had never seen this getup before, Josh thought there was something familiar about this particular Indian.

Halting his horse in front of Blackburn, the warrior hissed, "You sell the scalps of our people."

Blackburn opened his mouth, but no words came out. Twenty warriors placed arrows into their bows.

The warrior used the point of his lance to lift the necklace of rings around Blackburn's neck and said, "I knew the woman you took these from. Also, those robes you have came from the lodge of Kicking Horse. Give those rings to me. Now!"

Blackburn removed the necklace and placed it onto the lance, which was decorated with crow feathers. With a cracking voice, he asked, "What do you want?"

"Everything." The warrior gave him a threatening look and said, "You are riding my father's pinto."

Josh started to speak, but another warrior put a rifle to his face. "Keep quiet!"

"Now, wait a minute! You can't take that pinto; my horse won't hold us both," said Talbot.

"Get off those horses."

When Blackburn and Talbot dismounted, Josh did as well. The red-painted warrior grabbed the reins of the pinto and led it out of the way. The other horses were taken as well.

"You are fortunate to die a quick death, for we are in great haste," said a blue-painted warrior wearing one of the buffalo-head bonnets.

Blackburn raised his hand as if he were going to ask a question when the humming of bow strings sounded. Josh braced for the impact. Instead, he saw Blackburn and Talbot pitch over backwards from the flight of arrows. Each cried out at first, but went silent as they hit the ground.

The red-painted warrior handed Josh the necklace of rings. "These belong to you," he said in Cheyenne. He then instructed the others to return the Appaloosa to Josh, as well.

Taking the reins, Josh looked at the red-painted warrior. "Making Medicine, is that you?"

"Yes."

"Why are you with this war party? No good can come of it."

"We make war because the white men have broken their treaties and have killed our families. I watched your nephew take a bullet through his head when he was merely retrieving his grandfather's pony. You were there and saw him fall. I rode toward the morning sun to tell the warriors at their hunting camp of what took place."

Josh mounted the Appaloosa and looked the angry young warrior in the eyes. "I, too, have lost my family. I have also lost many friends. Do you wish me to lose another? Making Medicine, you know as well as I that Jesus loves you and has a different calling on your life. You cannot run from him forever."

"Do not mention that name again! He has not helped our people. It is the Sioux who will help us with our war against the blue coats." Making Medicine spoke with great emotion, quickly wiping a tear from his eye.

He then tossed a leather bag of pemmican to Josh. "Have

something to eat, Black Robe. You are hungry, alone, and have been betrayed. Now you know how it feels to be a Cheyenne."

The blue-painted warrior gripped Talbot's brass-plated Henry rifle. For a moment he studied Josh then suddenly tossed the rifle to him. With lightning reflexes, Josh caught the rifle with both hands, but was careful not to make any threatening moves. "It is loaded, but we cannot spare you any more ammunition," said Blue Face.

Another warrior, with three streaks of yellow paint on each cheek, handed Josh one of the decorated robes.

"That is the robe your mother-in-law, Hummingbird, gave to you. Those two dogs had it the whole time," Making Medicine said. "Did you not recognize it?"

"No, I didn't," Josh admitted, "but even if I had, they wouldn't have given it to me."

"This is the last time we shall see one another," said Making Medicine.

"I hope that is not true," replied Josh while putting on the robe. "I will keep you in my prayers, my friend."

Making Medicine angrily thrust his lance into the ground between Blackburn and Talbot. He gave a yelp, and the war party galloped off to the north.

Josh looked down at the lifeless bodies of Blackburn and Talbot, each impaled with ten arrows. He worked the lever action of the Henry, chambering a round, and said, "Well, boys, looks like you should've followed the Arkansas after all."

The feathers atop Making Medicine's lance, staked to the ground, fluttered in the breeze as Josh reined the horse to the left and began the long ride back to Denver.

# Chapter 14

## CAMPFIRE COFFEE

For the rest of the day, Josh followed the Arikaree River upstream. Every so often he would gnaw on a piece of the buffalo jerky. Mid afternoon he spotted a rider far in the distance. Unable to discern whether it was a friendly or hostile Indian or a trapper, he rode into one of the many groves of cottonwood trees along the south bank. He remained in the saddle, but could no longer see the rider. Slowly he pulled back the hammer of the Henry.

After about fifteen minutes the stranger headed past Josh's position. It was a mountain man dressed entirely in buckskins, wearing moccasin boots and a fur hat. Across his saddle was a Sharps rifle, and following his horse was a pack-mule. He spotted Josh and called, "Is that you, Flapjack?"

The mountain man had a little more gray in his beard, but Josh recognized him. He rode out of the trees. "Hey there, Porcupine, how were you able to see me?"

"That robe you're wearin' has got every color of the rainbow, but I smelt you before seein' you. There's not a grizzly in the world that would come within a hundred feet of you."

Josh scratched the razor stubble on his face. "Yeah, I suppose I could use a bath and a shave, but I've been preoccupied with other matters."

"That's what we figured." Porcupine returned the Sharps to its scabbard then shook hands with Josh. "Good to see you're still among us, Flapjack. You sure had us worried."

"Who's 'we'?"

"This here posse for starters," answered Porcupine when four men with wide-brimmed hats and repeating rifles galloped over to them. "Not to mention all the concerned folks back in Denver."

"What are you talking about? Nobody in Denver knows me."

"You couldn't be more wrong, young fella," said Sheriff Sopris, who reined his brown bay to the right of Porcupine. His two deputies stopped to the right of him. "Porcupine may not know his head from a cannonball, but he's right about all those people in town concerned for your safe return."

Porcupine flashed an annoyed look at the sheriff then said to Josh, "Folks were up in arms when they heard Cap'n Soule was killed the night before he was suppose to talk with them congressmen. Word soon got out you was kidnapped by the same rats that carried out that deed. Well, two of 'em anyway."

Josh scrunched his face. "Yeah, those two were Blackburn and Talbot. I was with Marshal Hunt when he brought them in to the sheriff here. There was another man left behind they called Squire. I know Silas put a round into him because of the way he was cussing. Blackburn figured Squire would tell the law they were going to California."

"That gutter trash Charlie Squire didn't tell us anything; he left town and headed south," said Sheriff Sopris. "Marshal Hunt went after him. He figured Squire would probably hide out with some rustler friends of his in New Mexico. What Birdbrain Blackburn didn't take into consideration was the Missus Soule. She told us that you were forced at gunpoint to leave with them. I got the county commissioners to allow me to hire Porcupine to pick up their trail. Shucks, I hate to admit it, but he did a darn good job."

"You couldn't have picked a better tracker," said Josh. "I'm glad he found me. My food is about out and I'm powerful hungry."

"Don't worry, Chaplain, we'll get you some grub after a few more miles," said the sheriff. "That old cantankerous-looking codger back yonder with his pack mule is our cook, Mister Taylor. On special occasions, he'll wash his hands, and I think finding you counts. You remember my deputies, J.W. Goodyear and Lester Belle?"

"I remember them dragging Blackburn and Talbot, in a not-so-gentle but appropriate manner, up the stairs of the jailhouse." Josh grinned.

"I recollect that day." The sheriff chuckled. "By the way, where are Blackburn and Talbot?"

"They're about fifteen miles down the trail, spread out on a piece of prairie like a couple giant-sized pin cushions."

"Cheyennes?" asked the sheriff.

"Yep."

"And they let you go unharmed?"

"Yes, they did."

Deputy J.W. Goodyear was a stocky man with pale-blue eyes and sandy-blond hair with some gray at the temples. After spitting out tobacco juice, he asked with a gravelly voice, "What do you think, Sheriff? Should we go retrieve their bodies?"

"Nah, coyotes need to eat like everyone else."


After riding seven miles in the reverse direction, Sheriff Sopris called a halt to make camp among some giant cottonwoods.

While removing his bedroll, Lester, a lean man with hair combed behind his ears, asked, "Say, Mister Taylor, what's for supper?"

"Beans. Just like we had last night and the night before that … and we'll have tomorrow night as well," answered the short, grouchy cook.

As darkness fell, everyone sat on gray, dead logs around the open fire while they waited for supper.

Porcupine scooped a large serving of cornbread and beans onto a metal plate and handed it to Josh. "Here ya go, Flapjack. Eat yerself a heapin' portion of these whistle-berries. They're good fer what ails ya."

Josh didn't ask about the medicinal properties of the beans, but he did find them delicious as he wolfed the food down with a large spoon. Afterwards, Porcupine brought him a piping-hot tin cup. "Careful, Flapjack. Taylor's coffee can float a horseshoe nail."

While each man sipped at the infamously strong coffee, Sheriff Sopris and Porcupine puffed on their pipes, and Lester spun one yarn after another. At the conclusion of each tale, the others would laugh in disbelief.

After one story about a large fish swimming off with his line and pole on the Yellowstone River, the sheriff said, "You know, Lester, every time you tell that story the trout gets a foot longer and ten pounds heavier."

"It's the honest truth," Lester assured everyone while picking his teeth with a long blade of grass. "If you don't believe me, you can ask Sam Dietrich. He saw the whole thing."

"Can't say that I know him," said the sheriff thinking hard while re-lighting his pipe.

"Nor do I, and that's the third time you told us to ask him about verifying one of your stories," J.W. said, pointing his finger at Lester.

"Come on, J.W., don't tell me you don't remember Sam Dietrich," pleaded Lester. "He was the big fellow with the glass eye I introduced you to at Mendenhall's Fourth of July picnic."

"That still doesn't ring any bells."

"He was the guy who catapulted Amarillo Bob through the front window of the Medicine Bow Saloon in Laramie for cheating at a game of Faro."

"Dog-gone-it, Lester! Who the heck is Amarillo Bob?"

On the trail the next morning after breakfast, Porcupine and Josh rode half a mile ahead of the others so they could speak privately. "Well, Flapjack, I heard about all you've been through since the last time we saw each other. I wanna let you know I feel just awful fer what happened to Sunflower and Little Dove."

"Thanks, Pete. I also know you've been praying for me and I appreciate that. I didn't realize what real evil looked like until that day by the creek. I was wondering how God could allow such terrible things to happen. Then I read in Ezekiel where it says that God does not delight in anyone's death. And according to John's Gospel, Jesus tells us the devil is a murderer and those who follow him share his desires."

"Yep," said Porcupine. "Fallen man in a fallible world."

"I also realized how foolish I was to put any stock in Colonel Chivington. He's an ordained minister, yet he's the one who orchestrated the massacre."

"Don't worry, Flapjack, you weren't the only one taken in by his pulpit pounding. Whether you took a likin' to him or not, there wasn't anything you coulda done to stop what happened that day."

Josh was silent for several minutes.

"Somethin' else is troublin' you, Flapjack. What's on your mind?"

"When we were in New Mexico, I killed a man. It was in the heat of battle and it was self-defense, but it still troubles me."

"Of course it does. When we get back to Denver, take some time off. Go up to my cabin in the mountains and spend some time prayin' and listenin'."

"That's not a bad idea. I'll take a few days off when we get back to town, but then I'm going to resign from my commission with the army and travel to Fort Stockton, Texas."

"Texas? The war only just ended. Are you sure about that?"

Josh smiled for the first time in a long time. "Yeah, I'm sure. I've got a letter to deliver."

# Epilogue

## ONE MORE CUP OF COFFEE

Darkness came early, and the roaring fire helped to ward off the chill. The clock over the hearth of the Colorado Stockmen's Association chimed eight times. T. Wright Mendenhall, in his portrait on the wall, seemed to be watching us. We sat on the comfortable furniture in front of the fireplace to enjoy our apple pie and coffee. I couldn't eat another bite, yet Pastor David showed no hesitation in taking a second piece.

Josh had stared at the flames intently while finishing his story. Figuratively speaking, Josh ended his story with his riding off into the sunset. He asked for one more cup of coffee and mentioned that it was getting late.

"Hey, wait a minute! What happened when you got to Texas? Did you find the parents of that Confederate soldier you shot? Did you deliver the letter?" I wanted to know.

"Hold on there," Josh said before taking a sip from his cup. "Yes, I found the Hislops in Fort Stockton and gave them their son's letter, although I never told them any details of how he died. They appreciated me coming down there, and we became good friends. Reverend Hislop, who presided over the Baptist church, introduced me to some stock buyers and that's how I got in the cattle business. That's another long story I won't get into, but I will say the Lord has greatly blessed me in that area."

"Yeah, it appears he has." Then I glanced at his big friend in the black priest suit enjoying a bite of pie he had just stuck into his mouth. "Okay, but at least tell me, where does Pastor David fit into all this?"

"In fact I was coming to that." Josh set his cup and saucer on the coffee table. "The new reservation for the Southern Cheyenne was established in Oklahoma. I built my ranch along the Canadian River there and was able to secure a government contract to provide beef for the tribe. My desire to help them never waned.

"I was introduced to Pastor David, who had started two churches on the reservation and was working on a third. Despite his priestly garb and haircut, I knew right away he was the young warrior I had known as Making Medicine. It reminded me of the last thing Sunflower had said to me: We may never know who is really listening when we share God's truth and love, and which of those 'seeds' we plant will germinate. In those dark days, Sunflower saw something I could not."

I was incredulous. "Are you kidding me? The big guy sitting here eating pie is Making Medicine?"

Josh and David had a good laugh, which helped to lighten the mood. Fumbling for my notebook, I got back to business. "Okay, Pastor David, or whatever your name is, what's your story?"

David wiped his mouth with a linen napkin while checking the time and said, "I'll make this brief. After the Sand Creek massacre, the other Cheyenne warriors and I went on a rampage against white settlers and the army. We fought for six more years along the Red River, until we became tired of being pursued, and finally surrendered at Fort Sill in 1874. Without a trial, eighteen of us were locked up at the notorious Fort Marion Prison in Florida. In my cell, I drew pictures of our war against the whites on a writing pad.

"Senator George Pendleton of Ohio and his wife visited me in prison. The Pendletons told me about Jesus and read several passages from the Bible. Alone in my cell one night, the words of Brother Joshua came back to me like a flash of lightning. I finally understood what he had been trying to teach me. I dropped to the floor and wept, wanting to know this God of love who sent his son, Jesus, to die for my sins. Right there in that dark prison cell, I took all my hate and desire for revenge, and nailed it to the cross. The senator helped secure my release from prison. Members of the Episcopal Church sponsored me, and I then studied for the ministry in Syracuse, New York. When I became a deacon, I returned to the reservation as a missionary. It was there I met my wife, Susie, and we started those churches. Every Sunday after the sermon I have an altar call and at least one, usually more, will respond. Sometimes Brother Joshua will visit one of the churches as a guest speaker."

"Absolutely amazing! How did your name change?" I asked.

"My full name is David Pendleton Oakenhater. My Cheyenne name is pronounced Oak-uh-hat-uh, which translates to Making Medicine. The army anglicized it to Oakenhater. David is for my favorite character in the Bible; and Pendleton, of course, comes from the family that adopted me."

I nodded then asked another question. "Do you know what became of Chivington after the massacre?"

Josh answered, "Nothing could be done to him or the members of the Third Regiment, since they had all been discharged. Other than that, I don't know."

"That was more of a rhetorical question," I confessed while taking out another notebook from inside my coat. "Since I was already in town when he died, I had time to do some research. Here's what I found: Chivington retained his position as presiding elder at the Methodist Church, but immediately after the guilty verdict, he was forced to resign. The next year, his son drowned while trying to haul a freight wagon out of a river. The year after that, his wife became ill and died. He then married his former daughter-in-law to get control of the money his dead son had left from the freight business. He got three-hundred dollars for his effort before walking out on his new bride, leaving her with nothing but a black eye and a box of unpaid bills. The Methodist Church revoked his membership on grounds of moral turpitude. When a grand jury looked into indicting him for assault and numerous claims of extortion, he fled the territory.

"In his home state of Ohio, he ran for legislator and lost in a landslide. In that same week, he was arrested for assaulting his third wife when she confronted him about his forging of her signature to obtain a bank loan.

"In the early '80s, he returned to Denver where he was welcomed by diehard supporters. He got himself a job as a deputy sheriff but was let go for perjury. His next job was at the coroner's office where he was soon fired for stealing money from the pockets of a corpse. A couple years later, he was investigated for insurance fraud after his house suspiciously burned down.

"Here's the kicker. Two years ago he filed an insurance claim against the Sioux Nation for thirty-thousand dollars because of some missing horses. The insurance company's investigator was Sam Tappan. While on his death bed last week, the colonel received notice that his claim was denied."

"Why are you telling us this?" Josh asked.

"Maybe he did not go unpunished after all." I returned the notebook to my coat pocket. "Would you agree he is not in Heaven?"

"That's not for me to decide," said Josh. "Only the Lord can judge his soul."

"Joshua is right," David added. "In the book of Romans, the Apostle Paul tells us that each of us will stand before the Lord and give an account of our lives, and that we are to stop passing judgment on one another. As Christians, it is our responsibility to forgive those who have wronged us, whether they ask for it or not, since the blood of Jesus has mercifully covered our own sins."

Convicting words! I had no answer to them. I simply thanked the two gentlemen for their time and hospitality, then bid them goodnight. How these two men could be so forgiving after losing everything was beyond my comprehension.

Here's my final conclusion: If the answers they found are in the Bible, then the answers I seek must be there too.

# Note to the Reader

*That Day By the Creek* is a work of historical fiction. This novel incorporates fictional characters (such as Joshua Frasier, Sunflower, and Porcupine Pete) and actual historical figures (such as John Chivington, Silas Soule, and Governor Evans). It does not purport to be an exact rendering of all the people, activity, and influences surrounding the Sand Creek Massacre, an historical event. However, the author has carefully researched those events and in his writing has sought to stay true to the known historical record and the tenor of the times. His description of the actual massacre at Sand Creek is based on historical documents such as those on the following pages, as readers can judge for themselves.

# Appendix

# Historical Documents

Consisting of documents collected by Major
Wynkoop as part of his report which was included in
the following:

1. *Sand Creek Massacre—United States Congress, Senate. Report of the Secretary of War, Sand Creek Massacre, Sen. Exec. Doc. No. 26, 39 Cong., 2 sess. Washington Government Printing Office, 1867. Report of the Secretary of War.*

2. *The War of the Rebellion: A Compilation of the Official Records of the Union and Confederate Armies. Four Series, 128 Volumes. Washington: Government Printing Office. 1880-1901.*

# I

# SWORN STATEMENT OF ROBERT BENT
1864

I am twenty-four years old; was born on the Arkansas River. I am
pretty well acquainted with the Indians of the plains, having spent
most my life among them. I was employed as guide and interpreter
at Fort Lyon by Major Anthony. Colonel Chivington ordered me to
accompany him on his way to Sand Creek. The command consisted
of from 900 to 1,000 men, principally Colorado volunteers. We left
Fort Lyon at eight o'clock in the evening and came to the Indian
camp at daylight the next morning. Colonel Chivington surrounded
the village with his troops. When we came in sight of the camp
I saw the American flag waving and heard Black Kettle tell the
Indians to stand around the flag, and there they were huddled—
men, women, and children. This was when we were within fifty
yards of the Indians. I also saw a white flag raised. These flags were
in so conspicuous a position that they must have been seen. When
the troops fired, the Indians ran, some of the men into their lodges,
probably to get their arms. They had time to get away if they had
wanted to. I remained on the field five hours, and when I left there
were shots being fired up the creek. I think there were 600 Indians
in all. I think there were 35 braves and some old men, about sixty
in all. All fought well. At the time the rest of the men were away
from the camp, hunting.

I visited the battle ground one month afterwards; saw the
remains of a good many; counted sixty-nine, but a number had
been eaten by the wolves and dogs. After the firing the warriors put
the squaws and children together, and surrounded them to protect
them. I saw five squaws under a bank for shelter. When the troops
came up to them they ran out and showed their persons to let
the soldiers know they were squaws and begged for mercy, but the

soldiers shot them all. I saw one squaw lying on the bank whose leg had been broken by a shell; a soldier came up to her with a drawn saber; she raised her arm to protect herself, when he struck breaking her arm she rolled over and raised her other arm, when he struck breaking it, and then left without killing her.

There were some thirty or forty squaws collected in a hole for protection; they sent out a little girl about six years old with a white flag on a stick; she had not proceeded but a few steps when she was shot and killed. All the squaws in that hole were afterwards killed, and four or five bucks outside. The squaws offered no resistance. Everyone I saw dead was scalped. I saw one squaw cut open with an unborn child, as I thought, lying by her side. Captain Soule said afterwards that such was the fact. I saw the body of White Antelope with his ------ cut off, and I heard a soldier say he was going to make a tobacco pouch out of them. I saw one squaw whose -------- had been cut out.

I heard Colonel Chivington say to the soldiers as they charged past him, "Remember our wives and children murdered on the Platte and Arkansas." He occupied a position where he could not have failed to have seen the American flag, which I think was a garrison flag, six-by-twelve. He was within fifty yards when he planted his battery. I saw a little girl of about five years of age who had been hid in the sand; two soldiers discovered her, drew their pistols and shot her, and then pulled her out of the sand by the arm. I saw quite a number of infants in arms killed with their mothers.

---

# II

## LETTER WRITTEN BY CAPTAIN SILAS SOULE (TO MAJOR EDWARD WYNKOOP)
Fort Lyon, ColoradoTerritory
December 14, 1864

Dear Ned:

Two days after you left here with the 3rd Reg't, a Battalion of the 1st arrived here, having moved so secretly that we were not aware of their approach until they Picketed around the Post, allowing no one to pass out! They arrested Captain Bent and John Vogle and placed guards around their houses. They then declared their intention to massacre the friendly Indians camped on Sand Creek. Major Anthony gave all information, and eagerly joined in with Chivington and Co. and ordered Lieutenant Cramer with his whole Co. to join the command. As soon as I knew of their movement I was indignant, as you would have been were you here, and went to Cannon's room, where a number of officers of the 1st and 3rd were congregated and told them that any man who would take part in the murders, knowing the circumstances as we did, was a low-lived cowardly son of a b----. Captain Y. J. Johnson and Lieutenant Harding went to camp and reported to Chiv, Downing and the whole outfit what I had said, and you can bet hell was to pay in camp.

Chiv and all hands swore they would hang me before they moved camp, but I stuck it out, and all the officers at the Post except Anthony backed me. I was then ordered with my whole company to Major A—with twenty days rations. I told him I would not take part in their intended murder, but if they were going after the Sioux, Kiowa's or any fighting Indians, I would go as far as any of them. They said that was what they were going for, and I joined them. We arrived at Black Kettle's and Left Hand's camp at daylight. Lieutenant Wilson with Co.s 'C', 'E' & 'G' were ordered in advance to cut off their herd. He made a circle to the rear and formed a line two hundred yards from the village, and opened fire.

Poor Old John Smith and Louderback ran out with white flags but they paid no attention to them, and they ran back into the tents. Anthony then [indecipherable word] with Co's 'D' 'K' & 'G', to within one hundred yards and commenced firing. I refused to fire and swore that none but a coward would, for by this time hundreds of women and children were coming toward us and getting on their knees for mercy. Anthony shouted, 'kill the sons of b-----s.' Smith and Louderback came to our command, although I am confident there were 200 shots fired at them, for I heard an officer say that Old Smith and anyone who sympathized with the Indians, ought to be killed and now was a good time to do it. The Battery then came up in our rear, and opened on them. I took my Comp'y across the creek, and by this time the whole of the 3rd and the Batteries were firing into them and you can form some idea of the slaughter.

When the Indians found there was no hope for them, they went for the creek and got under the banks and some of the bucks got their bows and a few rifles and defended themselves as well as they could. By this time there was no organization among our troops, they were a perfect mob—every man on his own hook. My Co. was the only one that kept their formation, and we did not fire a shot.

The massacre lasted six or eight hours, and a good many Indians escaped. I tell you Ned it was hard to see little children on their knees have their brains beat out by men professing to be civilized. One squaw was wounded and a fellow took a hatchet to finish her, and he cut one arm off, and held the other with one hand and dashed the hatchet through her brain. One squaw with her two children were on their knees, begging for their lives of a dozen soldiers, within ten feet of them all firing—when one succeeded in hitting the squaw in the thigh, she took a knife and cut the throats of both children and then killed herself. One Old Squaw hung herself in the lodge—there was not enough room for her to hang and she held up her knees and choked herself to death. Some tried to escape on the Prairie, but most of them were run down by horsemen. I saw two Indians hold one anothers hands, chased until they were exhausted, when they kneeled down, and clasped each other around the neck and both were shot together. They were all scalped, and as high as half a dozen taken from one head. They were all horribly mutilated. One woman was cut open and a child taken out of her, and scalped.

White Antelope, War Bonnet and a number of others had ears and privates cut off. Squaws' -------- were cut out for trophies. You would think it impossible for white men to butcher and mutilate human beings as they did there, but every word I have told you is the truth, which they do not deny. It was almost impossible to save any of them. Charly Autobee saved John Smith and Winser's squaw. I saved little Charlie Bent. George Bent was killed.

Jack Smith was taken prisoner, and murdered the next day in his tent by one of Denn's Co. 'E'. I understand the man received a horse for doing the job. They were going to murder Charlie Bent, but I run him into the Fort. They were going to kill Old Uncle John Smith, but Lieutenant Cannon and the boys of Ft. Lyon, interfered, and saved him. They would have murdered Old Bents family, if Colonel Tappan had not taken the matter in hand. Cramer went up with twenty men, and they did not like to buck against so many of the 1st.

Chivington has gone to Washington to be made General, I suppose, and get authority to raise a nine months Regiment to hunt Indians. He said Downing will have me cashiered if possible. If they do I want you to help me. I think they will try the same for Cramer for he has shot his mouth off a good deal, and did not shoot his pistol off in the Massacre. Joe has behaved first rate during this whole affair. Chivington reports five or six hundred killed, but there were not more than two hundred, about 140 women and children and 60 Bucks. A good many were out hunting buffalo. Our best

Indians were killed. Black Kettle, One Eye, Minnemic, and Left Hand. Geo. Pierce of Co. 'F' was killed trying to save John Smith. There was one other of the 1st killed and nine of the 3rd all through their own fault. They would get up to the edge of the bank and look over, to get a shot at an Indian under them. When the women were killed the Bucks did not seem to try and get away, but fought desperately. Charly Autobee wished me to write all about it to you. He says he would have given anything if you could have been there.

I suppose Cramer has written to you, all the particulars, so I will write half. Your family is well. Billy Wilker, Colonel Tappen, Wilson (who was wounded in the arm) start for Denver in the morning. There is no news I can think of. I expect we will have a hell of a time with Indians this winter. We have (200) men at the Post—Anthony in command. I think he will be dismissed when the facts are known in Washington. Give my regards to any friends you come across, and write as soon as possible.

Yours, SS
(signed) S.S. Soule

# III

# LETTER WRITTEN BY LIEUTENANT JOSEPH CRAMER (TO MAJOR EDWARD WYNKOOP)

Ft. Lyon, Colorado Territory
December 19, 1864

Dear Major:

This is the first opportunity I have had of writing you since the great Indian Massacre, and for a start, I will acknowledge I am ashamed to own I was in it with my Co. Colonel Chivington came down here with the gallant third known as Chivington Brigade, like a thief in the dark throwing his scouts around the post, with instructions to let no one out, without his orders, not even the Commander of the post, and for the shame, our Commanding Officer submitted. Colonel Chivington expected to find the Indians in camp below the Com [commissary] but the Major Comd'g told him all about where the Indians were, and volunteered to take a Battalion from the post and join the expedition.

Well Colonel Chivington got in about 10 a.m., Nov. 28th and at 8 p.m. we started with all of the 3rd parts of 'H,' 'O,' and 'E' of the First, in command of Lieutenant Wilson Co. 'K,' 'D,' and "G" in commanding of Major Anthony. Marched all night up Sand, to the big bend in Sanday, about 15 or 20 miles, above where we crossed on our trip to Smoky Hill and came on to Black Kettle's village of 103 lodges, containing not over 500 all told, 350 of which were women and children. Three days previous to our going out, Major Anthony gave John Smith, Louderback of Co. 'G' and a government driver, permission to go out there and trade with them, and they were in the village when the fight came off. John Smith came out holding up his hands and running toward us, when he was shot at by several, and the word was passed along to shoot him. He then turned back, and went to his tent and got behind some robes, and escaped unhurt. Louderback came out with a white flag, and was served the same as John Smith, the driver the same. Well I got so mad I swore I would not burn powder, and I did not. Captain Soule the same. It is no use for me to try to tell you how the fight was managed, only that I think the Officer in Command should be hung, and I know when the truth is known it will cashier him.

We lost 40 men wounded, and 10 killed. Not over 250 Indians mostly women and children, and I think not over 200 were killed, and not over 75 bucks. With proper management they could all have been killed and not lost over 10 men. After the fight there was a sight I hope I may never see again.

Bucks, women, and children were scalped, fingers cut off to get the rings on them, and this as much with officers as men, and one of those officers a Major, and a Lieutenant Colonel cut off ears, of all he came across, a squaw ripped open and a child taken from her, little children shot while begging for their lives (and all the indignities shown their bodies that was ever heard of) (women shot while on their knees, with their arms around soldiers a begging for their lives) things that Indians would be ashamed to do. To give you some little idea, squaws were known to kill their own children, and then themselves, rather than to have them taken prisoners. Most of the Indians yielded 4 or 5 scalps. But enough! for I know you are disgusted already. Black Kettle, White Antelope, War Bonnet, Left Hand, Little Robe and several other chiefs were killed. Black Kettle said when he saw us coming, that he was glad, for it was Major Wynkoop coming to make peace. Left Hand stood with his hands folded across his breast, until he was shot saying, "Soldiers no hurt me—soldiers my friends." One Eye was killed; was in the employ of Gov't as spy; came into the Post a few days before, and reported about the Sioux, were going to break out at Learned, which proved true.

After all the pledges made my Major A to these Indians, and then take the course he did. I think no comments are necessary from me; only I will say he has a face for every man he talks to. The actions taken by Captain Soule and myself were under protest. Colonel A was going to have Soule hung for saying there were all cowardly Sons of B----s; if Soule did not take it back, but nary take aback with Soule. I told the Colonel that I thought it murder to jump them friendly Indians. He says in reply, 'Damn any man or men who are in sympathy with them.' Such men as you and Major Wynkoop better leave the U. S. Service, so you can judge what a nice time we had on the trip. I expect Colonel C and Downing will do all in their power to have Soule, Cossitt and I dismissed. Well, let them work for what they damn please, I ask no favors of them. If you are in Washington, for God's sake, Major, keep Chivington from being a Bri'g Genl. which he expects. I will send you the Denver papers with this. Excuse this for I have been in much of a hurry.

Very Respectfully,
Your Well Wisher
(signed) Joe A. Cramer

(postscript) Jack Smith was taken prisoner and then murdered. One little child 3 months old was thrown in the feed box of a wagon and brought one days march, and there left on the ground to perish. Colonel Tappan is after them for all that is out. I am making out a report of all from beginning to end, to send to General Slough, in hopes that he will have the thing investigated, and if you should see him, please speak to him about it, for fear that he has forgotten me. I shall write him nothing but what can be proven.

Major I am ashamed of this. I have it gloriously mixed up, but in hopes I can explain it all to you before long. I would have given my right arm had you been here, when they arrived. Your family are all well.

(signed) Joe A. Cramer

---

Accessed from: www.kclonewolf.com/History/SandCreek/
(Note: This letter from Joseph Cramer was part of Major Wynkoop's investigation.)

# IV

## Major Edward Wynkoop's Report
THE CHIVINGTON MASSACRE, REPORT, JANUARY 16, 1865 PG. 63
FORT LYON, COLO. TER., JANUARY 15, 1865

SIR:

In pursuance of Special Orders, Numbers 43, headquarters District of Upper Arkansas, directing me to assume command of Fort Lyon, as well as to investigate and immediately report in regard to late Indian proceedings in this vicinity, I have the honor to state that I arrived at this post on the evening of the 14th of January, 1865, assumed command on the morning of the 15th of January, 1865, and the result of my investigation is as follows, viz:

As explanatory, I beg respectfully to state that while formerly in command of this post, on the 4th day of September, 1864, and after certain hostilities on the part of the Cheyenne and Arapahoe Indians, induced, as I have had ample proof, by the overt acts of white men, three Indians (Cheyennes) were brought as prisoners to me, who had been found coming toward the post, and who had in their possession a letter written, as I ascertained afterward, by a half-breed in the Cheyenne camp as coming from Black Kettle and other prominent chiefs of the Cheyenne and Arapahoe Nations, the purport of which was that they desired peace, had never desired to be at war with the whites, &c., as well as stating that they had in their possession some white prisoners, women and children, whom they were willing to deliver up provided that peace was granted them. Knowing that it was not in my power to insure and offer them the peace for which they sued, but at the same time anxious, if possible, to accomplish the rescue of the white prisoners in their possession, I finally concluded to risk an expedition with the command I could raise (numbering 127 men) to their rendezvous, where, I was informed, they were congregated to the number of 2,000, and endeavor by some means to procure to aforesaid white prisoners, and to be governed in my course in accomplishing the same entirely by circumstances. Having formerly made lengthy reports in regard to the details of my expedition, I have but to say that I succeeded—procured four white captives from the hands of these Indians—simply giving them in return a pledge that I would endeavor to procure for them the peace for which they so anxiously sued, feeling that under the proclamation issued by John Evans, Governor of Colorado and superintendent of Indian affairs (a copy of which becomes a portion of this report), even if not by virtue of my position as a U. S. officer, highest in authority in the country, included within the bounds prescribed as the country of the Arapahoe and Cheyenne Nations, that I could offer them protection until such time as some measures might be taken by those higher in authority than myself in regard to them, I took with me seven of the principal chiefs, including Black Kettle, to Denver city, for the purpose of allowing them an interview with the Governor of Colorado, by that means making a mistake, of which I have since become painfully aware—that of proceeding with chiefs to the Governor of Colorado Territory, instead of to the headquarters of my district to my commanding officer.

In the consultation with Governor Evans the matter was referred entirely to the military authorities. Colonel J. M. Chivington, at that time commander of the District of Colorado, was present at the council held with these Indian chiefs, and told them that the whole matter was referred to myself, who would act toward them according to the best of my judgment until such time as I could receive instructions from the proper authorities. Returning to Fort Lyon I allowed the Indians to bring their villages to the vicinity of the post, including their squaws and papooses, and in such a position that I could at any moment, with the garrison I had, have annihilated them had they given any evidence of hostility of any kind in any quarter. I then immediately dispatched my adjutant, Lieutenant W. W. Denison, with a full statement to the commanding general of the department asking for instructions, but in the meanwhile various false rumors having reached district headquarters in regard to my course, I was relieved from the command of Fort Lyon and ordered to report at headquarters. Major Scott J. Anthony, First Cavalry of Colorado, who had been ordered to assume command of Fort Lyon previous to my departure, held a consultation with the chiefs in my presence and told them that, though acting under strict orders, under the circumstances he could not materially differ from the course which I had adopted, and allowed them to remain in the vicinity of the post with their families, assuring them perfect safety until such time as positive orders should be received from headquarters in regard to them. I left the post on the 25th day of November for the purpose of reporting at district headquarters. On the second day after leaving Fort Lyon, while on the plains, I was approached by three Indians, one of whom stated to me that he had been sent by Black Kettle to warn me that about 200 Sioux warriors had proceeded down the road between where I was and Fort Larned to make war, and desired that I should be careful—another evidence of these Indians' good faith. All of his statement proved afterward to be correct. Having an escort of twenty-eight men, I proceeded on my way, but did not happen to fall in with them. From evidence of officers at this post I understand that on the 27th day of November, 1864, Colonel J. M. Chivington, with the Third Regiment of Colorado Cavalry (100-days' men) and a battalion of the First Colorado Cavalry, arrived at Fort Lyon, ordered a portion of the garrison to join him under the command of Major Scott J. Anthony, and against the remonstrance of the officers of the post, who stated to him the circumstances of which he was well aware, attacked the camp of friendly Indians, the major portion of which were composed of women and children.

The affidavits which become a portion of this report will show more particularly than I can state the full particulars of that massacre. Everyone … I have spoken to, either officers or soldiers, agree … that the most fearful atrocities were committed that ever was heard of. Women and children were killed and scalped, children shot at their mothers' breasts, and all the bodies mutilated in the most horrible manner. Numerous eye-witnesses have described scenes to me coming under the eye of Colonel Chivington of the most disgusting and horrible character. The dead bodies of females profaned in such a manner that the recital is sickening, Colonel J. M. Chivington all the time inciting his troops to these diabolical outrages. Previous to the slaughter commencing he addressed his command, arousing in them by his language all their worst passions, urging them on to the work of committing all these atrocities. Knowing himself all the circumstances of these Indians, resting on the assurances of protection from the Government given them by myself and Major Scott J. Anthony, he kept his command in entire ignorance of the same, and when it was suggested that such might be the case, he denied it positively, stating that they were still continuing their depredations, and laid there, threatening the fort. I beg leave to draw the attention of the colonel commanding to the fact established by the inclosed affidavits that two-thirds or more of that Indian village were women and children, and he is aware whether or not the Indians go to war taking with them their women and children. I desire also to state that Colonel J. M. Chivington is not my superior officer, but is a citizen mustered out of the U. S. service, and also that at the time this inhuman monster committed this unprecedented atrocity he was a citizen by reason of his term of service having expired, he having lost his regulation command some months previous.

Colonel Chivington reports officially that between 500 and 600 Indians were left dead upon the field. I have been informed by Captain Booth, district inspector, that he visited the field and counted but sixty-nine bodies, and by others who were present that but a few, if any, over that number were killed, and that two-thirds of them were women and children. I beg leave to further state for the information of the colonel commanding that I have talked to every officer in Fort Lyon, and many enlisted men, and that they unanimously agree that all the statements I have made in this report are correct.

In conclusion allow me to say that from the time I held the consultation with the Indian chiefs on the headwaters of Smoky Hill up to the date of the massacre by Colonel Chivington, not one single depredation had been committed by the Cheyenne and Arapahoe Indians. The settlers of the Arkansas Valley had returned to their ranches from which they had fled, had taken in their crops and had been resting in perfect security under assurances from myself that they would be in no danger for the present, by that means saving the country from what must inevitably become almost a famine, were they to lose their crops. The lines of communication to the States were opened and travel across the plains rendered perfectly safe through the Cheyenne and Arapahoe country. Since this last horrible murder by Colonel Chivington, the country presents a scene of desolation; all communication is cut off with the States except by sending large bodies of troops, and already over 100 whites have fallen as victims to the fearful vengeance of these betrayed Indians. All this country is ruined; there can be no such thing as peace in the future, but by the total annihilation of all the Indians on the plains. I have the most reliable information to the effect that the Cheyennes and Arapahoes have allied themselves with the Kiowas, Comanches, and Sioux, and are congregated to the number of 5,000 or 6,000 on the Smoky Hill. Let me also draw the attention of the colonel commanding to the fact stated by affidavit that John S. Smith, U. S. interpreter, a soldier, and citizen, were present, in the Indian camp by permission of the commanding officer of this post, another evidence to the fact of these same Indians being regarded as friendly, also that Colonel Chivington states in his official report that he fought from 900 to 1,000 Indians, and left from 500 to 600 dead upon the field—the sworn evidence being that there was but 500 souls in the village, two-thirds of them being women and children, and that there were but from 60 to 70 killed, the major portion of which were women and children. It will take many more troops to give security to travelers and settlers in this country, and to make any kind of successful warfare against these Indians. I am at work placing Fort Lyon in a state of defense, having all, both citizens and soldiers, located here, employed upon the works, and expect soon to have them completed, and of such a nature that a comparatively small garrison can hold the fort against any attack by Indians. Hoping that my report may receive the particular attention of the colonel commanding, I respectfully submit the same.

Your obedient servant,
E. W. WYNKOOP,
Major, Comdg First Colorado Vet. Cav. and Fort Lyon.

# ABOUT THE AUTHOR

John Buzzard's life experiences include serving in the United States Navy aboard the USS America during Operation Desert Storm in 1991, and being shot during an armored-car robbery in Berkeley, California.

John is also the author of the memoir *Storm Tossed* (Cladach, 2006), which he penned under the name Jake Porter.

John lives in Tucson, Arizona with his wife, Eva, and their German shepherd, Rocky.